The Heart of the Elf King

RACHEL LOUISE FINN

Copyright © Rachel Louise Finn
First Published, January 2025
Paperback ISBN: 979-8-89686-389-2

This is a work of fiction. Any resemblance to actual events or persons, living or dead, is entirely coincidental.

All rights reserved. No part of this publication may be reproduced, distributed, or transmitted in any form or by any means, including photocopying, recording, or other electronic or mechanical methods, without the prior written permission of the publisher, except in the case of brief quotations embodied in critical reviews and certain other noncommercial uses permitted by copyright law. For permission requests or anything else contact therachellouise@gmail.com

CONTENTS

The Golden Wood...7
The King..13
The King's Son...22
The Dinner Invitation.......................................36
Out Of Bounds...42
Rescue...52
Fallen..70
Awake...80
The Library..92
A Little Change...111
The Roses...122
Steps Forward...136
Something There...146
Realisation...153
Into The Wood.. 173
The Day In The Snow......................................180
A Silence Finally Broken................................199
The Great Massacre.. 212
Moments of Contemplation........................... 216
The Winter Festival.. 230
The Mirror...245
Enemies At The Door.....................................256
Intruders...263
The Confrontation.. 275
Beneath The Trees... 282

Safe 290
Reunited 301
The Question 311
Doubt 316
Loose Ends 322
The Big Day 335
Ever After 339

The Golden Wood

Amaya's father had gone missing five nights ago and had yet to return. He'd left their village of Feardenn to go trading with the nearby hamlet of Whitehall and nobody had seen or heard from him since. The worry had been coursing through her, steadily growing as each new day passed with no sign of him.

She tried to keep her mind busy by tending to the crops and animals around their small farm, but Amaya simply couldn't rid herself of her panic.

Her father had never been away for so long and she knew for sure that something had gone horribly wrong when his horse came back that same morning, alone and clearly spooked.

Amaya rushed into town, pushing her way into the local tavern and attempting to rally together some of the men to help, to go out and look for him. But they hadn't listened. They hadn't taken her seriously at all.

To them, Amaya was nothing but a silly girl who knew nothing of the world and spent too much time with her nose stuck between the pages of books that they deemed pointless. When her father wanted to come back, they said, he would.

Left with no other options, Amaya had saddled the horse back up, praying it would somehow know to take her along the same path that her father had gone.

When it came to a stop on the outskirts of the Golden Wood and stamped its feet, snorting in fear, Amaya knew. She knew that he had ventured into that accursed place.

A cold fear crept up her spine, and Amaya's heart leapt into her throat as she dismounted. She swallowed down her fear; her gaze fixated upon the dense treeline before her.

"Go home." She said gently to the horse, finally turning and nudging its nose away to try to send it back to the farm.

She knew it wouldn't go back in there and she wasn't cruel enough to force the animal past the boundary of the forest. She had no idea what had happened in here, what she might find, or what dangers she might encounter, but she knew that turning back wasn't an option. Her father was all that she had and she would not leave him here.

The Golden Wood was not a safe place to venture, especially alone. Amaya knew that.

The forest was covered in a dark enchantment that was in place to keep out any who dare enter. Even without such a thing, it was full of darkness in its own right and her people had long since learned to stay well clear of this place.

Monsters lurked in and beneath the trees. Tribes of dirroh some people said, horned beasts with foaming mouths of red saliva and claws big enough to slice you from head to toe in a single swipe. Groups of noopsall said others, vicious flesh eaters who skinned you alive.

Not only that but Amaya had been warned since she was a small child about the elves who dwelled in the kingdom just beyond this forest.

Rumours had always flown around the three human settlements of the Golden Isle about these beings. Beautiful and powerful but some said they were as dark and twisted as the forest itself. There were stories about them taking humans and killing or keeping them as slaves.

Amaya was in two minds about that because most of what she had read in her books said that elves were wise and kind and cared about all living things, but perhaps the poisoned air of the wood had infected the ones living on the other side of it?

There were all sorts of theories and tales and she had no proof either way but now that she was here, stepping into the suffocating forest, she was terrified that every single thing she had ever heard was true.

Still, she continued on. Her father was here, somewhere, she knew it. And she would not leave him.

~

It felt like Amaya had been walking for hours and she had lost the path some time ago.

The air itself felt like it was pressing down on her, trying to bury her in the earth beneath her feet but really it was just trying to push her out as the spell that lay upon this forest was intended to do.

Her head had grown heavy and she wanted to simply lie down on the ground and close her eyes. Every time she looked up, she couldn't even see the sun overhead to gauge the passage of time and she felt completely trapped and hemmed in. It was a beautiful forest otherwise but it was so claustrophobic and dizzying that she barely noticed.

Amaya had become so focused on the pressure attacking her from outside, the unsteadiness of her own feet, and the fact she had no idea which way she was travelling, that she hadn't even noticed the soft sounds echoing all around her.

Eyes had been on her from the moment she set foot in this forest, closely following her trail from the branches above. Bird-like creatures had Amaya in their sights and they were rapidly closing in. She was easy prey, especially considering she didn't even know that they were there.

Another half hour passed before something suddenly took hold of her from behind - no, not from behind, from *above* - and then her feet were suddenly lifted clean off the ground.

A fresh wave of panic ripped through her as Amaya twisted her head and caught a glimpse of the beast. A serutluv! A pale yellow bird of prey that dined upon flesh. It looked at her with greedy green eyes and she noted that its beak was larger than her entire head.

Before she could do or say anything,

however, it let out a piercing wail and released her. She landed hard back on her feet, her ankle twisting, the impact knocking her off balance and sending her tumbling to the forest floor. Sounds of a fight suddenly filled her ears, as well as a rushing of large wings, but she didn't look up. She was frozen in fear.

"Prince Valerian!" A voice cut through the air but Amaya thought that she had imagined it completely. Nothing felt real anymore and she was still reeling from her near death experience.

Suddenly, she felt the shadow of a new presence appear beside her right elbow.

Just as she was about to give in to the shaking of her arms, which were the only thing holding her upright, fingers clasped around her upper arm, pulling her back up onto her feet.

Shock rippled through her body at the very real feeling of contact and her head snapped up, her eyes landing on the brown-haired male who now stood in front of her, eyeing her with mild curiosity.

A human alone so far in these woods? It was a strange sight for him to see.

Amaya opened her mouth to speak but nothing came out and it probably wouldn't have mattered anyway.

She was pushed gently out of his grip and into the arms of another, whose grasp was tighter as they pulled her along, obviously wanting her to go with them and she had not the energy to refuse.

"Take her to the king." The voice of the

brown-haired one sounded once more from somewhere behind her, before he turned and disappeared through the trees to go after the rest of the serutluv that had escaped.

The King

A time later - who could say how long? – Amaya suddenly became aware that she was indoors and her mind was slowly released from the influence the forest had had over it.

How foolish she had been to enter these parts alone, without a single thought! But her father... *her father!*

Panic in her eyes, she turned to look at the one who had hold of her arm. Female, she noticed immediately. She was tall and her dark hair was neatly braided out of her face, revealing the pointed tips of her ears.

Elves.

"Please." Amaya began, her fear rising. "I have to..." One look from the elf beside her caused her to close her mouth immediately, any further words dying in her throat. She turned to look ahead with a frown as she was led - or, more aptly, dragged - along expansive twisting corridors. It took her breath away, the very sight of this place.

Where was she?

Amaya felt like her legs could give out beneath her at any moment as she mindlessly allowed herself to be led through the magnificent hallways. She was aware that she was being looked at by passing elves, mostly with curiosity she thought, though she couldn't be certain. For all she knew, it was well-concealed hostility.

Eventually, she was pulled into a large room and everyone around her came to a halt, forcing her to stop also.

She still felt slightly off balance and her mind was having a difficult time catching up to what exactly was happening. She couldn't believe that she had failed so spectacularly. Now that she was out of that unwelcoming forest, her thoughts had become clearer and she was growing terribly concerned. Her father was still out there somewhere, lost in that dreadful place, and she had gotten herself captured by elves of all things.

Though they had technically saved her from the serutluv, hadn't they? Still, she got the feeling that it wasn't exactly an intentional act, more just good luck on her part.

"What have we here?" A rich, powerful voice rang out from somewhere just above her, covering the room like velvet.

Frowning, Amaya lifted her gaze, finally noticing that she was standing beneath a throne that sat at the top of a small set of steps, and that the male sitting atop the throne, wearing a crown and draped in finery, had his predatory gaze fixed directly on her.

Her whole body went rigid and her heart felt like it dropped into her toes as her eyes locked with his. He tilted his head slightly as he regarded Amaya, watching her as she took in the sight of him.

His hair immediately confused her as it seemed to be both silver and gold to her eye and she had not the capacity to figure out how that could be. It cascaded in a long waterfall past his shoulders and down his broad chest. His eyes were golden and the look in them wasn't welcoming. Truthfully, this was the most beautiful creature Amaya had ever seen but a chill ran through her as she looked into those unfriendly eyes.

"A human." He mused as he rose from his seat and turned to move gracefully down the steps, towards her. His gaze was fixed upon her every second of his advance and she found herself unable to look away, not sure if she was more enthralled or terrified. "Why are you trespassing in my kingdom?"

Her eyes widened as she looked back at him, horror suddenly blooming white-hot in her chest. Trespassing? No! Amaya hadn't even known where she was!

Take her to the king, that elf had said.

The being now standing directly in front of her, looking down his stupidly perfect nose at her, was undeniably the king.

Elf. King.

This was Thalian, Elf King of the Golden Isle.

She was through the other side of the wood, in the Golden Castle, in the hands of the elves.

A deafening silence followed as Amaya lost her thoughts somewhere in the back of her head. Her tongue felt like concrete in her mouth and her throat was dry as sandpaper. The guard at her side shifted ever so slightly, uncomfortable, as she knew that the silence would do this human no favours.

"Speak, girl!" The king snapped, making

Amaya jump. He merely arched a brow at her, unimpressed.

"I..." The words needed to be forced out of her mouth. Fear had taken hold and she was no longer enamoured by his appearance, not really. He was *terrifying*. "I didn't mean.... y-your majesty, I did not know. I was..." She paused, swallowing past the lump in her throat, unable to meet the gaze of the king any longer, dropping her eyes to his chest to avoid his glare. "I was looking for my father, he... he is missing, I believe he is lost in the woods... forgive me, I... I did not..."

There wasn't much more that she had to say but Amaya was fairly sure that she wouldn't have been able to get anything else out even if she had tried.

The king straightened, turning away from her. His back to her now, he seemed to be deep in thought. Unbeknownst to Amaya, he was linking her words with the prisoner that had very recently come to dwell in his dungeon. He took so long to speak that Amaya thought that perhaps he had decided to say nothing at all. When his voice came, he was speaking words that she couldn't understand and she realised he was talking in the tongue of the elves.

The guard next to her suddenly came back to life again as she bowed and turned away, retreating back out of the heavy doors at the entrance to the throne room.

Another silence followed and a shiver ran through her as the king finally turned back to look at her, eyeing her slowly from head to toe. Amaya did her best not to squirm beneath his hawk-like gaze.

"You say you are looking for your father." He said, taking a step and beginning to walk around her, circling her like an animal would circle its prey before going in for the kill.

Nodding, Amaya did her best to stand still, to show no fear. "I-I... yes. Y-your grace, he left the village of Feardenn five days ago to trade with Whitehall and... and his horse returned alone, scared, and I... I just wanted to find him."

"You entered the forest alone?" He questioned, now standing on her left.

"Y-yes..." She nodded, clasping her hands in an attempt to stop herself fidgeting.

He hummed in response but Amaya couldn't decide what it was that he meant by it and she didn't dare ask. She didn't even turn her head to look at him. His entire presence frightened her and she wondered how she would ever get out of here. It didn't feel like he believed a single word that came out of her mouth. How could she reason with him?

The doors reopened behind her with a bang and the king stepped away from her, hands clasped behind his back, observing. Amaya finally turned to see the guard dragging something along with her. *Someone.*

"Father!" Amaya cried, unable to keep herself from moving then, flying towards him as he collapsed to the ground beside her. She cradled his head gently. He looked terrible. Had they even been feeding him? A flash of anger coursed through her and she turned to shoot a glare towards the king.

He stared impassively back at her.

"Amaya..." Her father's voice was low, his hand gripping her arm as she finally turned back to him. "My daughter, you should not be here."

"I came to find you. I *had* to find you!" She argued, thinking of the fear she had felt when his horse had returned home without him.

"It would appear that trespassing runs in the family." The king's voice once more filled the room and Amaya turned to look at him.

"We are not trespassing!" She suddenly raised her voice, unable to help it as his words sparked an anger in her.

Her father's fingers weakly squeezed her arm in warning but she ignored it, standing up again and taking a step towards the Elf King. "I told you! My father was obviously lost in those woods. Have you even felt what it's like out there? I barely knew where I was!"

No emotion showed on Thalian's face as he stared back at her. He was well aware of the enchantment meant to keep folk such as these out. It was of his own making, after all. If they had not entered, if they had stayed on their own side where they belonged, they would not have felt any ill effects.

"You hold him prisoner for what?" She continued her tirade, unable to stop. "For getting lost? For daring to tread a path that he did not know he shouldn't be on?"

"No." Came the king's simple reply. "For breaking and entering. For attacking the Crown Prince." He took another step towards her, leaning into her personal space, his voice low. "For spying."

"My father is not a spy." Amaya tried to reason, though the other things he had said sounded... troubling.

"That is what they all say." The king stepped back, waving his hand to dismiss the guard and her father, turning to take the steps back up to his throne once more. He was bored of this now. "You will return to your little village. You will tell the men to never enter this forest, to leave us be. Your father will remain here as our-"

"No." The word left her mouth before she could even realise that she had decided to speak at all.

The guard had been dragging her father away again, back in the direction of the doors. Amaya assumed he was probably to be locked in some dingy dungeon where they kept their prisoners, which is undoubtedly what he was right now.

At her response, the entire room seemed to freeze. It was as if there was an inaudible intake of breath which was not immediately released as all eyes remained locked upon the Elf King.

He had stilled mid step but hadn't yet turned back to look at the defiant little human standing down below the dais. He did so slowly, the slightest hint of intrigue in his cold gaze, though all

Amaya could see was the anger that briefly flashed across his expression before all emotion disappeared from his face entirely.

"No?"

Amaya felt like she had made a huge mistake but she had seemingly already made up her mind. "No." She repeated, hating how her voice shook.

She felt very small and very weak under the piercing gaze of the king, who was standing still as a statue in the middle of the staircase, staring at her unwaveringly.

"Let my father... go." She said, trying to ignore how her voice trembled as she did her utmost to hold his gaze. "You can... I will..." This was *not* going at all how she wanted it to. Not that she would be here doing any of this if she had her way. She would be safe at home with her father. He looked sick, he looked uncared for. He was getting older and he couldn't stay here, not like this. "I will stay here in his place. Take... take me instead."

Not a single flicker of emotion passed over his face as he regarded the girl. She looked back at him, feeling lightheaded and anxious but not backing down. Maybe he would just lock them both up and that would be the end of it, they would rot here for the rest of their lives. Which would be an eternity to them but nothing to an immortal being like an elf.

The silence stretched unbearably until Amaya finally broke eye contact, looking down at the floor.

Then, and only then, did The finally deign to answer her. "Very well."

Amaya was so surprised by the words that her head jerked back up so fast it was a wonder it didn't just snap off. He was no longer looking at her, speaking over her head to his guards in their own language. She could hear her father, who was vehemently disagreeing with her decision between coughs but his cries fell on deaf ears.

"See that he is escorted safely out of the forest." The king flicked his wrist, dismissing the guards, one of whom led her father away and the other taking hold of her arm and pulling her away from the throne.

Amaya chanced one last look at the king before the doors closed behind her.

He was seated back upon his throne, one leg lazily crossed over the other, staring icy daggers across the room at her retreat.

She shivered and turned away, the heavy door closing loudly behind her.

The King's Son

It all happened so quickly. Amaya and her father were allowed only the briefest of goodbyes in the hallway before they were torn apart.

He tried to beg and reason with her to change her mind but nothing would shift her decision. He needed to go home and she would be fine. She did her best to reassure him, knowing she would likely never see him again. Unless she found a way to escape...

Could they not even spare her a proper minute to say goodbye in exchange for forever? Can this king be so coldhearted that a daughter could not kiss her father goodbye for possibly the very last time in her life?

Amaya was assured by a guard that he would be taken to the other side of the forest and deposited safely. He would make it home and he would have to warn the rest of their people not to venture into these woods. Not to come near this castle. She wasn't sure if she truly believed a word any of these elves said, though most of them sounded sincere enough, but she didn't have much of a choice other than to just accept what she was being told and what was happening.

She was then dumped rather unceremoniously into a cell. The dark-haired she-elf who locked the door gave Amaya a slightly sad look before she turned and left her alone. She stood at the bars on tip-toes and craned her neck as best she could but she couldn't see too much past the cell. It appeared she was the only prisoner which actually surprised her. After the throne room encounter, she had expected the cells to be overflowing with poor innocents that the Elf King had locked up for no reason other than his own amusement.

Alone, the time passed far too slowly. Amaya almost wished she was still lost in the forest somewhere or that they had let that serutluv kill her. Though she reasoned that then her father would still be trapped here. Better that she was in this cell than he was and she stood by that.

Exhausted, she lay down on the floor and stared at the high ceiling, quickly and easily going out of her mind. Gods, she wished she had a book or something. She didn't dare consider asking someone for one.

As if that would even be allowed, she thought bitterly.

~

Some time must have gone by because she was suddenly opening her eyes, feeling herself gently shaken awake.

She had fallen asleep.

Groaning, Amaya stirred, forgetting where she was for a brief moment until her eyes met those of an elf guard and it all came rushing back. At least she had been allowed a brief respite in her dreams, she supposed.

She was led back to the throne room. When she realised where she was going her steps faltered but she was pushed gently through the doors and across the floor.

Coming to a stop in front of the throne, Amaya kept her gaze locked on the empty space in front of her, not daring to look up into the eyes of the king. She didn't want to be anywhere near him, let alone look at him or speak to him.

"You have traded your freedom for your father's." His smooth voice echoed around the room. She didn't respond. It wasn't a question. "Some would call you noble, even brave." Amaya lifted her eyes at that, finally looking at him in surprise. "I would call you foolish." He continued icily, reaching the bottom of the steps. She looked away again.

With surprising speed, he crossed the space between them, a long finger sliding beneath her chin and tilting her head back up to look at him. "Your manners are lacking, little human."

"I..." Amaya floundered, unsure what it was now that she had done wrong. She felt like even the smallest misstep would only make his disdain for her grow. Make him lock her in the deepest, darkest cell for the rest of her miserable days never to see the light, fed the bare minimum if she was lucky.

King Thalian straightened up, looming over her. "You will look me in the eye when I address you." Her heart jumped wildly around in her chest. He moved, pacing around her like before, like a wolf on the hunt. "You will live out your days here, in my kingdom. You will refer to me as 'my king', not 'your majesty', for that is what I am now. *Your* king. You are my *prisoner* and *subject* by default, by your own volition."

"What... what will you do with me?" Amaya somehow ventured, not sure where she even found the courage to speak to him.

He was so intimidating and the ghost of a smirk on his face seemed almost evil to her eyes. What kind of creature locked people up over misunderstandings and refused to listen to reason? What kind of king was he? Not much of one in her estimation.

When she got no answer, she continued. "Am I to rot away in your dungeons or would one such as yourself prefer a slave?"

A flash of something crossed his expression and before she could figure out what it was, his face was mere inches from her own, his voice low and dripping malice. "Hold your tongue, *girl.*"

Her chin lifted marginally, a tiny hint of defiance in her expression, as she found herself staring him down. The king's eyes sparkled just slightly with surprise.

The silence was deafening as Thalian stared down at Amaya and she stared back up at him.

Where this sudden rush of courage came from, she had no idea but she simply found herself so angry at her situation (and at him) that she couldn't control it.

No more words were spoken and, with a

simple flick of his wrist, a guard took Amaya gently by the upper arm and steered her back out of the room, returning her to her cold, lonely cell.

~

Amaya didn't know how many hours had passed this time but a while later she was woken again, a gentle voice rousing her from slumber.

Her eyes opened slowly and she looked up to see an elf with light brown hair and kind eyes.

She jolted upright in shock, half wondering where she thought she knew him from. It hit her a moment later - this was one of the elves from the forest. The one who said to take her to the king.

"Forgive me." He said, offering her a soft smile. "I did not mean to startle you." His tone and his words confused Amaya as she watched him straighten up to his full height. "I've come to show you to your room."

She blinked at him. "My... my room?" She asked, utterly incredulous.

There was a twinkle in his eye. Amusement? She couldn't decide.

"Yes. Your room. Please, come." He gestured for Amaya to go with him and, confused, she stood and hesitantly began to follow him away from the cell and up a nearby staircase.

Her attention was captured completely by her surroundings as she followed him through the vast corridors and up a winding staircase but they passed everything quite quickly and eventually came to a door which the elf pushed open, gesturing for her to enter first.

Amaya eyed him suspiciously before she took a hesitant step past the door and looked around. She found herself then faced with the most beautiful room she had ever seen, embellished with intricately carved furnishings, beautiful wall decor and muted colours.

"I-" She found herself speechless, turning to look at the elf who was now leaning in the doorway. "I don't understand."

He was smiling at her, arms crossed over his chest as he watched her. She couldn't figure out what was happening, why he had brought her here and given her a whole room with a proper bed and...

A room. A *bed*.

Suddenly, Amaya felt an ice cold fear creep up the back of her neck and her expression changed as she took a stumbling step away from him.

The backs of her knees hit the edge of the bed, nearly causing her to fall. Amaya wondered if there was something close enough to grab to fight him off.

He immediately stepped forward and held out his hands. "No... no." He seemed to catch on very quickly, probably reading her thoughts in her expression. "Oh, I am *so* sorry!"

Of course she might jump to such conclusions, he thought to himself. She had been held here practically against her will, what on earth was he thinking?

"I am not going to hurt you." He kept his hands up in front of him as if to let her know he was not going to attack and gave her such an earnest look that she quite quickly began to believe him.

He stayed where he was, not moving any closer. "Forgive me. I was not thinking." Humans had such things to fear, he knew this, and the thought unsettled him to no end. Forcing such a thing upon another? He could not comprehend it.

"My name is Valerian." He continued. "Prince Valerian. I mean you no harm, really. I simply wish you to be comfortable. Here, in this room. On your own." He gave her a careful look and Amaya could feel herself relaxing a little more, the thundering of her heart beginning to subside as she looked back into his eyes, seeing only sincerity. She nodded.

"I should not have assumed." She managed, swallowing thickly as she took another glance around the room. "Thank you."

He shrugged. "It was all I could set you up with on such short notice." Valerian sounded almost apologetic and Amaya shot him a curious look. This was the largest, prettiest room she had ever seen, what was there to be sorry for?

"It's beautiful, really." She told him, before becoming unsure again. "I just... I do not understand. The king..." His father? He'd said he was the prince. Her head was starting to swim with all this information, fighting to keep up.

She looked into this elf's eyes and didn't see the hostility she had seen in the eyes of the king. He didn't really seem to look much like him at all either. Their hair colour was different, though their eyes were similar. Valerian's were darker though. "You are his son?" Amaya inquired and he nodded. "Did..." Another troubled frown creased her brow as she thought back to what Thalian had said when her father had been brought from the cells. "Did my father hurt you?"

Valerian sighed, glancing down at his feet, and then looking back up at the girl before him. "It is complicated. He wasn't in his right mind when he reached us... I believe he ate the berries."

"The berries?"

Valerian explained that there was a bush of red berries in the forest that humans could not eat but he didn't go into too much detail and Amaya didn't think she would have understood much of it if he had.

This was all getting to be too much for her. Her whole life had been nothing but farming and reading and simplicity. She knew magic existed and other races were out there but she had never seen any, she had never travelled from the Golden Isle to the mainland. She had never even left her village, though she had dreamed of it. She had dreamed of adventure but she had never had the heart to leave her father. Besides, where would she even go? They were separated from the mainland and she'd never be able to afford a boat.

"I will leave you to get settled." The prince

said then, offering Amaya another smile. "Someone will check on you in a while to see if you are in need of anything."

Then he left the room, closing the door behind him, leaving her in confusion as she turned to fully take in her new, unexpected surroundings.

~

King Thalian's fast, furious footsteps carried him down the hall in the direction of the private dining area he shared with his children.

Upon his arrival he pushed the door roughly, causing it to bang loudly off the wall behind it as it swung open.

Valerian lifted his head at the intrusion but he didn't look surprised. He had been expecting this. However his sister, Camellia, sitting beside him practically jumped out of her chair at the almost violent appearance of their father.

"You gave her a *room?*" Thalian practically snarled, pacing towards the table. "Must you insist on disobeying and undermining me at every turn?"

"Father." Valerian sighed, shaking his head. "Be reasonable."

The king's eyes flashed with rage as he regarded his son. "Reasonable? Do not test me, my son. That *girl.* Her *father.* That man somehow got around my guards, broke into this castle, and *assaulted* you. Not to mention what he did to the..." He trailed off, not speaking of it, and Valerian did not push him. "And you wish to, what?" Thalian continued. "Reward his pitiful excuse of a daughter? For what purpose? She is my *prisoner* in his stead, my boy, she is not a guest here."

"Father." He said again, a moment after letting him rant on as he needed to. "That man was unwell, you know this, he had to have come along the river. The berry bush. He was not in his right mind. The wound he gave me was not deep, it has practically healed already." He gestured to his right arm, the top of which had been the victim of the man's dagger in his state.

"Excuses."

"Reasons." He said, ignoring the warning rise of his father's left eyebrow at the interruption.

Camellia shifted uncomfortably beside him, her gaze focused intently upon the spoon in her hand, though she made no move to continue eating.

"Listen to me." The prince continued, unperturbed. "This girl... she cannot go anywhere. She cannot get out of this castle. She is still, for all intents and purposes, your prisoner if that is what you wish." He paused, studying his father's face. "You said she was to live out her days in this kingdom, you did not specify that she was to be caged for the entire time in the dungeons."

Thalian's eyebrow arched even higher as he stared his son down. Valerian had stayed in the forest when the girl was brought in but Aurelia, his black-haired best friend and one of the king's soldiers, had obviously told him of the entire exchange in the throne room.

He could tell that his son was not going to back down on this for some bizarre reason that Thalian simply couldn't comprehend. Why all of this energy over mortals?

"There will be a guard posted outside of that room at all times." He stated, pinning his son with a glare. "If she so much as blinks in the wrong direction, you will *both* be punished. Do you understand me?"

"Yes father. Of course." Valerian forced himself not to smile at the win, bowing his head respectfully.

The older elf snorted, unsatisfied, before he turned and strode from the room, letting the door slam shut again.

Valerian allowed his expression to crack then, a small smirk appearing on his lips as he turned back to his plate.

Camellia finally lifted her head and shot her brother a reproachful look but he just smiled at her and resumed eating. A moment later, she left her meal untouched and rose from the table, leaving the room.

~

"Why are you doing this?" Aurelia wondered. "You're only going to antagonise him."

She and Valerian had met later that same day in the training grounds just behind the castle to practice with their weapons, something they liked to do quite often to keep their reflexes sharp and add a little excitement into their afternoons.

Valerian smirked, shifting his foot as he blocked a blow from Aurelia's sword. "As his son, I believe that is in my job description."

Aurelia gave him a pointed look, an amused smile beginning to tug at the corners of her mouth. "Valerian."

He shook his head. "Come on, Aurelia. The girl has done nothing wrong, she does not deserve to rot away in my father's cells. He says a lot of things when he is angry, that does not mean they must be set in stone."

"He is the king." She reminded him.

"Yes, he *is* the king." Valerian agreed, dodging another blow with a chuckle. "He is also my father and you and I both know that that is his greatest weakness."

Aurelia laughed at that, shaking her head at the prince as she sidestepped his blade.

It wasn't a lie, really. Since the death of the queen, everybody was fairly certain that the prince and princess had been what kept Thalian going, kept him holding on when he might have wanted to just let go and drown in his grief.

Valerian had been a child at the time and could barely even remember his mother, much to his own dismay. His sister was a little older than he and remembered much more, something he once resented her for, when he was young and foolish and trying to figure everything out. Soon, however, he'd realised it was a blessing considering his father would not even speak his mother's name, and

Camellia would talk to him of their mother in secret some nights before he drifted off to sleep.

Time and the festering memories had turned their father into this harsh, unyielding king with a reputation of being cruel, especially in the eyes of those outside of these lands.

Within the walls of this kingdom, however, despite his temper and his hardness, the elves of the Golden Isle knew that he was a good ruler. That he did what he did and made the choices he made for his people.

However, some things had perhaps gone a little too far. Valerian thought that perhaps his father had retreated too much into himself and pulled the kingdom with him. He thought that they were a little too isolated, too cut off, especially if they would ever be in dire need of help or aid. Who would come if his father continued to push away trade and allyship with most of the surrounding towns and realms? Even the messages sent by the Elf Chief, Haradir, from across the sea had gone unanswered for centuries.

Valerian understood his father but he didn't often agree with everything he said and did, and he certainly didn't agree with this.

His father's distrust of humans, of mortals, of the world itself, and his fear over his son being injured (and the harsh reminder that he too could be taken from him) had driven him to act, once more, in anger.

Valerian wanted to try and show him that there was another way, that his worry was unfounded, that he could not control every*one* and every*thing* around him.

He could not control the events of the world no matter how hard he might try to do so. Valerian wanted to try and help his father to understand things from his perspective and maybe this poor mortal girl would be a good starting point for him to try and get that to happen.

"I hope you know what you're doing." Aurelia told him. Her voice was serious but she was smiling even as she spun to dodge another downswing of his sword.

The Dinner Invitation

The room was much larger than the cell and Amaya spent a short time looking around it. No weapons stashed away, not that she really expected there to be, but she told herself that she'd had to at least look.

The door had actually been unlocked when she had tried the handle but there was obviously somebody standing guard outside so she didn't have much hope of escaping that way. She would be grabbed before she could get two paces and probably thrown back into the dungeon.

Amaya still couldn't understand what she was doing here. Why was she in this room? Why had the prince let her come here? Did the king approve? She didn't think anything could really happen without the king's consent but she also couldn't imagine him suggesting or simply allowing this to happen, especially not with the reception he'd given her. Or the fact that her father had obviously been locked up for all the days since his capture and she'd been moved to this room the very same day. She assumed, at least. Time had been a little difficult to track properly without the sun.

A female elf had come to the room to offer her some tea and ask if she needed anything else. Amaya had been too shocked to do or say much of anything, still completely confused about where she had found herself but her mind was slowly forming the beginnings of a plan. She *would* get out of this room and she *would* return back to her village, to her father.

Once the elf had left and the door had once again firmly closed Amaya inside, she turned around and got to work.

Gathering every sheet she possibly could from the bed (and some spares from a nearby dresser) she began to tie them all together by their ends, creating a kind of rope ladder that she was going to try to use to get out of the window.

Though, from the height that she had seen as she'd glanced outside earlier, Amaya thought she'd probably need many, *many* more sheets. However, there was a ledge that she thought she could reach and for now that was her goal.

She would figure the rest out after. She just had to get out of this room first.

~

A while later, the sheet ladder was reaching quite a decent length. It had taken a little longer than anticipated, however, as it was harder to tie proper knots in the sheets than she had imagined.

Amaya pushed open the window to her room and sat by it so that she could more easily gauge the distance as she worked.

This castle was quite intricately built and she was concerned that she was going to end up getting lost before she found her way out of here but she told herself to focus on one problem at a time.

Her main priority was escaping this room. She hadn't thought she had any chance down in the cells but here there was a definite opportunity to escape.

As she worked, her thoughts kept straying to her father, hoping he had been safely taken to the edge of the forest like the elves had promised her. He would find his way home from there but from the look of him he would need a doctor. What had they done to him? What kind of monster didn't help a man in clear need of aid? He'd looked ill and uncared for. Surely even if somebody kept prisoners, there was a standard to which they must care for them? Her heart filled with more and more anger as she thought of that wretched Elf King, her fingers tugging a little more violently at the sheets as she tied the material together.

The sudden sound of knocking at the door caused her to freeze in place before she turned hesitantly away from the task at hand.

Valerian stood on the other side. He'd lifted his hand to knock, not wanting to just stride into the room and make Amaya feel uncomfortable. She was most likely uncomfortable enough and he still felt bad for having scared her earlier. He was too gentle and kind a soul for that and he would probably feel bad about it for a good many days yet.

"My lady?" He ventured, unable to see the way her eyes narrowed at how he'd addressed her. Amaya didn't speak but he knew she was in there. There was no way she could have gotten past the guard and he had heard a shuffling sound from inside the room just before he knocked. He deduced that she must still be scared and therefore was ignoring him.

"Are you hungry?" Valerian continued, pausing briefly to see if she would grace him with a response. None came. "I've come with an invitation to dine. Would you not like a different view for a while?"

Valerian knew that this was probably just going to get him in some sort of trouble with his father, and he couldn't really say that right now he had much of a reason for doing this other than feeling badly, but sometimes he thought that was a good enough reason on its own.

There was still no response from inside the room as Amaya stared at the door, her thoughts a mess. If she didn't agree, would he have it opened and have her dragged out regardless? Why was the prince inviting her personally to dine? Amaya was a prisoner, was she not?

"Please, I mean you no-"

"You *will* join us for dinner." A new voice interrupted, cutting Valerian off.

Valerian and the guard standing sentry at the door turned to see the king taking slow, deliberate steps towards the end of the hall where the girl's room was located.

Amaya recognised the smooth baritone of the voice immediately and her blood ran cold.

"That is *not* a request." King Thalian continued, addressing Amaya but pinning his son with a venomous glare.

He simply could not understand what Valerian was doing or thinking but he had to admit that part of him, small as that part may be, was beginning to get curious. Curious enough to go along with his son's ridiculous scheme and see how this would play out.

Besides, maybe if Amaya joined them for a meal he would be able to give her some more rules about her new place here. Perhaps he could assign her some lowly job so she was not just sitting around taking up space and resources... since Valerian was *so insistent* on her not being locked up in a cell for whatever bizarre reason.

Anger rushed through Amaya's veins at his command and she frowned at the still closed door. "You have taken me as your *prisoner*." Amaya spat back at him. "And now you want me to have dinner with you? That, *my king*, is completely insane!"

Thalian's composure slipped a little, genuinely shocked at not only her ungrateful tone but her words. Surely she had the good sense to show more respect and common courtesy? He was the king of this land after all and Amaya had been afforded more than she should have, considering the situation. Yes, perhaps his son was mainly the one to actually thank for the room but nothing could happen without his approval. Was she so foolish to believe she could speak to him in this way?

"You have been afforded your *own room*, a comfortable *bed*." He stated, voice low, tone just bordering on dangerous. "One would think that you would be a little more *grateful*."

"Grateful!" Amaya could hardly believe her ears. How arrogant! "I would rather starve before I *ever* eat with you!" Came her reply, her tone plainly conveying her bitterness towards him.

"Very well!" The words were hissed through the door, accompanied by the sound of a palm smacking hard against the wood that caused Amaya to jump. "Be my guest!" Thalian snapped. "Starve."

Then the Elf King turned from the door, looking down at the others in the corridor. Anger flashed in his eyes and not even Valerian thought to continue to push the situation.

"If she does not eat with *us*, then she does not eat *at all.*" He said, loud enough for Amaya to be able to hear him on the other side of the door, and then he turned on his heel and disappeared around the corner.

Out Of Bounds

The silence that followed the king's retreat from outside the door was deafening. Amaya had visions of him barging into the room and dragging her, kicking and screaming, back into the cell to rot for the rest of her days but luckily he didn't even attempt to enter - just left her with the memory of his fury.

He was incredibly swift to anger and Amaya had to admit that the speed with which his ire had sparked scared her.

Nobody else had disturbed her since he took his leave and she was fairly certain he meant what he said. That she wasn't going to be given any food unless she decided to eat with him.

"Over my dead body." She muttered, wondering if she was going to start talking to herself all the time now. If she would turn into Lady Enry from her village, who had lost her husband and children to a dirroh attack and gone quite mad. She spent most of her time shut up in the large house her husband had built but when she did venture into town, she was often seen conversing with herself by the fountain or outside the bakery, like she was talking to the ghosts in her own head. Amaya found it quite sad but most people just called Lady Enry crazy, or said that she was a witch and everybody tended to stay away.

Amaya still had the window open and was now focusing on lowering the sheets she had tied together out of it, watching their descent as they moved closer to the ledge that she was aiming for below. One end had been tied to a post on the, in her opinion, rather overly grand bed behind her. From there it trailed across the room and out the window.

When the door suddenly opened without warning, Amaya jumped a mile and turned to face it, looking like a rabbit caught in a trap.

The female elf from earlier walked into the room carrying a little tray upon which sat what she assumed to be another pot of tea. She crossed the room and set the tray down on a table in the corner, her gaze moving from the tea to the girl and then to the sheets hanging out the window. The tiniest of smiles tugged at the corners of her mouth before she went back to the tray.

"How about some tea first?" She asked, pouring some into a cup which she then held out towards Amaya with barely concealed amusement shining in her eyes. "It's cold out there."

Colour flooded into Amaya's cheeks as she moved slowly away from the window, going to sit on the edge of the bed with a soft sigh. She supposed she was thankful this elf lady wasn't running immediately out of the room to call the guard she knew would still be out there, or even the king himself. She shuddered a little at the thought of him and she knew that the elf noticed but she didn't say anything, just handed her the cup and watched as she had a sip.

"Uh. Thank you…" She murmured, looking back at the now slightly familiar face of the elf in front of her. "What's your name?"

"Myleth." The elf smiled.

Amaya returned the favour, giving her own name and Myleth seemed like she was genuinely interested in knowing it which surprised her.

She had a few more sips of the tea, which she had to admit was very nice, and then Myleth picked the tray back up and spoke again.

"I am to take you to get dinner." She said, causing Amaya to tense up. Myleth noticed this as she turned back with the tray and she gave the girl a kind look. "Don't worry. The king will not be there."

What had transpired since her arrival appeared to no longer be secret in the castle.

The knowledge caused Amaya to frown as she stood from the bed, carefully placing the teacup on the tray as Myleth held it out towards her. "I don't understand. He said-"

Myleth turned back to the door, gesturing for Amaya to follow her out into the hallway. "He says a lot of things, dearie." Was all she said as she led the human girl down the corridor towards a set of stairs.

Amaya simply trailed along beside her, trying to keep her expression neutral but she couldn't quite hide her wonder as she gazed at her surroundings. This place was something beautiful to behold, she had to admit.

Myleth smiled as she glanced at the girl beside her, noticing her looking around at the statues and wall hangings as they passed by. "And you haven't even seen the half of this place."

Amaya smiled slightly, though it quickly disappeared. "I don't suppose I ever will." She found herself saying.

"Nonsense." Myleth waved her hand. "You will see everything soon enough, I am sure."

Amaya gave her a curious look. How could she if she was locked away in a room for the rest of her life? She didn't ask, simply letting the topic lie. She was too tired to argue.

"What's up there?" She found herself asking after a moment of silence in which her wandering gaze found a set of stairs that were set against a wall and wound up several floors, half concealed by a thick ruby red curtain as if someone was attempting to hide it.

"Oh. Nothing." Myleth did her best to shrug and wave off the question as if it was nothing at all but something in her tone caught Amaya's attention. "That area's private, dear. Out of bounds." The elf continued walking, her steps seeming to quicken as she hurried the girl away from the half hidden stairs.

Amaya glanced back over her shoulder as they rounded the next corner, her curiosity piqued.

Myleth continued to lead her in the direction of what she soon discovered to be some sort of large dining hall.

She was still confused about being allowed out of her room and part of her wondered if this was some elaborate trap and the king was going to jump out from around the corner and drag her away to personally turn the key to the cell in the dungeons.

However, he was nowhere to be seen. Instead, the room was practically empty apart from a few other elves.

Two males sat at a table talking over plates of bread and cheese. They looked up when the doors opened and offered Myleth friendly smiles. She led Amaya over to the table and gestured for her to sit. She did so, still wholly rattled that any of this was happening, the confusion she felt only growing each second that nothing bad happened.

From the conversation, Amaya managed to glean that the two elves she and Myleth had joined were called Doronion (the king's butler) and Elion (one of the guards) and she got the impression that the two of them were usually thick as thieves.

Amaya was given a plate of her own and eventually felt herself relaxing just a bit, even smiling slightly as she listened to the three of them talking about their day with each other, laughing and joking like old friends.

The joy and animation she saw in their expressions as they joked around together was unexpected to her, especially here in this place, with a king like that on the throne. She had kind of built up an image in her mind of this place and the people in it but maybe they were just as trapped with their cruel king as she was.

The doors opened again and Amaya flinched, swinging her head round to look. Her gaze fell upon the face of the prince and he saw her a moment later, his fair features breaking into a smile as he did. He made a beeline for the table, seating himself as a female elf Amaya hadn't seen before quietly followed him over and sat beside him.

"It is good to see you out and about, my friend." Valerian smiled, causing even more surprise to bleed into her expression. Friend? Amaya couldn't for the life of her understand why he - why everyone, really - was being so kind to her.

Was this all some kind of an elaborate joke that she wasn't in on? Or was it simply that the king was out of sight and therefore it was safe?

Amaya ate slowly, savouring the meal in case it was one of the only ones she was going to get. She was asked a few questions and she answered them politely but mostly she just listened to the chatter going on at the table, finding a little comfort in it somehow. It felt... nice. It almost made her feel less alone.

When the conversation eventually shifted to the topic of the king, Amaya found herself rolling her eyes, an unintentional scoff leaving her lips.

Everyone at the table turned to look at her and she ducked her head, feeling her cheeks heat up with shame. "I..." She shook her head, unable to get the words to come out.

His son was sitting right there and, as kind as he had been to her, she felt guilty for her reaction and she also still couldn't be sure he wouldn't go running right to him.

"You know... the king is not as terrible as he appears." The words stunned Amaya as she lifted her face, gaze landing on Doronion who was looking back at her with an expression so soft it surprised her.

Shaking her head, she looked around at them all, eyes flickering from one to the other. "He is not here. You do not have to lie for him. I certainly won't be saying anything to him if that is your concern."

Valerian chuckled and Amaya turned to him, startled. "My father can be temperamental, yes, but truly-"

"He locked *my* father up and intended to keep him that way forever!" She argued. "He was unwell when I saw him!"

"He was refusing treatment from our healers!" The female elf next to Valerian suddenly insisted.

Amaya looked at her with some degree of surprise, having almost forgotten she was there at all. She was so quiet. Reserved. Almost shy.

"My sister is right." Valerian said after a brief, mildly awkward pause.

Amaya looked at Valerian again. Sister? Thalian had another child? It was difficult sometimes to even think of Thalian being fatherly, now it turned out he had a daughter too?

Valerian sounded like he was being sincere and it gave Amaya pause, providing him room to continue. "Your father *did* attack me with a dagger. The king was upset that his son got hurt." He tried to explain but he knew that it had to look and feel like everything he said was a lie and that everything Amaya believed about his father was the truth. He couldn't blame her for it, not really. He knew how his father behaved, how he could come across. He'd known his father his whole life. He was privy to many things that Amaya was not.

She just assumed that perhaps they were all sticking to the story of Thalian not being as bad as he seemed because the prince and princess were sitting right here at the table with them, which she supposed she could understand. As sincere as they all sounded, it wasn't something she felt that she could believe. She simply nodded and went quiet, saying no more about it.

Time wore on and Amaya began to relax a little more with every second that the king did not appear to rain hell down upon her. The conversation between the five elves at the table (which had moved on again from Thalian) was nice enough and she enjoyed their company more than she wanted to admit.

Eventually, they all began to drift away and Valerian's sister - who Amaya had learned was named Camellia - asked if she could escort her back to her room. It relieved her to know the princess didn't seem to harbour ill feelings towards her after her comments regarding her father.

Myleth smiled and offered her a half hug goodnight. Amaya kept waiting for the other shoe to drop but it never did. She turned to leave the room and walked quietly through the corridors with Camellia.

Camellia was quite unlike her brother. She was a very quiet elf, seemingly quite shy or timid. She walked with her hands clasped, her eyes a little downcast, not much like a princess at all. Amaya wouldn't have guessed it to look at her, though she was dressed finely enough. She had grey eyes, not golden, and her hair was a similar colour to Thalian's, though a little lighter, leaning more silver than gold.

"Is there anything you need before I leave you for the night?" Camellia asked softly, offering her a polite smile.

"No. Thank you." Amaya shook her head, attention turning to that mysterious staircase again as they passed by. "Myleth said... that way is out of bounds." She ventured. "What's up there?"

Camellia stopped, her eyes widening slightly. "That is... the rooms up there belong to my father. You must never go there." She took Amaya by the elbow and gently urged the girl onwards.

Amaya wordlessly let Camellia guide her along the corridor back towards the room she'd been given... but there was something in the tone of her voice, some edge that only heightened her curiosity.

It looked like that way was rarely used and it seemed to be a strange place for the king's private chambers to be for some reason, a little too... out in the open. She'd have thought that someone with his cold demeanour would have liked to sleep and exist further away from the more central areas of the castle. But it was mostly the way everybody was talking about it that made her suspicious. Myleth answered too quickly and seemed to be trying too hard to be casual. Camellia had looked startled at the mention of it, perhaps even a little frightened, and quickly steered her away.

"I'm told Myleth will bring you breakfast in the morning." Camellia told her with a smile once they reached the room, giving her arm a gentle, almost friendly squeeze before she took her leave, disappearing back the way she had come.

The princess's footsteps receded and Amaya stayed standing outside the door. For some reason the guard had vanished and had not yet returned, perhaps having gone for dinner himself while the prisoner was gone.

She stood debating with herself for another long, long moment... and then she turned and began to slowly and carefully venture back down the hall.

Rescue

The only sound Amaya could hear was the echo of her own quiet footsteps as she tiptoed down the corridor, keeping close to the wall and peering carefully around each corner she came to.

Her heart was in her throat, anticipating capture with every step she took. Thankfully, the Gods appeared to be on her side as she didn't run into anybody else the entire way.

She treaded carefully back down the vaguely familiar hallway that Myleth had taken her to dinner, figuring that she could decide her next move from there.

Rounding another corner, her eyes were once more drawn towards that red curtain at the bottom of the half concealed staircase. She stopped and lingered, staring. She couldn't deny how curious she was about this place. Everybody's reactions towards the mere mention of it had only furthered her belief that they were hiding something. Camellia had told Amaya the rooms up those stairs belonged to her father but something just rang false about it and, before she really knew what she was doing, she was hurrying towards the staircase and gently easing back the curtain.

With one last look over her shoulder, Amaya slipped past the fabric and began to ascend.

It was so quiet she could have heard an arrow being nocked into a bow from a distance away.

Her feet carried her up the stairs and over

the threshold of this hidden wing, looking around as she started her quiet exploration.

Elegant paintings sat upon the walls and the bed Amaya found through one of the doors was one of the grandest things she had ever seen. Fit for a king indeed but it didn't look slept in.

In fact, nothing in here looked as though it had been touched in a long while despite how well taken care of it all looked. There was a distinct lack of dust and she could tell these rooms, while perhaps unused, were well maintained.

Upon the wall near the entrance, she saw a framed portrait of a beautiful elven woman. Her light brown hair had a shimmer to it even in a painting, cascading around her face like a waterfall, and her features were nothing short of *perfect* - she took Amaya's breath away. However, the portrait looked to have been viciously slashed, as though somebody had taken a knife to it in a fit of rage. It was perhaps the only thing up here that didn't seem well looked after.

Amaya moved on, finding books and papers, sparkling necklaces and rings adorned with beautiful gems. In the wardrobe nearby she found a collection of beautiful dresses and she wondered who they belonged to. Camellia, perhaps, but why would they be in rooms she claimed to belong to her father?

A large ornate mirror sat upon a dresser and she moved towards it, peering at her tired reflection before her gaze lowered to the items laid out on top of the dresser. Her fingers ghosted over a silver hairbrush, tracing the intricate pattern on the handle.

"What do you think you are doing?" A furious hiss from the doorway caused Amaya to spin on her heel, knocking the hairbrush to the floor.

Thalian stood glaring at her, fury etched across his face. He came up here quite often. Sometimes just for a moment, sometimes for hours.

These were his late wife's private rooms, after all.

He hadn't intended to come up here tonight but something had pulled him this way and now he was very glad that he did. How Amaya had even gotten up here was completely beyond him but that wasn't his immediate concern. No, his concern was on the fact that she was in here at all, touching things, sticking her nose where it did not belong.

Every single item in these rooms was precious to him and he had found *her* - his *prisoner* - in here putting her dirty little human fingers all over everything.

Amaya's mouth opened but no sound came out. Fear had taken hold of her at the mere sight of his face and the sound of his voice. She shuffled further away, her back hitting the wall as he advanced on her, pacing closer with terrifying speed and a dangerous glint in his eye.

"I was only..." Amaya started but the words died in her throat.

"You were only, *what?*" His voice was low

and even and, somehow, that was far more terrifying than if he had been screaming at her.

He was close now, too close, and Amaya felt like she was in terrible danger. What was he going to do?

"Looking for something to *steal*, I wager." Thalian continued on when she offered him nothing else.

He glared at her for a moment longer before he suddenly bent down to pick up the hairbrush from where Amaya had knocked it to the floor. With surprising care, he moved to set it back in its place on the dresser, his expression softening and becoming sad for just a second before he rounded back on the girl, fire in his eyes once more.

That's not what terrified Amaya most, however. When he turned his face back to her, much of it was no longer the pristine alabaster skin that she had seen previously.

Thalian had become so furious that he had accidentally let go of a magic spell that he used to keep some terrifyingly graphic wounds on his face concealed. Long, thick, jagged strips had been carved out of the delicate flesh of his face and neck, leaving nothing but gaping holes in their wake.

What Amaya saw was horrifying and only added to her vision of the king as a terrifying monster, and she couldn't hold back her fearful gasp if she'd tried.

"Who do you think you are?" Thalian raged, scowling down at her, not yet fully registering her look of revulsion for what it was.

His arm shot out, taking hold of her wrist in a vice-like grip, eyes blazing.

Amaya's fear spiked further, believing that this was it, that he was about to hurt her... maybe even kill her. Her wrist ached and in the back of her mind she was aware she would likely have bruises there the next day. If she survived to see the next day, that is.

Thalian had suddenly become aware that he had let the concealment spell go, something he rarely (if ever) did as it was second nature to him these days to hold it in place and the realisation only served to make him angrier. He felt much more vulnerable this way and that wasn't a feeling he cared for.

"Get out." His voice suddenly seemed a little strained as he released her wrist and turned his head away from her, long silver-gold hair falling across his face as he did so.

Amaya stood where she was, frozen in place. She kept willing her feet to move, to get away from him. She kept willing for her mouth to open, to grovel for forgiveness. Absolutely nothing happened and she found herself just staring at him in pure horror.

"Get! Out!" He roared when Amaya made no movement, rounding on her once more. His face was back to normal, having regained full control of himself.

She didn't have any more time to think, not that there was anything left to think about. She pushed away from the wall, brushing past him, and took off running. She raced back down the stairs and past that stupid red curtain, along the hall.

She just kept running until she came to what was very obviously the front doors of the castle. They were standing open and the two elves on guard were startled by her sudden appearance.

She rushed past them before they could even think and then she just kept going, praying that her legs wouldn't give out as she fled through the castle grounds and into the forest.

~

The forest was dark and the trees felt like they were pressing in on her.

The further Amaya ran, branches pulling at her hair and scratching her face, the worse she started to feel and the more turned around and lost she became.

The suffocating weight of the forest itself came back in full force, settling over her like a heavy, scratchy blanket. Tears were blurring her vision as she continued to fight her way through the trees and the bushes, eventually stumbling out somewhere along a path.

Amaya briefly wondered where the serutluv were, memories of her previous journey through this wretched place coming back to her in full force. The thoughts were pushed from her mind by the memory of the king. He'd been so angry and she had been so scared.

And his face...

She quickly shook the image from her mind, focusing on the woods around her. She wished she had somehow been able to steal a horse but she would just have to manage on foot.

She felt like she was running for ages when she eventually came to a stop, though by this point she had as much sense of time as she did direction. None.

For a moment she just stood where she was, trying to get her bearings but it seemed impossible as, everywhere she turned, everything just looked exactly the same.

Amaya had no idea which direction led back to her village and she had no idea which part of this forest the bird-like serutluv nested. She had no idea if she was running from danger or running towards it.

She was tired, having spent all day tying stupid sheets together and in a high state of anxiety, which hadn't been helped by Thalian finding her poking around in those forbidden rooms.

Her thoughts turned briefly to Myleth and the others, wishing she had listened to their warnings. She found that she also wished she had been able to say goodbye to them but Amaya pushed that to the back of her mind. She needed to focus. She had to find her way back to the village. Her father must be going out of his mind with worry.

As she looked around, she started to

become aware of noises a short distance ahead. Cautiously, she took a few more steps and parted the foliage, peering between the branches and the leaves. It was dark, being late in the night by now and the forest seemed to be a dark place in general, so Amaya couldn't quite make out the source of the noise right away. When she finally did, her blood ran cold.

Dirroh.

Dirroh were disturbing creatures, all sharp fangs and red saliva. Three huge horns sat on the top of their heads, and their claws could slice through flesh as easily as a knife through butter. They travelled in packs of usually six or seven but sometimes more.

As she looked, she could make out a group of five lurking beneath the trees a short distance away, talking amongst themselves in a language Amaya couldn't understand, all grunts and snarls. Despite this, the 'words' still made her shudder.

She could see their fangs glinting through the dark and her heart started to beat so fast she could feel it in her ears as she backed away in fear. Silence was paramount and she moved slowly, carefully... but it wasn't enough as her foot came into contact with a fallen twig, the snapping sound seeming to echo loudly through the entire forest.

A deafening silence fell and Amaya knew they were listening now, waiting, trying to ascertain what had made the noise and from which direction it had come.

Then she heard them moving and before

she could react, the large shapes of them suddenly sprang through the bushes. They were snarling, charging straight towards her.

Amaya might have screamed but she couldn't be sure. One lunged at her and without giving it too much thought she snatched a thick branch from the ground and did her best to use it to defend herself. She got a blow in, fending off the beast only once before the branch was split in half and the splintered pieces scattered across the forest floor. The dirroh grinned menacingly at her as all of them now began to advance again, seeing the easy kill right before their eyes.

This was it.

She was about to die.

Then, at the very last moment, there was a sudden rush of noise through the trees on her right. A thunder of hooves and a clash of steel saw Thalian appear from the undergrowth and dismount gracefully from a large horse at speed, drawing his blade in the same moment.

As Amaya watched, he placed himself between her and the band of dirroh, sword in hand. He started swinging instantly, attacking the creatures with a graceful skill that she had never seen before in her entire life.

She stood, stunned, as he fought the dirroh back. She was still reeling from how close she had just come to death and now the very king she'd feared would kill her was in front of her, saving her life.

One of the dirroh got around him and

started to come for Amaya again but Thalian was quicker, spinning and taking the creature down.

His eyes met hers briefly as the animal fell and she stood frozen, staring at him in shock. The moment lasted only a few seconds before the remaining dirroh rushed up on him from behind, sinking its fangs deep into the king's shoulder.

He let out a pained grunt, forcing himself into a full body swing, his sword swiftly cutting the dirroh's head from its shoulders.

His chest heaved as he caught his breath, staring at the bloody remains of the creatures around them.

Thalian turned slowly, facing Amaya again, but in only a moment he was falling. He landed hard on his knees, gritting his teeth in pain. He hadn't been able to don his armour before he left the halls and the fangs had pierced him deeply. He could already feel the venom that had been in the animal's fangs working its way into his system. It must have been the leader of the pack, he realised, as only they held the toxic substance in their teeth.

Amaya, on the other hand, had taken the opportunity to turn back to the horse he had chased after her on, taking hold of its reins and readying herself to jump onto the saddle and get the hell out of here once and for all.

However, she found that her feet wouldn't move as she stood there, tightly clutching the reins in her shaking hands. Her head felt heavy and her thoughts were tangled and confused, though this was not entirely the work of the forest like before.

No, this time she was grappling with her conscience.

Amaya could hear the king behind her, his breathing shaky, and found herself glancing over her shoulder. He was in the same position but he had his eyes closed now and he already looked quite pale. She looked once more from him to the horse and back again… before making a decision she had absolutely no doubt she would regret.

When she stepped back towards Thalian, he opened his eyes, not bothering to hide the surprise written all over his face. He was frowning and she knew that he had expected her to get on that horse and flee, but she found that she just couldn't. Truthfully, it wasn't in her to leave him there injured as he was, after he had saved her from certain death, no matter how he had treated her before.

"You have to stand…" She told him gently, knowing that she wasn't able to lift him onto the horse herself but she knew from the look of him, the fact his arm now seemed to be going limp, that he wouldn't be able to ride by himself… and she didn't know if he had the strength to make it back to the castle alone.

Amaya didn't know that the fangs that had pierced him had been laced with venom, none of the night raids by dirroh on her own village in the past having had a leader involved, and she knew he was an elf king (warrior, even, from the looks of it) but it wasn't in her to turn and leave him. Especially after he saved her life.

After a long moment in which he simply stared at her in disbelief, Thalian nodded.

She reached out carefully for his uninjured arm, not sure if she could really do much to help, but he didn't object as he gritted his teeth and forced himself to his feet.

~

When Thalian and his horse had thundered past the guards at the gate in pursuit of Amaya, every elf in the castle had been left trying to catch up with whatever had just transpired.

After the human girl had gone running out into the night, fleeing into the forest, they hadn't even been certain if she had been released or not because it didn't make sense to them that she would be able to be roaming around by herself in the first place.

Then, when the king himself had raced after her like a madman, even more confusion rippled through the elves of the kingdom.

Once Harlynn - the head of the king's guard - heard what happened, she leapt to her feet at once and started throwing orders around. She was preparing a group to go after the king and was standing at the head of them about to give the order to leave when the pair returned.

The sight of Amaya walking alongside the horse with Thalian in the saddle was one she hadn't expected to see when she turned her head. Harlynn's eyes nearly bugged out of their sockets in surprise but she forced her feet to move, rushing over to the king.

She gave Amaya a look of confusion, unable to understand what was happening because it was immediately clear that Thalian had been injured out there somehow and... the girl was no longer running.

"My king!" She moved to help Thalian down from the horse but he waved her away and insisted on dismounting himself, biting back a wince as his feet hit the ground.

"Take the horse back to the stables." He ordered, turning for the entrance. He didn't say a word to or about Amaya. He didn't even look at her as he continued on, making his way inside. "There was a pack of dirroh out there. Northwest. Send archers immediately. I want to know if there are any more and what they were doing in this part of the forest." They did not usually come so close.

"Of course." Harlynn said quickly, turning to gesture to a nearby guard, who nodded and scampered away. "I will fetch the healers." She then added.

"No." Thalian gritted out. "I am fine. Leave me be." He could feel the toxins working its way into his system and he had a few other more superficial wounds but he would see to them himself.

He wanted to be alone.

He was still angry and now he was in pain which, if possible, only served to make him angrier still.

Amaya watched him sweep away towards the stairs that led to his own rooms with a frown. He was really going to just walk off and not see anybody? She had seen the fight and as amazing as he had been, as skilled as he was, she wasn't stupid. She still had no inkling that the fangs that pierced his shoulder had contained venom but Amaya was aware that he definitely had at least one other cut on his forearm where his tunic had been ripped by a very large, dirty claw.

Before she could even really fully realise what she was doing, her feet had started moving, carrying her up the stairs and down the hall, following the king as he escaped to the privacy of his chambers.

Nobody stopped her.

Thalian soon became aware of her footsteps behind him and he rolled his eyes, throwing her a dark glare over his shoulder. "You are either lost, *girl*, or incredibly stupid."

"Well, I know which one *you* are." Amaya muttered under her breath before she could stop herself.

He whirled on her, her mutterings no match for the hearing of the elves, turning with terrifying speed. "Excuse me?"

Fear shot through her for a moment but this time she was quick to get it under control. If he wanted her dead, he would have just let those dirroh kill her. Right?

"You are hurt and yet you refuse to let anybody help."

"I do not *need* any help." Thalian sneered in reply, turning on his heel and striding away from her, his long legs carrying him so fast that she almost had to run to keep up with him.

This elf was so stubborn and arrogant, so utterly foolish, that she almost could not believe it. "Your son told me that my father refused help from the healers too and look at the state he ended up in!"

Thalian eyed Amaya, unamused that his son had once again been seemingly sharing every little thing with *her*, a random human who should still be rotting in the dungeons to prevent this headache. Why was Valerian spending all his time and energy on - what? - making a *friend* out of her? The idea might have made Thalian laugh if it wasn't so ridiculous.

"Unlike your fool of a father, I actually have skill in healing myself." He pushed the door to his bedchamber open and strode in, not holding it open for her to follow because of course she was not invited and he wanted her to simply go away. She could go back to her own room and stay there forever for all he cared. He didn't want to see her, she had caused him far too much trouble and anguish tonight.

Amaya hesitated for a moment, aware that she was absolutely pushing her luck right now, but then she nudged the door open and followed him inside.

Thalian, already in the process of shrugging his tunic off, turned to her with an incredulous look on his face. "In case I wasn't clear," he hissed at her. "You are unwelcome here."

"In case *I* wasn't clear." Amaya replied, taking slow, cautious steps towards him, not wanting him to lash out despite how very clear it was that she was crossing many boundaries. "You need help. So *let* me."

Amaya had traded her freedom once more to get him back here and she wasn't going to let his stubbornness see him not take care of his wounds properly. She seemed to forget for a moment that he was a king, an elf, and a warrior who had seen far more than she could ever hope to see in her short lifespan.

The noise that left Thalian next was practically a growl as he filled up a goblet with what she could only assume was some sort of alcohol before downing the entire thing in one swift motion. He then moved to sit down on a chair beside a small table where he continued shrugging himself from his tunic in deathly silence.

Amaya hovered by the door, watching with uncertainty before it became apparent to her that he had agreed without actually letting her know that he had agreed.

With the briefest roll of her eyes, she crossed the room towards him before jumping slightly as the door behind her opened again.

Valerian rushed in, worry etched across his face. He stopped short when he saw Amaya, his expression turning to surprise to see her here of all places, though he recovered quickly enough.

"Father. The healers instructed me to bring these to you." Since he was being stubborn and refusing their direct aid, though Valerian had enough sense to keep that part unspoken.

He set a few items on the table next to his father's goblet and Amaya followed his movements. She saw there were various herbs, a little jar of ointment, and some damp towels.

She moved forward and picked up one of the towels, turning to look at Thalian. He glared back at her in complete silence before a huff of air came from his nose and he practically ripped the rest of his tunic sleeve away from his arm. He held back a wince at the pain that rippled through his shoulder but Amaya saw it all the same and she knew Valerian would have too.

The prince was standing in slightly stunned silence, watching the human girl and his father as he tried to figure out what he had walked in on. Last time he had seen Amaya she had been clear that she was not his father's biggest fan and from what he'd heard she had also made a run for it.

Thalian's eyes were practically burning holes in her face as he stared at her but he didn't move or speak and so she tentatively stepped towards him. His gaze was almost like a dare and Amaya wasn't going to let him win whatever game they were now playing.

Lifting the cloth, she began to clean his wounds, starting with the one on his arm.

His sharp hiss made it clear to her that it hurt and part of her did feel some satisfaction at that. After all, he deserved it. A little.

Fallen

"*Must* you press so hard?" Thalian growled through gritted teeth, curling his hand into a fist against the armrest of the chair.

Amaya had cleaned the wound on his forearm without much issue but the one on his shoulder that had, still unbeknownst to her, been struck by the poison was causing him to become more and more aggressive as the seconds ticked past.

Secretly, she thought that he was acting a little bit like a baby and she was getting frustrated.

"You know, it wouldn't hurt this much if you would just sit still!" She couldn't help but snap at him, though she did her best to keep her voice soft despite her irritation. She was still wary of him and also quite upset that she had given up her one chance at freedom, at getting back home to her father.

"Well, this would not have happened at all if you had not been so foolish as to run away." He shot back at her, his tone laced with disdain.

Amaya blinked, her fingers pausing their work for a moment. "If you hadn't frightened me so badly, I wouldn't have run off like that!"

Maybe there was a little bit of a lie in her words because what else did she think she was trying to do, creeping through the hallways like she had late at night? Though, truthfully, she was sure that she wouldn't have gotten out of the front gates if she hadn't been fleeing for her life in a way that had stunned the guards, so maybe it wasn't a complete lie.

Regardless, Amaya had been so terrified by Thalian's awful temper... and the look on his face. She quickly pushed the memories away.

Thalian scoffed, turning his head to look at her properly. "None of this would have happened if you had kept your thieving little nose out of places it does not belong!"

"I was not stealing!" Amaya cried. "Maybe you should learn to control your foul temper and not always jump to conclusions!"

Silence fell as they both glared at each other for a few moments. His eyes flashed with rage as he regarded her and she thought maybe he was going to do or say something else but eventually he simply turned away and poured himself some more liquor with his free hand.

Amaya went back to tending his wound, using the herbs that Valerian had placed on the table, and then she stepped away from him and quietly left the room without another word, closing the door gently behind her even though she was tempted to slam it just to spite him.

He was still the king and she was still scared of him and his temper and what he could do, even if he had seemed to give in to her just now. Even if he had saved her life in the forest. She was still stuck in this castle as a prisoner and she didn't want to give him more reasons to throw her back into a cage.

When she left the king's room, Valerian was waiting at the end of the hall and he turned towards her.

Unbeknownst to Amaya, he had heard every word she and his father had exchanged in the room, and he was amused beyond belief. However, he hid it well, planning to keep it in until he could tell Aurelia or Camellia all about it later on.

"So. How is his prognosis, *doctor?*" He asked teasingly, using the word he knew most of the humans on the isle seemed to prefer over 'healer'.

It actually made a smile tug at her lips as she half rolled her eyes at him. "I do believe he will live."

"That was nice of you." He said a moment later, not mentioning how strange he found it that his father had even allowed any of it to happen. "I know you are uncomfortable here."

"Not uncomfortable... just stuck." Amaya murmured, trailing her fingertips over the intricate pattern on the wall as she walked down the hallway with him. "But I suppose everybody is."

"What do you mean?" He wondered, looking at her curiously.

She immediately felt as if she had overstepped. She felt strangely comfortable in Valerian's presence and had forgotten that he was the prince for a moment. That Thalian was his father. "I, uh, nothing. Please... forget it."

Valerian stopped, reaching to gently place a hand on her arm. He shook his head, his expression gentle. "You can tell me, you know. You can *trust* me."

With a sigh, she shrugged. "I don't know!" She exclaimed softly, because she truly felt as though she knew nothing anymore. "I just... forgive me, but your father, he is... horrible! Are you and the others not just... trapped here with him as much as I am? This whole castle feels cursed."

Her outburst was met with silence and dread instantly began to writhe like worms in her stomach as she felt like she had made a serious mistake.

However, Valerian simply sighed and shook his head. "I know he can seem difficult and hot-headed but he is a *good* king, he is a good *person*." He wished he could explain it to her fully but there wasn't really any way that he could do so. There was no way she would ever understand. Amaya didn't know any of them well enough and as nice as she was to him and Aurelia and Myleth and everyone else, he wasn't sure that she actually trusted anybody here or believed a word they said. For which he couldn't blame her in the slightest.

"I swear to you, he means no harm. Despite some of his actions... some of his words." He gave her a slightly pointed look before continuing to lead her down the hallway. "Believe me. Nobody is trapped here."

Amaya was quiet for a minute, coming to a stop outside the room she had previously been given. "Except me." She murmured, catching Valerian looking at her sadly. "I am not to be locked back in the dungeons?" She then ventured, eyeing the door of the room. Though the king hadn't actually given any verbal instructions to that effect, she was sure he could have given the order with but a simple look.

Valerian chuckled softly, shaking his head. "No." He smiled at her, lifting her hand and pressing a light kiss to the back of it. "Sleep well. You have had quite a day."

Then he took his leave and Amaya turned away, noting the guard was firmly back in place as she pushed open the door to her room with a heavy sigh.

However, a sudden commotion at the end of the hall had her turning again. Aurelia had come rushing up the corridor looking for the prince.

"Valerian!" She cried, forgetting titles in her rush, brows knitted together in concern. "It is the king! He has fallen!"

~

Thalian had been pouring himself another drink when it had happened. He had left it too long and the venom had worked its way through his system quicker than he had expected it to.

He had indulged Amaya's little hero complex but intended, after she was gone, to use the correct herbs and a little of his own magic to help dispel the poison from his wound. However, the poison took him quicker than he had thought it would and before he knew it, he was unconscious.

Doronion had rushed in from his place outside the room, alerted by the smashing of glass as Thalian knocked liquor bottles and goblets off the table when he fell.

The king's butler had been stricken with worry and had immediately called for help before moving to pull Thalian up off the floor and onto the bed.

"Get the prince!" He shouted as a guard came in to see what all the fuss was about. "And send for a healer!"

The guard in question had run headfirst into Aurelia, who took it upon herself to get Valerian while the guard made for the healer's chambers.

Without so much as a second's hesitation, Valerian took off back towards his father's room.

Amaya found herself following on some kind of autopilot and the guard posted outside her room did not even try to stop her. Indeed, he himself was too caught up in reaching the king's quarters.

When she got there, Amaya lingered in the doorway, peering in as best she could past the bodies of healers and guards all rushing to assist. Her mind was racing with confusion. He had been fine, had he not? She had *just* left him! He had been his usual arrogant, angry self but physically he had been fine. At least, he had seemed fine.

She could see that Valerian was worried and, as she watched all of the elves running around tending to their king, she could see the looks of concern written upon all of their faces too. She didn't think they could fake it that well. Indeed, there would be no reason to fake it at all with Thalian unconscious.

Did they truly *care* for the Elf King? Why?

She didn't have much time to dwell on it as the chaos around her continued.

Healers flitted around the bed, inspecting the king's wounds, the same wounds Amaya had tended to not even ten minutes ago. Would the blame for this fall upon her?

Fear coursed through her at the thought and she wondered if she should once more try and run for it while everyone was distracted. However, her feet stayed rooted to the spot as she hovered in the doorway of Thalian's bedchamber.

Amaya heard various conversations happening at once as orders were thrown around but what stuck out to her the most was that the wound on his shoulder had been full of venom and the venom was quickly working its way through his system.

She felt something she couldn't name pull at her from within as she stood wringing her hands together. She hadn't known! If she had known she wouldn't have even been able to do anything. She didn't have any experience with venom.

Had Thalian known? Surely not. Right? He surely would have gone to his healers, he would have been more forceful in throwing her out of the room... or at least he would have told her what to do for a venomous wound. Wouldn't he?

"I didn't know." Amaya said, reaching out to catch Valerian's arm as he passed by her on his way back out of the room. He was momentarily startled, not having known she was even there. "I'm sorry."

Valerian's gaze softened. "It is not your fault." He told her simply. "My father should have acted quicker."

"He knew?" Amaya wondered aloud, looking from Valerian to the king lying out on the bed, surrounded by healers and guards.

The prince nodded, following her gaze towards his stubborn father. "Yes. He will have. He would have been able to feel it."

"Then why-?" Amaya cried, frowning as she looked back up at him. "Why did he not say anything? He sat there and allowed me... I should not have pushed so hard!"

Valerian, truthfully, didn't know why his father had sat there and allowed Amaya to continue tending him as he had. It was a mystery that he wasn't sure he would ever get the answer for but he was quick to shake his head again, looking down at the human in front of him.

"If my father truly did not want to allow you to continue then you would not have had the chance." He told her firmly, knowing it to be the truth. He couldn't explain to her why but he knew that Thalian would have dragged her from the room himself if he truly hadn't been inclined to allow it to continue. His father had reacted much more violently over much less. "Do not blame yourself." He told her, giving her hand a reassuring squeeze before he turned and left to go and tell his sister what had happened.

~

The rest of the night passed slowly and Amaya eventually wandered back to her room, lying on the bed and thinking back over the events that had transpired that day.

She still grieved her chance of escape but she knew that she wouldn't have been able to leave King Thalian in the woods injured. And now that she knew he'd been exposed to venom she found that she was actually glad not to have fled.

As terrified as he'd made her, as badly as he'd scared and hurt her, that wasn't who she was at her core. He saved her life out there when he could have let her die and be rid of his problem once and for all and it seemed that she had returned the favour.

Not that that thought gave her much hope for him deciding to set her free out of the 'goodness of his heart', but still.

Eventually, she drifted off into a light sleep, rising late the next afternoon. When she sat up she noticed a tray of food by the door - breakfast - and figured that Myleth had been in and had taken care not to wake her.

Amaya smiled to herself, moving over to nibble at some of the fruit on the tray before she got washed and dressed and then hesitantly cracked open the door of her room.

The guard was still standing outside but he turned his head towards her when the door opened and nodded to her. He made no objection and didn't try to stop her when she stepped out of the room and started down the hall.

Amaya wasn't planning to run away this time. She was looking for Myleth or perhaps Valerian. Still, she kept glancing back over her shoulder and giving the guard a confused little look until she turned the corner and he was out of sight.

The guard watched Amaya go, having been told overnight by Valerian to allow her the freedom to leave but he'd been kept there at his post in case the king recovered enough to take notice.

He hadn't.

Awake

"You should have heard her, Aurelia!" Valerian insisted, grinning as his friend looked back at him with disbelieving eyes.

His father would recover, he had been told that morning, but he might not wake for another night or two at the most. It was just a waiting game and Valerian was relieved that Thalian was not gravely injured.

Aurelia had joined him that afternoon for lunch and he had finally regaled her with the story of Amaya and Thalian in his father's room when she had tended to his injuries. He told her of the back and forth between the two, the way Amaya hadn't held her tongue when Thalian challenged her.

Aurelia just shook her head, unable to picture it. Surely he would have thrown the human girl straight back in the dungeons if she had said even half of that to his face!

She said this out loud, watching Valerian laugh, seemingly unable to explain it himself but adamant that it had happened. Aurelia was more than a little stunned but Valerian seemed kind of overjoyed about it and that fact made her smile.

"Well, I don't believe it." An elf piped in from Aurelia's side.

The prince turned to look at him, quirking an amused brow. "Come on, Elion!" He chuckled, giving the other elf a look of amusement. "Have I ever lied to you?"

"Well, there was that time when you were a child and you told me you *hadn't* set foot in the armoury and sent every piece of weaponry crashing to the floor even though Harlynn *saw* you sneaking out of the room, but–"

"Oh, come on! Still holding onto that after all these years?" Valerian laughed.

Elion sniffed. "Well, you weren't the one who had to clean it up, my prince."

"I keep telling you, my father would not have cut your hand off if he had seen it before you managed to get it all tidied."

"Well, that is easy for you to say."

Aurelia sniggered, lifting her hand to try and smother the sound behind a cough but Elion caught it and shot her a withering look.

Valerian was laughing again. "Regardless! My childhood is long behind me and this is very much true."

Their conversation was cut short as the door opened and the three of them turned their heads to see Amaya walking into the dining hall, arm in arm with Myleth.

~

Back in the village, Amaya's father was frantic.

He had spent the time since being home barely conscious since falling into his bed, recovering from his illness, but his strength had at last returned and so today he made his way to the local tavern. He all but crashed through the doors, silencing the room with a single action and turning many startled pairs of eyes his way.

"Ah, Gideon! We were beginning to think you had moved away, old man." A voice he knew well, belonging to a man named Vermund, called from the corner. "Come. Have a drink."

"There is no time!" Gideon cried, shaking his head as he stood at the door, his face twisted in panic.

He hadn't been able to calm himself since leaving his daughter with the elves, guilt and worry torturing his addled mind in every half-conscious moment he was able to find. He had been too weak and unwell to act before now and he knew for sure that he couldn't do anything to rescue Amaya alone.

"My daughter has been taken! Someone *must* help me! We have to go now!"

"How much have you had to drink today?" The man behind the bar asked with a laugh.

Vermund spoke up from his corner again. "What do you mean, taken?" His legs stretched out in front of him lazily as he lifted the ale in his hand and took a long drink.

Vermund was a well respected man in this town, a skilled hunter and warrior, but he was vain and superficial.

He had had his sights set on Amaya since he moved to this town from Whitehall years ago, finding her outward looks pleasing to him. It matched well with his own, he had decided, and he was adamant that she was the woman he was going to take as his wife. He had cornered her multiple times over the last few years, asking for her hand and she had managed to brush him off every time but Vermund was relentless. He refused to understand that the last thing she would ever want is to marry him.

Gideon turned his attention to Vermund, eyes full of his worry for her, for his only child. Vermund was a warrior. Surely if anyone could help it was him!

"She followed me into the forest! The elves! The king! He took her, he's holding her captive!"

"The Elf King..." Vermund gazed back at him, disbelief written all over his face, but he stood up all the same. He hadn't seen Amaya in a few days now that he thought about it and he was eager to find her again so that he could get his hands on her once and for all.

He glanced at his friend Oeric, who was sitting beside him, and held his arms out as he turned back to Gideon. "Well, hey. Lead the way, we will help you!" He wasn't sure that he truly believed Amaya was in the forest with the elves but he would go along with this for a time, just in case. It was a little odd, after all, that nobody had seen her sitting by the fountain or in the stables with one of her books the last while. Besides, he was willing to indulge her father a little, thinking it would be a good way to get the man on his side when he insisted upon Amaya's hand for the final time.

Oeric rolled his eyes, not wanting to leave his ale, but he dutifully stood up and followed Vermund and Gideon out of the tavern.

There was a brief pause before the three men started walking towards the town border, heading in the direction of the Golden Wood.

~

Amaya had found Myleth on her way down the corridor and the elf had greeted her like an old friend, linking their arms together like it was the most natural thing in the world and leading her to the dining hall.

The way she talked and her mere presence had a way of putting Amaya instantly at ease. She was quite possibly her favourite elf here, the prince a close second. The king, of course, was right down at the very bottom of the list.

Myleth steered Amaya to the table where Aurelia and Valerian were sitting. Harlynn drifted over to join her brother Elion soon after, and there followed a comfortable buzz of conversation as they all ate.

Amaya picked at the food, not feeling entirely hungry but she knew that she had to keep her strength up the best she could.

Valerian watched Amaya quietly for a few moments, studying her movements and her expression. He thought back to his father, the way she stood up to him, the way she had brought him back from the forest seriously injured even though it meant forfeiting her freedom once more. He also thought about the way Amaya had insisted on tending Thalian's wounds for him when the stubborn king had refused a healer. She hadn't had to do any of that and the fact that she had made Valerian believe her to be a woman of real integrity.

"So, Amaya." He finally spoke up, smiling at her. "What sort of things do you do? Back in your village?"

Everyone turned their attention to her, eyes full of apparent interest as they waited for her response.

Amaya was a little taken aback by the very genuine expressions she saw looking back at her. Did they truly want to know the answer? Why? She was almost as confused by their interest in her as she had been by their concern and worry for the king.

"Well." She began, having a sip of water before continuing on. "I helped my father run our farm. We grew crops and raised animals. That's where all of our trade came from. My father would ride out to the other two villages and sell our goods. But mostly... I just liked to read."

She spoke in the past tense, telling them what she *did*, whereas Valerian had asked her what she would *do,* as if she still had the chance to be there doing the things she normally did. She didn't comment on it but she certainly noticed it.

"You like reading?" Valerian smiled brightly. "Would you like me to arrange for some books to be brought to your room? I am sure you would like more things to pass your time with while you are here."

Eagerly, Amaya nodded, an excited smile instantly appearing on her face.

Books!

She had been going slightly stir crazy shut up in that room all the time with absolutely nothing but her thoughts to entertain her. She had been missing her books so much. Her stories and her knowledge.

"Yes please!" She said quickly, as if the offer would expire.

"Consider it done." Valerian grinned, nodding before he moved to stand.

Aurelia followed suit after nudging Elion who had whispered something in her ear that Amaya assumed was a joke of some kind. She briefly wondered if it was at her expense but she tried not to dwell upon it.

"I will see you later." Valerian took his leave, the black-haired female following him.

Eventually, Myleth stood and took her leave as well, needing to go and get some work done, and Elion and Harlynn drifted away soon after that, leaving Amaya alone. She felt quite awkward about this because she was a prisoner so why hadn't anyone escorted her back to her room?

Still, she reminded herself that the guard hadn't jumped on her when she left and Valerian hadn't seemed eager to chase her back upstairs. She wondered when the king would wake up and these small freedoms would once again be taken away.

For the next few hours, she entertained herself as she walked through the twisting hallways, taking in the wonder of the Golden Castle now that she seemingly had the time to properly savour it.

It truly was breathtaking. Amaya could never have thought up anything so intricate and beautiful in her wildest dreams. Large ornately carved doorways stood at the entrance to every room, little leaves and vines cut delicately into the wood. Huge embossed windows which let in plenty of natural light. Greenery at every windowsill and corner. It was truly a place of great beauty. Such a shame that it was so shrouded in darkness.

Eventually, Amaya headed back in the direction of her room, slipping inside with a sigh. Though when she spotted the little pile of books on the table, she brightened. Valerian had been true to his word and she moved over quickly, picking up the one at the very top of the pile and opening it.

It was a book of poetry and Amaya began devouring it page by page, eventually drifting off into the most peaceful slumber she had experienced since her arrival in this place.

~

When she opened her eyes again it was incredibly dark and she figured that it must now be quite late into the night.

The book she had been reading had fallen shut beside her, looking like it was just about to fall off onto the floor. She rescued it from its precarious position and swung her legs over the edge of the bed, sitting up and looking around the room.

There was a tray of bread, cheese, and fruit on the table by the door which told Amaya that Myleth had probably come along while she was sleeping again.

She stood up and walked over to the table, nibbling gratefully at some cheese as she took the time to fully wake up.

A short while later, Amaya found herself going a little stir crazy again. She wanted to read a bit more but she found that she also wanted a change of scenery. She wanted to stay out of the confines of this room as much as she could for however long she was going to be allowed to do so.

Venturing to the door, book in hand, she eased it open and peeked out. A guard was standing there still and her heart jumped into her throat out of instinct but they made no move to stop her as she took tentative steps out into the hall, gathering the courage to keep moving.

Amaya breathed a sigh of relief when she rounded the corner, her shoulders relaxing. Her sense of direction in this place was still not perfect but it was just nice to be able to roam freely. She wondered if Valerian had said something to the guard when his father had gotten injured but she couldn't figure out why he would have bothered. Or why he would care enough to do so.

She let her feet carry her without much conscious thought, briefly noticing how quiet it was as she once more admired all the architecture and the wall decor around the building.

When Amaya finally blinked herself fully back to the present moment she realised that she recognised the hallway she had found herself in... and the door she was now standing outside of.

This was the king's room.

She immediately turned, panicking as she realised where she had ended up, desperate to get away at once but then something within her caused her to hesitate.

Amaya eyed the door, curious to actually see how he was recovering. She hadn't seen him or asked about him since the venom took him. Nobody had told her anything either and she didn't blame them considering the fact that she had made her dislike of the king quite plain.

Hesitating momentarily before deciding to just do it, Amaya reached for the handle and eased the door open.

A healer inside the room who was checking on the king looked up in surprise but they didn't say anything after they recognised her. They finished up and eventually left her there without a word.

Inexplicably, she found herself moving to take a seat in the chair next to the bed. She told herself not to, told herself to just turn and go back out into the hall and get as far away from here as she could. Go and read her book somewhere quiet and forget about him.

For some reason, she didn't.

Staring at Thalian, Amaya shook her head slightly. He was such an idiot for getting himself into this position. And for what? His own hubris?

Sighing, her fingers pried opened the book and flicked through the pages. She told herself that she would stay here for another minute and then she would leave, maybe find somewhere pretty to sit and finish reading, perhaps beside a large window so she could pretend that she was outside.

However, she ended up perched there for quite a while.

When Valerian came to check on his father later, he found Amaya still sitting there, now actually reading aloud from the book in her hands. He was stunned as he watched her, his attention moving between the two of them before he eased the door closed again without Amaya ever knowing he was there. Then he hurried off to tell Camellia what he just witnessed with a sort of perplexed smile on his face.

Amaya's voice continued to fill the room with its soft melody as she read aloud from *The Verse of The Great Massacre*, an ancient rhyme about a terrible war in Amarar's history.

> "--and through Amarar, in days of old
> the legend of the wizard passed on--"

A second later, her head shot up as a voice suddenly interrupted the flow of her own, finishing the verse as if they had it memorised.

> "...across the lands, just as foretold,
> the evil that there was; now gone."

The book nearly dropped out of her hands altogether as she looked over at the bed, finding Thalian's eyes now open, his intense gaze fixed on her.

The Library

Thalian's eyes held Amaya in place as she stared back at him, finding herself both too scared and too enthralled to look away.

There was a softness in his gaze that she hadn't seen before, though it was so slight that she wondered if she was just imagining it.

She swallowed past the lump forming in her throat, doing her best to gain self control even as her thoughts floundered. "I'm sorry." She began. "I just-"

"Sorry for what?"

Truthfully, she didn't know quite what she was apologising for - being in here, or getting caught - and it showed plainly on her face if Thalian's briefly amused expression was anything to go by. Colour crept into her cheeks and she stood quickly from the chair, remembering to bow her head just slightly before she turned to the door. "I will leave you to rest."

"You like to read?" The king's voice came again, just as she was at the door reaching for the handle.

Turning around in surprise, Amaya nodded. "Uh, yes... I... actually, I love to read."

Thalian stared at her for a long moment, looking as though he were thinking very hard about something. She couldn't help but wonder what it was but then he was moving, pulling himself into a sitting position and swinging his legs over the side of the bed.

Her eyes widened as the sheets fell, bunching around his waist as he reached for a shirt on a nearby wall hook. He was undressed beneath the sheet and she took in his broad shoulders, eyes travelling down his torso as though outwith her control entirely.

His attention turned back to Amaya as he moved to stand. The sheet began to fall away from his body and she immediately forced herself into a spin, her cheeks suddenly feeling hot as she stood burning a hole into the wooden grain of the door.

She wasn't sure how many moments passed but eventually she became aware of Thalian's presence lingering in the space behind her. He reached out a hand and she visibly flinched, unable to stop herself.

Thalian hesitated at that, pulling his hand back and sucking in a soft breath which he released in a sigh. He had frightened her terribly, he knew that. He studied her for a second before he moved again, his fingers finally grasping the door handle and pulling it open.

"Follow me." He said, his face set into a neutral expression once more, stepping past her and out into the hall.

Clutching the book like a lifeline, she followed him, her legs suddenly feeling like they were full of lead. Was he going to lock her away again once and for all? He must be wondering what she had been doing in his room at all, especially unescorted.

The silence was deafening as Amaya trailed

after Thalian, keeping up with his long strides as best she could.

Everyone they passed in the hallways bowed to their king, glad to see him better, before continuing with their tasks. Amaya was either looked upon with mild curiosity or ignored altogether and she wasn't sure which one she preferred.

When she finally paid more attention to her surroundings than to Thalian's long legs ahead of her, she recognised the hallway they were in and came to an immediate halt.

Thalian continued to move, completely unaware for a few moments that she had stopped, before he realised that she was no longer behind him.

He turned, a flicker of irritation beginning to bubble up within him. Why did she always have to make things so difficult? He glowered at Amaya for a long moment before his eyes followed the girl's wide gaze and he finally understood what the problem was.

She was staring at the ruby red curtain at the bottom of the forbidden staircase.

Thalian's shoulders deflated and he bit back another sigh before he took two long strides back towards the girl.

"You have nothing to fear." He told her.

Amaya, on the other hand, felt like she actually had very much to fear. She was panicking beyond belief. Her mind had quickly convinced her that Thalian had brought her back here so he could finish what he started when he'd found her snooping around up there before running off into the forest. She had gone where she wasn't allowed to go and she was the reason he had gotten hurt by those dirroh in the first place. He probably couldn't wait another moment to punish her properly. He was going to shout at her, hurt her, lock her back up...

When his deep voice reached her ears, she tore her eyes away from the curtain and turned to look at him. Where she expected to see steel, she saw something a little softer in his expression (this time definitely real) and it surprised her so much that some of her panic instantly dissipated.

"Please." He said, gesturing behind him to a door that was hidden away, tucked right underneath the staircase. It was so easy to miss at first glance, Amaya hadn't even known it was there. "I only want to show you something."

After another long moment during which she hesitated, wondering whether she could run fast enough to hide from him, she nodded and took a step forward. She tilted her chin, doing her best to look like she wasn't scared in the slightest despite knowing that her reaction had already given it all away.

Thalian hid a smile at that, secretly thinking it quite admirable. Truthfully, he had felt a little guilty about what happened when he found Amaya up in those rooms. He had just been *so* angry.

When Thalian was angry about anything to

do with that room and the things in it he sometimes had a habit of acting before thinking. He knew this and everybody else in his kingdom knew this too. But not Amaya, of course. The topic of his wife and her fate and his grief was forbidden in this realm and had been since she died.

Still, he had scared the girl beyond what he had truly ever intended and he had put her in danger. He had immediately followed her trail into the woods that night in case she ran into any serutluv like she had on her way here.

Amaya was his prisoner, yes, but the elves of the Golden Castle treated their prisoners well enough. Contrary to what was now popular belief in the human villages, they were not savages.

He had been incredibly surprised when Amaya had not turned and fled with his horse after the dirroh were all slain, instead helping him return to the castle in one piece. He had been further surprised when she stormed after him into his bedchamber and insisted on personally tending his wounds.

He'd been furious with her that night but the guilt had already started to bubble its way slowly up to the surface so he had found himself indulging her... to his detriment, yes, but that was his own fault. It was not hers.

Waking up to Amaya at his bedside reading to him, however, was the thing that surprised him the most. Why she was there, he couldn't for the life of him figure out and he didn't plan to spend much time doing so. However, he decided she was probably deserving of a little kindness in return... especially if she was to be here for the rest of her life.

Thalian was not one for apologies, not really, so this was as close as Amaya would get for now. He pushed the door open and stepped into the room, waiting for the girl to follow him. He watched her face as she walked in, noting the way her eyes almost immediately lit up.

Thalian had led Amaya into the largest, most beautiful library she had ever seen in her entire life. The elaborately carved wooden shelves reached towards high ceilings embossed with a subtle floral texture, each one full to bursting with *books*. More books than Amaya had ever seen or would ever have hoped to see. She had only ever dreamed of being able to look upon so many books, let alone hope to ever read this many.

Her village had no real library and only the smallest selection of books was available to her. She had read and reread her sad little collection over and over, reliving the same stories and relearning the same information as the years passed.

Her father had traded for a new book every so often, when he left to sell their wares in the other villages, but that was all. What Amaya was looking upon right now was beyond her wildest dreams.

After a moment of staring, she remembered Thalian and turned back towards him. He was watching her and she suddenly felt a little embarrassed. She shook her head and gestured to the room. "This is... it's incredible."

Thalian inclined his head slightly, letting his gaze drift from Amaya as he looked around the room himself. His hands were clasped behind his back and he was standing tall, proud, every inch the king she remembered yet somehow not quite as harsh.

"You may use it as you see fit." He said, turning back just in time to see the surprised look on her face. "Come here whenever you wish."

Without another glance at her, Thalian turned and strode from the room, disappearing back out into the hall and down the corridor. The door clicked shut behind him and Amaya was left standing in stunned silence as she tried to make sense of what had just happened.

~

The next few days passed slowly but not uncomfortably as Amaya began to get used to her new normal.

A guard was no longer posted outside her room but she had heard that there were a few extra stationed at the castle entrance... which she supposed was expected considering how easily she had been able to slip out into the forest after the king found her in the forbidden rooms. She hoped none of the guards on duty that night had gotten into trouble on her account.

She spent plenty of time in the library that Thalian had taken her to. Amaya had been cautious at first, worried that it was all part of some elaborate ruse, however she had relaxed as the time passed and nothing bad happened.

She spent a lot of her time curled up in the corners of the library, lost in whatever book she had picked up that day, finding in between those pages a sense of solace and freedom for the first time since she found herself stuck in this place.

When Amaya was not in the library she was usually with Myleth or walking around the castle exploring. Tentatively, of course.

However, she had not actually seen the king since the night he allowed her access to the library and she thought that, with some more luck, she simply just wouldn't see him ever again.

Maybe he would forget all about her and she could blend into the background of his kingdom, living out the rest of her days in exactly the way she was now.

Despite it all, Amaya couldn't fully shake how... *nice* it had been of Thalian to allow her access to this lifeline of a room and, much to her own frustration, she found him to be a more regular thought in her mind than she would like.

~

Valerian had been in the forest for the last two days with Aurelia and the rest of their group, scouting to make sure there were no more dirroh lurking too close to the castle.

He felt better about leaving Amaya there

without him now that his father seemed to have relaxed a little since his recovery. He felt secure enough in the knowledge that Thalian wouldn't throw her in the dungeon again, at least.

Valerian was also pleased that his father had recovered from the venom, though the speed with which it had affected him worried the prince. Even a dirroh tribe leader did not usually take down a being as powerful as his father so swiftly. He could feel something in the air, some darkness that he could not see, and he couldn't help but wonder, for one of the few times in his life, about the world beyond this isle.

Still, things were better for now so Valerian could focus fully on his task of scouting the woods, keeping the border of their home safe. The group were travelling back to the castle and would hopefully return home by the end of the next night.

Aurelia turned to him during their final camp set up, the two of them having chosen to be first on watch while the others rested. "Do you think he is really going to keep her here forever?" She asked, having been working up the courage to get the words out.

Sometimes Aurelia didn't know quite how to take the king. She respected him as a ruler but she did not always agree with him. In fact, Aurelia found she more often than not *disagreed* with him but she was not in a position to disobey in the way Valerian could sometimes get away with.

The prince sighed, shrugging as he fiddled

thoughtfully with a stick between his fingers. "I have honestly given up trying to understand the inner workings of my father's mind." Though he did think that he was actually pretty good at understanding his father and his... complications. Far better than any other in the realm, except perhaps his sister. "I do not see him keeping her prisoner forever." He said after a pause. "It is not his way."

"He seemed to be pretty set on it." She couldn't help but mutter, gaining a look from Valerian but he always appreciated whatever Aurelia had to say to him. He liked that she didn't hold back simply because of who he was and that she wasn't afraid to speak her mind. "She does not deserve to be a prisoner *at all.*"

"Trust me, Aurelia. She will not be here forever." He assured her, though he found himself feeling ever so slightly sad about that fact. He had come to see Amaya as something close to a friend already.

Valerian liked the human and thought that she was a person of true kindness and strength. She had given her freedom for her father's and then she had given it again for his own.

Amaya had shown the Elf King kindness where nobody would have blamed her for not doing so. Many would probably even agree that Thalian did not deserve it.

Something about her actions had even seemed to get through to his father in some way, though he knew the king was loath to admit it.

Still, after being graced with hers he had shown his own kindness in return.

"Did you hear that?" Aurelia's voice pulled him back from his thoughts.

Valerian became alert again at once, the sound of various voices reaching his ears from a distance away.

Aurelia was already up on her feet and he gave her a firm nod before the two of them crept away from the camp to find the owners of the voices.

~

The library was quiet. Peaceful, even, as the night descended. The curtains at the large window were open but Amaya couldn't see much of the sky from where she sat. She wished she could go outside and sit under the stars but she knew she could not.

Sighing, she turned back to the book in her hands, quickly getting lost again in the pages. She had stayed quite late here tonight, not yet feeling able or ready to sleep. She had even missed dinner, choosing instead to continue to hide away in her beloved words.

When the door opened, Amaya jumped, startled by the sudden noise. Looking up, she expected to see Myleth having sought her out with a tray of food much like she had done the first night Amaya had come here. Instead, she met the king's steely gaze once more.

An array of emotions she could barely name instantly flooded through her as she stared at him. He stared back at her for a long moment before he finally walked towards her, setting a tray of food down on a nearby side table.

"A servant was on her way with this. Apparently you have not yet eaten despite the hour being so late."

He probably meant Myleth so Amaya just nodded, though wondered why he would now be here instead of her but she didn't dare question him. It almost felt like he was telling her off for skipping meals but she decided she was being ridiculous to even entertain the notion that he would care about something like that.

Amaya tentatively reached towards the tray and popped a berry into her mouth, wanting to look like she was grateful and not just completely confused and intimidated by his presence.

They were both quiet for another few seconds before Thalian started moving again, his long legs carrying him across the room.

Amaya's shoulders relaxed and she let out a tiny breath of relief.

However, he did not move back towards the door as she had expected and hoped. Instead he made his way towards a bookcase, plucked a book from the shelf, and moved to sprawl out in a large armchair nearby.

All Amaya could do was stare at him, wide eyed, as he studied the page of the book in his lap as though she no longer existed.

It seemed that he was intending to stay here. With her.

Swallowing down her unease, she forced her gaze away from him and back down to the book on her own lap, though she now found that she was completely unable to focus on anything at all, the words on the page as jumbled as the thoughts in her head.

~

"We have been in this damned forest for two days!" Oeric cried, kicking at a large tree root that was sticking up from the ground beneath his dirty boots.

He had followed Gideon and Vermund in here to look for Amaya, though he didn't particularly care whether she was in town or she wasn't. Still, he was one to blindly follow Vermund wherever he was told, never having it in him to say no to the other man.

"Come, Oeric. Keep your wits about you. We must be getting close." Vermund stated, though he was secretly frustrated himself as he eyed the back of Gideon's head in front of him.

"Keep my wits..." Oeric muttered darkly, scowling at the ground as he continued to put one foot in front of the other. He could barely see and his head felt all heavy, like some enormous weight was pressing down upon him, trying to make the earth beneath these trees his final resting place. "We'll be lucky if we last another night. We're running out of water. And food."

"Ah, there's a river somewhere, I'm pretty sure." Vermund said loudly over his shoulder as his large black boots crunched on the dead leaves littering the ground. "And berry bushes, if the tales are true."

Despite being a skilled hunter, he hadn't bothered to try and practise any stealth since coming into these woods, though he didn't really want to run into any of the creatures that might be lurking... or the elves, particularly. He was merely entertaining Gideon's apparent delusions for his own personal gain.

He was pretty certain that Amaya was not with the elves. From all the tales the village had heard about elves, Vermund knew they would not have let her father go if they'd had him. He was pretty sure Gideon was just losing his mind. He'd been cracking for years now in the eyes of the townspeople, and Amaya had been following in his footsteps with all her *thinking* and the things she read in those silly books. He'd be sure to knock that out of her when he finally found and married her.

Gideon, who had been frantically staring ahead of him trying to keep his mind steady and remember the way to the Golden Castle, came to a sudden halt and whipped around at the words that left the other man's mouth.

His memory took him back to the river he'd crossed and then the berry bush that he'd eaten from shortly before he felt like he'd lost his mind entirely.

"No!" He practically shouted. "Those berries are *cursed*, you must not eat them!" He insisted. "You will go mad!"

"Hey, hey. No need to shout, old man." Vermund held his hands up in mock defeat, really just wanting to strike the man across the face but that would only get in the way of his plans to take Amaya as his wife. "It is only berries, do not-"

"No!" Gideon shouted again, desperation in his eyes as he stepped forward and grabbed hold of the collar of Vermund's shirt to give him a shake. He had to make him understand that would only lead to madness! It had caused him to do things that he would never have done, things he sorely regretted.

"Get your hands-!" Vermund never finished his sentence because in the next instant an arrow appeared out of nowhere, aimed directly at his left eye and another pressed lightly against the back of Oeric's head.

~

The library was unbearably silent and Amaya kept shifting uncomfortably in her chair, fidgeting as she did her best to keep her eyes trained upon the book she was holding.

She had been entirely engrossed in it before Thalian had come into the room and she probably would still be if he had actually left her alone.

She knew that she could stand up and leave any time she liked (right?) but some part of her was determined not to give him the satisfaction of knowing she was uncomfortable in his presence.

He had allowed her access to this library and had let her wander fairly freely after returning to his castle but she still wasn't sure if she could actually trust him.

Amaya was having a terribly hard time matching up the arrogant, cruel king who she had first met, with the kindness that that very same being had shown her only days ago. Still, she registered with some surprise that she was no longer deathly afraid of him.

Thalian was watching her from the corner of his eye, though she would not have been able to tell. He was thoroughly amused by the way she seemed completely unable to sit still and, yes, he knew that his presence was unnerving her.

Truthfully, he couldn't have given a reason for his staying here if he had been asked. He wasn't sure if he would have been able to give a reason for his intercepting Myleth and the tray of food either. He could easily have allowed her to continue and deliver the meal to Amaya herself and the girl would have been none the wiser. So, as with all things that he could not or would not answer, he pushed it to the back of his mind and pretended it simply did not exist.

Eventually, Amaya could take it no longer and gave up the fight, closing the book and standing up to return it to the shelf where she'd found it.

Thalian didn't move a muscle as she moved

around, glancing at him just briefly. She hoped he didn't notice but he absolutely did, though the only movement he made was to lazily turn the page of the book in his hands.

Hesitating, Amaya eyed the food tray and decided that she shouldn't leave it there. It was something he might deem rude, even disrespectful. She wasn't here to live, she knew she was still technically a prisoner and even if that weren't the case, he likely viewed her as beneath even his lowest ranking staff member.

She leaned down and picked the tray up, careful as she turned around to make for the door. She didn't think she would be able to find her way back to the kitchens alone just yet so she decided she would take it to her room and Myleth could help her in the morning.

Once she was actually up on her feet, she was suddenly aware of just how tired she was and how late it must be.

Stifling a yawn was her undoing.

Before Amaya even knew what was happening, the tray slipped from her grasp and she felt her legs give out beneath her. She let out a curse, doing her best to try and steady herself before she hit the floor.

However she needn't have bothered because, not even a second after she started to go down, a strong arm was suddenly circling her waist and hauling her backwards while the contents of the tray scattered across the floor.

After a brief shock, Amaya looked up to

once more meet Thalian's stare, this time seeing what she could only describe as mirth shining in his eyes.

At least he doesn't look angry, she thought. With any luck, he wouldn't tell her off too badly for the tray. She felt her cheeks start to turn red with embarrassment as she looked at him, suddenly realising just how close he was actually holding her. When he'd caught her, her hands had come up to clutch his forearms and Amaya hadn't let go yet.

When she realised she was still gripping onto him and that too many seconds had passed to make it appropriate, she immediately let go and lowered her eyes.

Holding in a chuckle, Thalian released his hold on her. He stepped back and turned his head, surveying the mess. "Perhaps it would have been wiser for you to have retired for the night sooner?"

Biting her lip, Amaya willed her cheeks not to flush an even brighter red and turned in the direction of the mess. "I... I apologise, your maj--*my king.*" She quickly corrected herself in a panic, remembering his words to her in the throne room about manners. She did not need to give him any more reasons to hate her. She needed her life here to be as easy as it possibly could be. For somebody who was trapped against her will. "I will clean it immediately." She added quickly.

Thalian winced inwardly as he listened to her nervous rambling, though his face remained impassive as he studied the human before him.

He watched her move as if to bend down so

she could clean up the tray she had spilled but he stepped forward again, taking hold of her upper arm - *gently* - and pulling her back.

When Amaya looked up, he shook his head. "Somebody else will see to it." He told her. "You should rest." There was another silence as he let go and walked towards the door. When he reached it, he turned back to her. "I shall escort you to your room."

A Little Change

The walk down the hall from the library was one of the longest of Amaya's life as she tried to figure out whether or not the king had some ulterior motive.

Was he lulling her into a false sense of security? She couldn't come up with any reason why he would need to do that, other than the fact that she had built up such an image of him in her head that everything about him seemed to trigger paranoia. It was maddening but she focused on keeping herself upright on shaky legs as she trailed beside him in the direction of her room. No need for a repeat of the library, she thought.

"How many in your village can read?" Thalian asked after a long silence, turning his head so he could look at her.

The question took Amaya off guard and she looked up at him, eyebrows shooting up in surprise. "Uh." She shrugged and shook her head, grasping for words. "Not many."

"But you can." It was not a question. Thalian knew lots about the villages on the other side of the Golden Wood and hers in particular - Feardenn - was quite a poor one. Not many people prioritised learning to read and write and he was quite intrigued to find that Amaya was different.

Nodding, she clasped her hands in front of her, looking around at the grand architecture of the castle once more, unable to help herself. The magnificence of the place still overwhelmed her.

"Yes. My father taught me when I was small." Her expression fell slightly at the thought of her father. Amaya missed him. A lot.

Thalian sighed when she mentioned her father and she immediately took it negatively, turning to look at him with a frown. "My father is a good man." She said firmly.

"I said nothing to the contrary." Thalian replied, waving a dismissive hand.

"You did not need to!" Amaya said as she stopped walking. She stood there, half-glaring up at him as she watched him turn around, irritation clear in his eyes. She found that she didn't care. She loved her father, he was all she had and she was all he had.

Valerian had told Amaya he had not been in his right mind when he had stumbled upon this kingdom and she believed him. Her father was not at fault - he would never hurt anybody, not intentionally.

"How can you be so cold?" She heard herself saying.

"That is not how you address your king, *girl*." Thalian's voice had dropped considerably, a clear warning laced through his tone like ice.

Now *this* was the king Amaya recognised.

"I have a name, you know." She half-snapped in return.

Another silence fell over them both. Amaya was sure she could have heard a pin drop in that hallway as Thalian stared her down and she stared back, not wanting to give in to him. She had never met anyone more frustrating or more confusing in her entire life. How did he switch so rapidly from mean to kind and back again? Was it all false? A lie? It seemed very possible.

Thalian's face was as blank as a fresh sheet of parchment but his mind was working on overdrive. He was faced with the fact that Amaya was being outrageously disrespectful, to a king no less. Her - his *prisoner* - who he had *allowed* to roam freely in *his* kingdom!

He was also faced with the fact that he actually understood where this ire was coming from and hadn't he been *trying* to be nicer? To 'control his foul temper' as she had once so ineloquently put it?

He had been determined to, in his own way, make some sort of amends - show gratitude for what Amaya had done after the encounter with the beasts in the forest.

So why was she making it so difficult?

"You are right." Thalian said after another long moment of agonising silence, once more surprising her.

Her frown disappeared and she looked up at him in disbelief, having been anticipating an argument or for him to grab her arm like he'd done after finding her in those forbidden rooms.

Thalian said her name then and Amaya blinked, not having believed that he'd actually even known it.

"I apologise." And with that, he turned

away and continued down the hall towards the room she was staying in.

Amaya stood where she was for a second longer than necessary, staring dumbly at the back of his head, and then she forced herself to move.

Walking after him, she found the anger had gone out of her. Instead of continuing to glare at him, she simply eyed him with curiosity as they walked.

Finally coming to her room, she held in a sigh of relief, reaching for the door handle so she could let herself in. Her previous irritation at the Elf King had all but waned after his apology.

Apology!

Amaya could scarcely believe the words had actually left his mouth!

She turned to look at him once she had stepped through the doorway, to bid him goodnight in an attempt to keep hold of this civility, and found him studying her.

Thalian couldn't deny that he was curious. To himself, that is. If anyone were to ask him outright he would act as if it was the most ridiculous notion in the entire world.

He had been full of frustration and derision when his son had decided to take Amaya under his wing like a little mortal pet but he couldn't quite shake that there was something... he couldn't put his finger on it but he quite wanted to figure out what was bothering him so much about this girl.

"Meet me here after lunch on the morrow." He said before she could shut the door in his face.

"I wish to show you something."

Then, as usual, he turned without another word and left Amaya standing there, staring after him in a by now familiar confusion as he swept away.

~

Hours later, Gideon opened his eyes slowly, groaning at the sharp pain shooting through his head.

It was no longer dark. He could see the sky above him clearly as he rolled over and pulled himself upright. It appeared to be morning now.

Confused, he looked around, slowly coming to terms with his new surroundings. The grass beneath him, the trees at his back. The last thing he remembered was being *in* the very forest that he was now waking up beside.

What happened?

He stood and turned on shaky legs, peering through the treeline but he couldn't see anything.

Where had Vermund and Oeric gone? They had been with him, had they not?

It came back to him in flashes. The arrows had belonged to elves, one of which he had recognised as the one he had attacked when he had been captured and imprisoned.

Then what?

Then... darkness.

But the elves had been in his line of vision, because as soon as the arrows had appeared, he'd spun away from Vermund to the side so he could see them. The blow had come from Vermund himself, that was the only thing that made sense, right across the back of his head. Rendering him unconscious.

He turned, full of anger, and started off over the field. He recognised the way back to Feardenn from here.

He had not been able to retrieve Amaya, his mission failing, but he would try to get more help and he would return.

He *would* rescue his daughter.

Two pairs of eyes watched his shaky, angry retreat from just beyond the treeline.

Aurelia shook her head sadly as she watched the man go. At least he was physically alright but she had been worried for a while there that the blow to the head would prove to be too much. It had all happened so fast. The voices she and Valerian had gone off in search of had come from the three men and they'd easily been able to approach and sneak up on them without alerting the humans to their presence.

Valerian had recognised one as Gideon, Amaya's father, and it didn't take a genius to figure out what he was doing back in this forest. Coming for his daughter. Trying to 'save' her. Valerian would gladly have reassured him that his daughter was being cared for if it had not all kicked off quite so quickly.

The larger of the other two men had started swinging, but not at the elves. He had struck poor

Gideon over the head and pushed him directly into Aurelia, knocking her off balance. Neither of the two elves had expected the men to attack one of their own.

Vermund had drawn his sword and fought his way back, half using the other, smaller man as a shield.

Valerian had wanted to go after them but he had been torn when he realised that Amaya's father was actually unconscious and could be gravely injured. So he'd let them go, something he did not plan on telling his father.

The two of them had done for him what they could, Aurelia using a little bit of a healing mixture on his head wound, though unfortunately he would be left with dreadful pain.

"He will come back." Aurelia said, grabbing her bow and quiver of arrows as she readied herself for the return journey to the camp they had left.

"I know." Valerian shrugged, sighing as he moved to follow her. "He is reckless. He will not make it through the forest alone."

Plus, from the look of it, he did not have many true allies that he could rally together and bring with him. Valerian worried he would get himself killed. Amaya would be heartbroken.

"Come, Aurelia. The others will be wondering where we have gotten to."

"He is just scared for his only daughter." Aurelia added, walking ahead through the trees back towards the camp.

The detour to the humans had cost them

another delay in getting back to the castle. She was *so* ready to be back there after this gruelling patrol. She could not wait to be able to properly bathe.

Valerian simply hummed distractedly in response as he followed her through the trees.

~

As tired as Amaya had been back in the library, she still found herself unable to sleep for a good few hours, tossing and turning as the time crawled past.

She had never been so confused and frustrated in her entire life. It was the Elf King's doing, of course. She wasn't foolish enough not to realise that but she just simply could not figure him out.

One moment he was terrifying her, practically to tears. The next he was acting... she didn't even know what to call it. Nice. Kind. He even *apologised*. He said the words *'I apologise.'* Out loud! To her face!

Amaya tried not to think about it but she was a little anxious about the coming day. Scratch that. She was *a lot* anxious about the coming day.

Why did he want to see her after lunch? What was he going to show her? The last thing she was in the mood for was another argument but, truthfully, despite the ups and downs of his emotions she found herself almost... excited about it. Maybe excited was the wrong word, she didn't know. She was *something* about it and that would be as much as she would touch upon that for now.

Rolling onto her side, she squeezed her eyes shut and willed herself off to sleep, doing her very best *not* to think about Thalian's arms around her as he saved her from falling flat on her face in the library that evening.

~

The morning seemed to come far too quickly after Amaya had finally drifted off, Myleth waking her with a tray of breakfast as had become routine.

Her eyes opened slowly and she groaned, burrowing back beneath the thick blankets, gaining a chuckle from Myleth as the elf threw open the curtains.

"Come now, it's a beautiful day." She trilled, moving to pull some clothes from the small wardrobe and setting them on the edge of the bed. Where the new clothing had come from, Amaya wasn't sure at all but she had been grateful for it considering she had come here with only the clothes on her back.

Peeking out from the blankets, she huffed and threw them off. While it did seem to be a beautiful day outside, it was clearly freezing and she would much rather stay in bed.

Myleth chuckled again as she watched the girl move to the small adjoining washroom to freshen herself up, coming back to dress a short time later.

Myleth was now sitting in a chair across the room, nibbling one of the breakfast biscuits from the tray she had brought, and Amaya couldn't help the amused smile as she watched her.

"A little bird told me that the king escorted you to your room last night." Myleth said, causing the girl to drop the skirt that she had been admiring.

"What!" Amaya whipped around to look at her, eyes wide, unsure who could have seen and why it was even a big deal. Though she wasn't sure that it *wasn't* a big deal. For some reason, it sort of felt like one.

Myleth clapped her hands together with a short laugh. "Oh, it's true!" She said, sounding excited. "I was worried when he took your dinner tray from me and insisted on bringing it to you himself but I see no harm came from it at all!"

"It is no big thing." Amaya muttered, turning away to focus on dressing so the other wouldn't be able to see her face flushing.

"No big thing!" Myleth practically squealed, watching the back of Amaya's head curiously. "The king does not make a habit of walking everybody in the castle back to their rooms. Least of all those he insists are prisoners."

Amaya turned back to Myleth with a slightly stunned expression, shaking her head. "I do not think I like what you are implying!" She balled up her sleep shirt and threw it across the room at her. "Let's not make a big deal out of nothing."

Myleth held her hands up, amused, not put

out at all by the girl's shock. "Do not worry. I am simply gossiping."

Amaya knew by now that Myleth was most definitely considered a gossip around here but she hoped that this particular notion of hers would stay locked up tight in her head and not be gossiped about with anybody else.

Still, all through the rest of the day her own mind was completely distracted by it even as she tried to engage in conversation with the others, and she could not help but wonder...

The Roses

Lunch came and went and Amaya trailed back to her room, dragging her feet, the knot in her stomach a tangible weight.

She wasn't entirely sure what she was feeling but anxiety was definitely there. Quite a lot of it. Almost every time Amaya ended up in Thalian's presence they only ended up arguing and she was not in the mood for it.

When she rounded the corner to her room he was already there, standing looking up at a painting of the forest on the wall.

He turned towards her when she approached. He was wearing black slacks and a deep burgundy tunic. His hair fell free as usual and he wore no crown, no circlet upon his brow. He somehow looked both casual and regal all at the same time.

"Oh, my king, have I kept you waiting?" Amaya wondered, thinking she was late and already starting on a bad note. "I am sorry, forgive me."

A small smile graced his lips as he looked at her and shook his head. "Please." He lifted his hand and waved off the apology. "No. I admit, I was early."

Amaya did her best not to show it but she was confused by that. If anything, she had expected him to arrive late. She still couldn't figure out what he could possibly want to show her. Or why he would want to spend any time around her at all.

She was both curious and apprehensive considering her past interactions with the king.

She simply nodded and worked up a polite smile of her own in response, unsure what to say.

"Come. This way." Thalian said, all business again as he turned and swept along the corridor, leading her back the way she had just come.

There were more elves out and about in the halls today and the two of them were met with more than a few curious looks but Thalian paid them no heed as he strode along. He was used to being looked at.

When Amaya realised they were coming to the library, she started to form an idea in her mind. He must want to show her a specific book or something in there, surely. She felt herself relax as she fixed her gaze on the door that led to the library.

However, confusion immediately washed over her as Thalian veered away before he even reached it, hardly sparing the room a glance. The tension within her returned in full force as she watched him approach the staircase that led up to those forbidden rooms.

The king turned at the bottom of the steps and beckoned Amaya to him. "It is alright." His voice was soft and he did not seem angry so she found herself walking towards him and following as he turned again, passing the curtain and starting up the stairs.

The memory of her last time in this part of the castle flashed back into her mind as Amaya reached the top step.

Her eyes were drawn to that painting of the beautiful elven woman again, the one with the deep slash running through it.

She stopped, unable to help herself and Thalian turned, following her gaze to the portrait. If Amaya had been able to hear it, the way his heart was hammering away in his chest would have given away the heartache he kept hidden beneath his expression of steel.

She turned and caught him staring but he did not appear to have noticed her move yet. A second too late, he lowered his gaze from the portrait to her face and cleared his throat.

"My wife." He said simply and turned, walking quickly away from the painting. It was the first time he had looked upon it, upon her likeness, in many years. He avoided it despite coming up here often enough. He could handle her items, specific ones and specific parts of these rooms at least, but he found he could not always handle seeing *her*. He no longer felt like taking a dagger to it as he had those first few weeks after her passing, but his heart still shattered anew at the sight. The guilt was still far too much to bear.

His wife? Amaya stared at the back of his head, slightly dumbfounded for a moment, before she hurried after him.

Amaya had never thought of him having a wife, which she supposed was stupid when she thought of Valerian and Camellia's entire existence. They had to have come from somewhere. Elves did not just pop out of the ground...

Did they?

No.

Amaya didn't know a lot about elves but that made no sense. So... the Elf King had an Elf Queen? Amaya wondered why she had not met her, though she supposed meeting prisoners wasn't high on a queen's to-do list.

"These rooms and the items in them belong to her." Thalian added over his shoulder, not looking back as he led her past the room he had found her poking around in the night she had run away.

Amaya crossed her arms as she trailed after him. These were the queen's chambers? The forbidden rooms belonged to her? She supposed that put everyone warning her away from here, and his anger at finding her snooping around, into a little more perspective.

"My king, forgive me, but why am I here then?" She wondered, looking over her shoulder as if she were about to get caught and seized despite the fact the king himself was here with her. "I am sure your queen would not like the idea of a mere prisoner in her private rooms..." The word *again* did not pass her lips though it bounced around in her mind.

Thalian stopped moving.

Amaya paused too and stared once more at the back of his head, with which she was becoming very familiar.

He did not turn around.

"She is no longer with us." He murmured, his deep voice laced with sadness at having to speak the words.

Before Amaya could reply he was off again, leading her towards a large set of balcony doors.

He did not need to tell her in words that his wife was *dead*. The tone of his voice said it all and, as Amaya followed after him, she found herself feeling a little sad.

Her own mother had died when she was only a small baby and she had seen how the grief had chewed away at her father over the years. She was pretty sure that elves did not simply pass away as easily as humans and she couldn't help but wonder what had happened to her. Not that she would dare ask.

She walked through the doors and was pulled from her thoughts as she found herself on a large balcony overlooking a garden.

A garden!

To the left there was a set of stairs which Thalian moved towards, walking gracefully down them as Amaya followed like an obedient little puppy, though her attention was now completely captured by her surroundings.

The sun shone above them and there were trees and grass and a little pond and so many flowers. However, she was not allowed much time to linger on any one thing as Thalian led her to a very specific part of the small garden.

He gestured to a bench for Amaya to sit and

followed suit after she did, gesturing to the flowers that were blooming nearby.

They were clearly roses but they were somehow unlike any rose Amaya had ever seen before in her life. They were a beautiful, deep red colour but something about them seemed to shine like the stars in the night sky and she found herself utterly drawn to them. She began reaching a hand out towards one of the flowers.

Then, with a gasp, she quickly snatched her hand back again as the rose suddenly began to move of its own accord. She watched as it opened itself up fully, turning in her direction as if it knew she was there, as if it knew she had been about to touch it. It was almost as though the flower was *looking* at her.

Amaya glanced up at Thalian in surprise and found him watching her.

He couldn't help allowing himself the smallest of smiles, his gaze shifting back to the roses. His fingers brushed gently over the petals of one of the blooms and Amaya watched the flower move, almost shivering as it turned its stem towards Thalian.

"What are they?" Amaya asked in amazement.

"Starfire Roses. They are less merely simple flowers, more so little creatures in their own right." Thalian said softly, looking back up at her. "They were my wife's favourite. She adored them."

His eyes had softened as he spoke and Amaya found herself smiling as she watched his mind tread tentatively into the past.

"They have all but gone extinct in the world. These few could even be the very last of their kind in the whole of Amarar." He admitted, a soft frown creasing his brow.

"That's so sad." Amaya murmured, turning to look at the roses again and slowly reaching her hand back out, fingers ghosting the edges of one of the flowers. It opened up and turned towards her, almost nuzzling to get closer. They had to be the sweetest little things she had ever seen. She felt sad to think that they had almost gone extinct from this world.

"Yes." Thalian agreed, falling silent for a brief moment before he cleared his throat slightly. "I must confess something."

Amaya looked up at him expectantly but he had gone quiet again, frowning a little more deeply as he stared at the roses.

"What is it?" She eventually asked.

He looked back up at her. "These flowers are part of the reason your father was treated... quite so forcefully by me when he came to us."

"What do you mean?"

"Do you remember me telling you why he was imprisoned?" He asked.

Amaya blinked and nodded. "Um..." She didn't much like thinking of her first day in this castle but she could recall it clearly. "Breaking and entering... attacking Valerian... spying."

Thalian nodded, sighing. "I was not entirely honest."

Surprise, surprise, Amaya thought sarcastically but she had the good sense not to say it out loud. She merely sat and waited for him to continue.

"Your father did break into this kingdom, though it is still beyond my understanding how he managed such a feat in his state."

She assumed he was talking about the fact that her father had supposedly eaten some enchanted berries. She still did not understand it but there were many things beyond her village she did not understand.

"It was my belief that this side of the castle wall-" Thalian gestured behind them both to the wall that surrounded the garden. "-was kept very carefully guarded but apparently not that night."

He had his own suspicions that because the queen was dead that the guarding of her side of the castle had become quite lax, creating a gap for Amaya's father to slip past. This displeased him but Harlynn had assured the king that she would make it explicitly clear to the guards that it was not to happen again.

"He was found here. By these roses. He had ripped one from the soil, breaking its stem. Killing it." He frowned, his fingers dancing gently across the petals of one of the flowers again, watching it move. "Its petals blackened and all life faded away. He was found in the process of attempting to take another. Luckily, he was stopped."

Amaya was quiet, frowning to herself as her attention moved back and forth between Thalian and the roses. These roses that were more alive than any other flower or plant she had ever seen. These roses that the wife he'd lost had so loved. These roses that her father, in his apparent madness, had desecrated and attempted to steal away.

"I'm sorry." She whispered.

Thalian looked up at her again and shook his head. "It is not your doing."

"It might be." Amaya said, surprising him.

"What do you mean?" He asked, looking at her in confusion. She had not even been here then, after all.

"My father... when he leaves, goes to trade with other villages, he always brings me back something." Amaya told him, looking at the roses as they danced. "I always ask him for a book. Any book." A slight smile at the fond memory. "And he often brings one back... but he always brings me something else too. A rose." She looked up at Thalian with sad eyes. "I think... I think maybe he was so confused with whatever those berries did to him... that when he found his way in here and saw roses..."

"All his mind could think was that he wished to take one home to the beloved daughter who was waiting for him. Like he always does." Thalian's voice took over as he finished the thought. He sighed again, shaking his head. "I was angry. This place... these flowers..."

"I understand." Amaya said, before he could say any more. They were his wife's and his wife was... gone. It was so sad and she could see that he struggled with it. Maybe... maybe he acted in anger out of grief. Maybe that was a trigger.

Thalian looked at her quietly for a moment before offering her a gentle smile.

"I'm... I'm sorry I came up here." Amaya continued after a beat, swallowing down her anxiety. "That... that night."

Thalian's smile faded and she felt a pang of anxiety shoot through her but he simply shook his head. "I am sorry that I reacted as I did. I should not have hurt you. I should not have frightened you."

Surprisingly Amaya found that, as she thought about it now, she forgave him.

"What happened?" She asked suddenly. His look of confusion gave her pause as she second guessed herself but she continued anyway. "Your... your face."

Thalian's expression dropped, pain flashing in his eyes for just a second before he collected himself, the blank slate returning once more.

Amaya regretted asking immediately and shook her head, opening her mouth to take it back, maybe even beg his forgiveness but Thalian was already talking.

"Long ago... there was a war. A terrible war. The Great Massacre, they called it." He took in a breath then, steeling himself against the memories. "I faced down some terrible foes... but I was distracted." He did not say it was the sight of his queen falling to her knees, blood pooling from a deep wound in her chest, that drew his attention for he just could not form the words. "They split my flesh so badly and so deeply that it could not be fully stitched back together. I learned how to use my powers to conceal it. Most do not have the stomach to bear witness."

Her eyes widened as she stared at him. *"You fought in the Great Massacre?"* That was a thousand years ago! Amaya knew that elves lived long, long lives but she had never truly given it a lot of thought. For the first time, she wondered just how old he actually was.

Thalian nodded, pain creeping back into his expression as he thought back to that day. That dreadful, awful, painful day. "Yes. I faced down the Dark Wizard's foul creations. The grath."

The history of the world was known by most, if not all, of course. Amaya had actually read many books with first-hand accounts of the war in them and she recalled the details now; the multitude of deaths, the Dark Wizard himself, the grath - the vicious, deadly beasts he had created.

Her heart filled with pity for the king as she looked at him, stitching everything she had just learned about him together, weaving a newer image of him in her mind.

"Show me again?" She ventured, the words slipping past her lips before she could stop them.

Thalian's eyes snapped back up to her face, staring at her in complete shock. He had not intended to show her the first time. It was a complete accident brought on by his intense anger.

It had been brought about by a severe loss of control and he had felt completely shamed by her reaction to seeing it. The fear in her eyes. The *horror*.

"I cannot, I..."

"Please." Amaya whispered, not even sure why she was pushing this.

She thought back to that night. The way he'd grabbed her. The dangerous sound of his voice. The way the wounds on his face had revealed themselves. She had thought him a monster but looking at him and listening to him now, Amaya wasn't so sure that was true.

He hesitated for a long time before he finally inclined his head, lowering his gaze from her face so he did not have to see the shock and disgust that would surely be written all over it. Then he allowed the glamour that concealed his wounds from the world to drop, the perfect pale skin melting away to reveal the terror beneath. Deep gouges where his skin used to be allowed her glimpses of the fat and muscle beneath, the whole canvas of his face angry and painful looking. However, it did not seem to cause him much physical pain and Amaya could not figure out how such an injury would even heal to that point. It seemed even elves, with all the advanced magic they possessed, could not regrow or cover skin.

She watched, breath hitching as the magic faded away. This time however, instead of fear and dread, she found herself filled with sorrow and compassion.

She reached out, almost as if she were going to touch his face but she was quick to stop herself, drawing her hand back and cringing at her own mistake. That would have been so far over the line. Still, Amaya did not feel that words would be quite enough.

Her hand moved again, reaching out to gently cover one of his own.

Thalian's head jolted back up in shock, his eyes locking on her face. What he saw written in her expression this time could have floored him.

How Amaya could even stand to touch him looking like this was beyond him. He stared back at her, committing the look on her face to memory, this time not seeing one trace of disgust and it surprised him more than he could ever put into words. He also felt the stirrings of something else that he couldn't quite put a name to.

The king carefully allowed the glamour to slip back into place and offered Amaya a small, tight smile.

She withdrew her hand and smiled back, cheeks flushing slightly as she turned her attention back to the roses.

She watched them quietly for a long while as Thalian did the same with her.

Today, it seemed, they had both given each other much to think about.

~

A while later, Thalian walked Amaya back

through the halls of the castle to her room (after a brief stop at the library to grab a book for the night, of course, though she doubted she would be able to concentrate.)

It was much more comfortable now, being in his presence, though she was still concerned that he could turn on her at any moment. Still, she thought that she understood him a lot more now than she did before and it made her feel better.

Thalian opened the door and Amaya stepped into the room, turning to bid him goodnight.

"Take dinner with me tomorrow." He said, before Amaya could close the door on him.

She blinked up at him in surprise, thinking back to the night Valerian had asked her to dine with him and his father, and the argument that had ensued between Amaya and Thalian when he ordered her to comply and she outright refused.

"This..." He added, looking at her with the smallest ghost of a smirk on his face, as he too was thinking back over that same moment. "...*is* a request, *not* an order."

Amaya couldn't help but laugh at that, strangely pleased when his smile brightened just a little at the sound. "Yes, of course." She told him, deciding that after today she would not mind at all.

"Good. I will see you then." He inclined his head to her before he straightened his shoulders and turned to leave her to her thoughts.

Steps Forward

Myleth had been waiting impatiently to ask Amaya how her afternoon with the king had gone the previous day. She had come to find her at dinner but the girl had fallen into a deep sleep a short while after Thalian had returned her to her room, so Myleth had left her to rest.

The next morning, however, the elf maid shook her awake early, simply unable to wait any longer.

She had been watching much more closely than Amaya had even realised and had gotten it into her head that something with the king had changed since the human girl arrived.

Just like Valerian, she had picked up on... *something*. Something was changing and it certainly did not feel like a bad thing.

Myleth admired her king. He was good to his people. He cared about his realm, even the forest beyond and everything in it.

Over the years, she had watched him shut himself off but everybody in this kingdom knew about the king's past. They knew about the loss of their queen and the darkness that descended not only over the realm but the very halls of the castle itself.

Things were not as they once were and the elves of the Golden Isle were quite a lot more isolated than they used to be many long years ago. She knew most wished for those days to return, even the prince who could not fully recall them.

Amaya crawled from beneath the blankets, rubbing at her tired eyes as Myleth woke her with a tray of toasted bread and jasmine tea, which she had never drank before but was incredibly floral and sweet. It soothed her inside and out and she was soon wide awake and readying herself for the day ahead.

Myleth's questioning both amused and embarrassed her in turn but what made her flush bright red was the excited squeal the elf let out when Amaya told her that she had been invited to dine with the king that evening and that, this time, she had agreed to go.

She stared at Myleth with wide eyes, shaking her head slightly. The she-elf only chuckled back, waving a hand.

"We must find you something to wear." She said, moving to the little wardrobe in the corner and rifling through it. A moment later, she huffed, finding nothing there that satisfied her.

"I could just wear that." Amaya gestured to the first thing that she saw, some drab looking dress, shrugging as she turned to continue fixing her hair for the day ahead before picking up a piece of the toasted bread and turning back to Myleth.

The other female was looking back at her as if she had suddenly sprouted an extra head. "You cannot wear *that* to dinner with the king!" She exclaimed, before she waved Amaya off and made for the door. "I will find you something suitable and be back in time to help you get ready."

Before Amaya could say anything more,

Myleth was gone. She shook her head at the big deal the other was making over this entire thing. Then she turned and picked up the book she had grabbed from the library the previous night and finally opened it to start reading. After her day with the king, Amaya most definitely had not had the attention span to take in a single word the night before and she intended to make up for lost time now.

~

Myleth, true to her word, returned an hour before dinner. She found Amaya still tucked up on a chair, now many chapters into the book. She had spent the whole day devouring it to keep her mind occupied, becoming so wrapped up in it that she had even forgotten to go to lunch.

As much as Amaya herself was trying to not make it out to be a big thing, she had to admit that she was nervous. Valerian had not returned from his patrol in the woods yet, and apparently Camellia mostly ate alone, so it would just be her and the king and, even with how well yesterday seemed to have gone, Amaya was still unsure exactly what to expect. Things could switch up at any moment, she had learned that already, but she found herself hoping that it didn't.

The dress Myleth returned with looked far too grand, too expensive. Amaya had never worn such an item of clothing in her life. Truthfully, she didn't think she had even *seen* such an item of clothing in her life. It was the type of fabric that only the incredibly rich could afford and wear, at least where she came from.

The little farm where she lived with her father didn't pull enough silver to provide as much necessary food some seasons, never mind pretty dresses.

Myleth helped her dress and then sat her down so she could put a few braids into her hair. Amaya usually just let it fall how it wanted, wild and messy, or tied the curls back with a ribbon, and she wondered if maybe too much effort might be going into one dinner.

Still, she reminded herself that he was a king - of elves no less - and he probably had certain expectations. What did Amaya know about dining with royalty, after all?

Just as Myleth's magic fingers ceased working on her hair there was a knock at the door and it opened to reveal Doronion standing there.

"I have been sent by King Thalian to fetch you for dinner." He told Amaya, smiling kindly at her.

Myleth pulled her to her feet and practically pushed her out of the door and down the hall. The nerves she had been pushing down suddenly came crashing down upon her in full force.

Amaya glanced over her shoulder at Myleth as she followed Doronion in the direction of the royal chambers.

Seeing her nervous expression, Myleth gave her a reassuring smile before she scurried off to find

Elion to tell him all about this new development.

~

Thalian turned when the door to the dining room that he shared with his children opened, greeted by the sight of Doronion bowing and announcing that he had brought his guest for dinner.

The king saw something pass Amaya's expression at the word 'guest' and he knew it was probably because she was now confused about her role here in his kingdom, having come as a prisoner, but he was quickly distracted from these thoughts by the sight of her.

His eyes took in her dress and her hair and the nervous expression that she was doing her very best to hide. He could not recall the last time he had thought a mortal beautiful but that was the word that echoed in his mind when he saw her.

True to form, Thalian recovered quickly, collecting himself and dismissing Doronion with a nod of gratitude and a brief word about checking on Camellia before he turned back to Amaya.

"I am pleased you could make it." He gestured to the seat near him, indicating that she should sit.

Amaya was curious as to whatever it was she had seen flickering in Thalian's gaze when she'd walked in but it had passed too quickly for her to really study it and maybe she had simply imagined it after all.

She sat down, ignoring his choice of words, as if she would have been busy or something. Amaya was his prisoner, she was always available... though it did feel recently that she was being treated more like a guest than a prisoner. Had been for a little while, she supposed, and she didn't feel totally trapped anymore. Though she still longed for the outside. And to see her father again.

Banishing those thoughts from her mind before the melancholy could settle upon her shoulders once more, she offered him a smile, reaching for the drink that was placed in front of her by a servant before they left the room to fetch the meal Thalian had called for.

"Thank you for inviting me." Amaya said politely. The events of the previous day were still filling her thoughts and she felt a slightly warm feeling coursing through her as she looked at him over the rim of her chalice.

"Did you get the chance to start that book?" He asked, slender fingers closing around the stem of his own goblet as he brought it to his lips, the sweet wine warming his very blood.

Amaya looked at him, a little surprised that he had even cared to remember she had grabbed a book before retiring the previous evening and even more surprised that he had thought to ask.

"Uh, yes... though I will admit I did not get around to it until this very morning." She told him, glancing down at the table briefly. She felt embarrassed but unable to pinpoint the exact reason for it. Maybe she did not want him to figure out that she had been thinking about *him* instead and had found herself unable to concentrate on reading.

Thalian said nothing about it, merely smiled at her and turned his attention to the food that had appeared thanks to the servants, who scuttled off through a curtain again, leaving their king with his unusual dinner guest.

The meal passed as the two of them settled into a conversation that was surprisingly comfortable and far easier than Amaya would have expected it to be. Neither of them talked about the previous day but she asked him about the library, if he had really read *all* of those books and he chuckled at her amazement when he told her that he had indeed.

"I have never even seen that many books, let alone read a fraction of the amount you have in that one room!" Amaya told him.

"Well, I expect you shall work your way through them quickly enough." He smiled, refilling his wine. "You are quite the voracious reader."

She smiled, taking another bite of her dinner. She hadn't been aware he had been paying that much attention to notice just how much she liked to read. He had seemed incredibly interested in the fact that she read at all from the first moment he'd seen her with the book in her hand, reading out loud as he awoke from his toxic slumber.

"I am far more used to being ridiculed, not encouraged." Amaya admitted out loud, the words slipping out before she could really stop them.

Thalian looked at her curiously for a moment. "Why is that?"

Amaya looked back at him with a little shrug. "The people in my village… they think me strange." She felt embarrassed to admit it out loud to him and usually she could brush it off but it was true what they say - if you are told something often enough you are usually inclined to start believing it.

"Strange?"

She nodded. "Mostly because I read, or at least that is the main reason they give. Because of my ideas and my thoughts… my mind is always travelling so far from home, from what is right in front of my nose, and they don't like it. Don't like that I 'waste my time' in silly stories and on expanding my knowledge. I don't know… they just think I am odd, I have heard them. Whispering and laughing." The only things Amaya really missed about the village was her father and her farm, most of the other people in it were no great loss to her. "I once tried to teach some of the village children to read a few words and I was practically chased out of the square and threatened to never try again." She shook her head. "The men think I get too many ideas in my head and that is not good. For a woman. Especially just a foolish farmgirl. You know."

But Thalian shook his head because he truly did not know. He held no such beliefs that the womenfolk should not engage in things such as arts and bettering themselves, taking part in things they simply enjoyed. He did not even believe that only the men should be the ones defending and fighting, Aurelia and Harlynn being prime examples of such.

"Your village sounds rather terrible." He said.

"It is almost as lonely there as it seems to be in your castle." Amaya replied without really thinking and then she looked at him with slightly wide eyes. "I... sorry..."

Thalian didn't say anything, simply moved past her slip, steering the conversation elsewhere but the truth was... it *was* lonely. *He* was lonely.

It had not always been this way. He hadn't always been this way. But the tragedies of his long life had only added up. While some may have come out the other side of such bitter loss, Thalian did not seem to fare quite the same.

He shut himself off and he shut the rest of the world out. He even kept his own son and daughter at arms length at times which he sorely regretted but it felt like too much time had passed and he could not go back and change it. Not any of it.

However, he could not dwell on it. It would do him and his people no good at all.

After dinner, Thalian led Amaya through the winding corridors back to her room and bid her goodnight, leaving her to her thoughts once more.

Myleth had passed them both in the corridor on the way and she had given Amaya a secret little smile that caused the poor girl to practically blush right down to her toes.

Thalian acted like he did not notice, keeping his gaze straight ahead as he walked but Amaya felt like he must have.

Indeed, he did notice, both Myleth's look and Amaya's blush. For some reason, the sight made him smile to himself on the brisk walk back to his own room.

Something There

The next day, on her way to the dining hall for lunch, Amaya was surprised to find Thalian walking towards her.

"Ah!" He came to a stop in front of her. "I had hoped to catch you before you left your room."

"Is something the matter?" She asked, slightly concerned.

"No, no." In truth, he was a little frazzled due to having expected Valerian and the others back that very morning but there had yet been no sign of their return. Still, he knew that it was too early to fear the worst. There were all sorts of possible reasons for a delay. "I was wondering if you would like to have lunch with me. In my garden." He paused before hurriedly adding. "I thought that perhaps you might be missing the fresh air."

Amaya was quite taken aback but she was quick to recover, nodding as she worked up a smile. "That... that sounds lovely! Thank you. Uh, my king." She added, remembering herself in her excitement.

"Please." He said, turning and gesturing for her to follow him along the corridors in the direction of his private gardens. "You may call me Thalian."

Her footsteps faltered at these words and she stared at the back of his head for a long moment in disbelief. A bewildered smile tugged at the corners of her mouth as she forced her feet to move again, following after him as he disappeared through the doorway that led to his own chambers.

With his back to Amaya, it was easy to conceal his own amused smirk as he fought the urge to turn and see the look on her face.

~

Thalian's garden was nothing short of beautiful.

Amaya followed him through the hallways towards his private rooms and into the little outdoor area that he called his own.

There was once a time when Thalian had walked for hours through the Golden Wood as the sun trickled through the leaves overhead, caressing his skin. Now, the wood was much too full of nasty dirroh and serutluv to enjoy it fully. You could hardly let your guard down for a second. The enchantment upon it, however, had no effect on the elves, for the magic that strove to keep others out of the Golden Wood was of Thalian's own making. He had cast it many years ago now, wishing to keep the other folk who dwelled on the Golden Isle away from his kingdom.

While he had shut himself away inside these walls this space was a lifesaver for him. Thalian, as all elves do, needed the outdoors. The sun and the stars. The trees and the flowers. The animals and the air.

Amaya followed him over to a large tree where, on the grass beneath the branches, there was a small meal set out to greet the two of them.

He settled himself gracefully and Amaya followed, watching him curiously though she did her best not to be too obvious about it. Did he really mean for her to call him by his name? It felt too intimate somehow. As if they were *friends*. Though she had to admit that she was feeling much more comfortable in his presence lately.

She felt as though she somehow understood the king a lot more now than she had before. Amaya understood and she even found that she *cared*.

The two of them passed lunch making light conversation. Amaya asked him questions about his kingdom and about elves in general and he answered, enjoying the eager way she ate up the information. She was so curious about elves and it was quite endearing to him.

Returning the favour, Amaya told him of the rumours that had passed round her village about the elves who lived beyond the Golden Wood, from the kidnapping of humans and keeping them as slaves, to the dark magic that they supposedly cast upon the beings around them. The men said they bewitched their women, some even saying they murdered their children and used their bones for their dark spells.

Thalian was quite horrified, having never really heard quite so many disturbingly untrue things about his race before. He knew that men and elves were very different and he knew that he had shut his kingdom off to them and gained quite the reputation but this bordered well on the extreme.

"I must say, I have been insulted in a lot of ways but this most certainly might be quite high up on the list." He said, shaking his head. If anybody was likely to do those sorts of things, it was mortals themselves, or dark witches, not elves.

Amaya couldn't help but laugh when he said that he had been insulted in many ways, able to believe that quite readily.

He seemed to know what she was laughing at and couldn't resist shooting her an amused smirk as he lifted his cup to take a sip before the frown returned.

"These people in your village." He continued, thinking back to their conversation over dinner the previous night coupled with what she had just told him. "They are awfully small minded."

Amaya found herself nodding, humming in agreement as she popped a grape into her mouth. "And I have not yet even told you about Vermund!" She exclaimed, unable to fully suppress the shudder that ran through her.

Thalian raised an eyebrow, curious as he watched her. "Who is Vermund?" He wondered, pouring himself a little more of the sweet honey mead provided with lunch.

"He is a hunter. He's a rich man and he is very respected back home but... oh, he is an awful, awful person." Amaya muttered darkly, scrunching her nose as she thought back over the years since he had come to the village. "The worst thing is that he continually tries to practically force me to wed him!" Her tone made her displeasure clear as day. Amaya simply could not imagine being the wife of that boorish oaf. "He does not take no for an answer. And trust me, he has heard it plenty."

Thalian frowned at that, studying her face for rather a long moment. "This man. Has he harmed you?" He found himself asking, watching her very carefully.

He did his best to keep his tone level but there was a bite to it and, as Amaya lifted her gaze, she could swear she saw something flicker in his expression. Anger? Maybe but she found that she was not scared by it. It was not directed towards her.

She shook her head. "No, no." She assured him quickly. Luckily, Vermund had never been alone with Amaya long enough for anything like what Thalian seemed to be implying and Amaya would have liked to think that he would not go to such lengths... but truthfully, if anybody was going to take what was not theirs, it would be Vermund.

Thalian relaxed a little, though the change was so slight in general that Amaya didn't really notice.

Having a little sip of her own mead, reminding herself to not overdo the alcohol, Amaya continued on. "He is simply insistent that he wishes me to be *his*. He is just so shallow, so vain. He has never read a book in his life. I don't think he had ever even *seen* one until he met me." There was a brief pause as a memory came upon her. "Do you know, he once ripped the pages out of my favourite story! Ruined the entire book, I have not been able to read it again since!"

"Which one?" Thalian asked, curious.

"It was the story of Nymeria." Amaya replied after a beat, focusing a little too intently on the food in front of her. She was a little embarrassed to admit it to him.

It was a beautiful story about one of the merfolk who fell in love with a human man and they fought against all the odds to be together. When he died, rather than outliving him for many hundreds of years, Nymeria surrendered her own life to the sea from whence she came. Despite the tragedy, Amaya found the romance aspect beautiful. It was not often that races mingled in such a way, some even holding onto prejudices against others, and thus the story had passed into something of a legend.

"Anyway." She continued quickly. "If I hadn't hated him before then, that would have certainly done it."

Thalian smiled slightly at the look on her face. "Well, thankfully, you do not have to see that dreadful man ever again."

As the seconds passed and the silence grew thicker, he realised that he had probably said the wrong thing. He hadn't meant it quite how it had sounded, not really. He hadn't meant to once more confirm her status as a prisoner. He didn't know what to say to remedy the situation so he simply... didn't say anything.

Amaya did her best not to look too unhappy. It *was* a good thing that she wouldn't see Vermund again, she agreed with that, but it just reminded her that she was not truly free and she never really would be again.

When the two of them had finished lunch, Thalian took Amaya on a tour around his gardens and then back into the castle before returning her to her room once more.

He surprised her by sending for her once more that very same evening, to join him again for dinner, which she did quite gladly.

The next day, this routine continued on quite naturally and the two of them fell into it happily enough.

At one point, Myleth and Elion watched from a window high above as Amaya sat in the garden with Thalian, both of them simply enjoying being in each other's silent company as they sat engrossed in different books.

Myleth gave Elion a nudge which he returned with a wide grin before they turned and left Amaya and Thalian to the rest of their afternoon.

This was a surprising development indeed.

Realisation

Late the following day, Valerian and Aurelia arrived back at the castle, the rest of their group in tow.

After they left Gideon to make his way home, they had expected to return to the realm the previous night. However, a surprise dirroh attack waylaid them for another evening. If they had not detoured to follow those voices they might not have caught this tribe for a long time. The delay was a good thing in the end and they cleared the spot of the creatures entirely but by this point everybody was exhausted and cold and beyond ready to be home. Winter was passing quickly but Valerian could tell that there was still snow on the way and he wouldn't like to get stuck out in it.

He walked Aurelia to her room and left her to clean up and rest before going off in search of his father.

His first stop, the hall where the king held court, proved - much to his surprise - to be a dead end. It was getting late, a few hours past lunch, and he wondered why his father would not be back taking care of business as usual. He was normally always so prompt and quite rigid in his schedule.

"Myleth!" Valerian called when he spotted her walking down the corridor towards the kitchens. "Do you happen to know where my father is?"

Myleth nodded and flashed him a smile but there was a look in her eyes that he couldn't quite place.

"Oh, he is still taking lunch, my prince." She told him with a little bow of her head before hurrying off around the corner.

Valerian watched her go with a frown and then turned on his heel to head for the royal quarters, moving directly to the dining room he shared with his father and sister. He thought it a little odd that Thalian would still be there at this time of day but he was the king and he supposed he could do as he wished. Perhaps today's workload had been extra stressful.

When he pushed open the door and stepped into the room, the last thing Valerian expected was to find his father sitting at the table, laughing over his chalice at something Amaya had apparently said to him.

The sight of Amaya at the table at all, chuckling along with his father, caused Valerian to stop and stare dumbly at the scene as if he couldn't quite comprehend it.

It was as though the two of them didn't even notice him for a minute, too lost in whatever had been so hilarious. When Thalian eventually looked up he offered his son a small smile, though his relief at Valerian's return was obvious to the prince.

"Ah! You are back. Pray tell, why the delay?" He inquired, not bothering to explain Amaya's presence, acting as though it were a perfectly normal occurrence. Which, to Amaya and himself, it was much closer to that now than it had been when Valerian first left for the forest.

"Uh." The prince floundered briefly before he regained control of himself and filled his father in on their rounds, telling him about the dirroh ambush and leaving out the three humans in the forest that he had allowed to run off uncaptured.

Thalian nodded, finishing the rest of his tea in a single gulp and moving to stand from the table. "I am afraid I must now take my leave." He said to Amaya, offering an apologetic smile. "I think I have tarried too long and neglected my duties."

"I certainly did not wish to keep you from your important business, my king."

He stopped mid step and gave her a look which Valerian could not decipher but which made Amaya look at him with a gentle, slightly embarrassed smile.

"Thalian." She acquiesced, though it still felt a little strange on her tongue.

Thalian raised his eyebrows, giving Amaya a satisfied smile before he turned and strode out of the room, leaving her alone with his rather confused son.

The last the prince had been aware of, the girl had simply been allowed access to a library and his father no longer wanted to chain her up in the cells.

Amaya put down her now empty cup and looked back up at Valerian. He had turned from his father's retreat and was watching her with a half-confused, half-amused glint in his eye. "Well, I am pleased to see that you have kept yourself busy while I have not been here to entertain you." He watched her blush slightly as he moved to sit down opposite her, leaning across the table with sparkling eyes. "It would appear we have much to catch up on."

He was beyond intrigued at the situation he had walked back in on. He hadn't expected Amaya and his father to be quite as close as they had looked when he came into the room.

He wondered just how much he had missed and found himself almost wishing he could have been here to witness such a miracle as his father befriending the human he had been so utterly annoyed to see Valerian doing the same with.

It was most amusing, as was Amaya's apparent embarrassment as he watched her squirm under his gaze. She stumbled over her words, telling him how his father had explained some things to her and invited her to spend time with him.

She left out a few details, not wanting to let go of every one of her little moments with Thalian, like some of the things that he had said in the queen's garden or the way he had looked when he showed her his old scars again. Some things were just for them alone, as much as she wasn't fully sure yet just *why* she wanted to hold these moments so close.

Valerian listened with rapt attention, picking at some of the food that was still sitting out on the table. He couldn't help feeling just the slightest bit smug about the whole thing. He had *known* that if his father just gave it a chance, he would see that there was so much more to Amaya and that there was so much more to the world beyond their kingdom that was not all bad.

There was *good* out there that could shine brighter than even the intensity with which his father focused on *evil*. It was not as black and white as the king always seemed to believe.

"I daresay you *have* been busy." He chuckled, watching her cheeks flush. "I should thank you. I feel your company has distracted my father from what would have been a terrible amount of strain due to my late return."

He chose his words carefully because he knew his father's fear for his safety would have come out as anger and Gods help the poor servants who would have found themselves on the end of it this time.

Amaya smiled a little, shrugging as she set her now empty tea cup back down on the table. "I don't need gratitude, my prince. As I was told not so long ago... the king is not quite as bad as he might appear."

Valerian smiled back, a playful look on his face. "If you are able to call said king by his given name, I must insist that you do the same for me."

~

Amaya spent the rest of the day wandering the halls, much more acquainted with the winding corridors of the Golden Castle than she had been when she first arrived.

She just loved the architecture of the place. It was absolutely beautiful, with its tall ivy-covered pillars and intricately carved ceilings.

As much as Amaya missed roaming free outside, not being confined to one small space was manageable and she was starting to feel as if she could deal with it. As if she could see out the rest of her days here as well as could be expected.

A moment later, she saw Camellia walking down the hall towards her.

The princess made a beeline for Amaya when she noticed her and she gave her a smile, which the girl returned easily. Amaya liked Camellia. Despite not having spent quite as much time with her as she had with others, she had been nothing but kind to her, just like her brother, though she seemed far more reserved than Valerian.

"Not in the library today?" Camellia inquired, falling into step beside her.

Amaya shook her head, slightly amused as it seemed that was now what she was known for, even amongst those she didn't interact with as often. She had always been 'that girl with the books' but it felt a lot better here than it had in her village. There was no derision in anybody's eyes here when it was brought up.

"I will be later on, don't worry." She laughed. "I just felt like taking a walk."

"Do you mind if I join you for a moment?"

Camellia asked and Amaya shook her head quickly because of course she didn't mind.

Truthfully, Amaya had never really had many friends before. Maybe one or two girls back in her village over the years but it never lasted for very long. The whispering about her would always prove too much for them sooner or later. Being associated with her as a friend didn't seem to be a good thing and so she would always find herself alone again.

Well, not alone, not truly. Amaya had her books, after all, along with her father and the animals on their farm. But still. Somehow, here in this place where she had started out as nothing but a prisoner, she felt that she had *friends*.

Myleth felt like a friend. Valerian felt like a friend. Even Thalian himself was now starting to feel like something close to a friend.

The two walked for a while, talking easily enough together. Amaya filled the princess in on some of the things she'd missed while being absent at lunch. Despite sharing the royal dining area with her father and brother, Camellia rarely took a meal there, preferring to dine alone in her bedroom, or in her own garden.

Camellia had been surprised, too, by the developing affinity between her father and the human girl. She loved her father very much but there was a little more strain in their relationship than there was in his relationship with her brother. He was a complicated figure and seeing him befriend a human after so many years of warnings and isolation had never been in her mind as a possibility.

She was pulled out of her thoughts by Amaya suddenly asking something about her and Doronion. Heat rushed to the tips of her ears as Amaya wondered whether or not the two of them were *together*. How the girl had even gleaned anything between her and Doronion was beyond the princess, she had not thought Amaya was paying that much attention to her comings and goings. Yes, there was something there, between her and Doronion, but it was not to be.

"He is my father's butler." She said simply, though Amaya could practically see her squirming inside. "He does a lot for my family, that is all. Besides..." A soft frown found its way onto her face before the next words seemed to slip unbidden from her lips, almost in a whisper. "Father would never allow..."

It was Amaya's turn to frown at that, the implication of Camellia's words not lost on her. "What do you mean?" She exclaimed, unable to help herself. "Why not?"

She couldn't fathom any reason at all. Camellia was beautiful, kind and courageous, a princess, the king's only daughter. The king would be lucky if she and his butler became more than just friends.

"He is a servant." She said simply, turning to Amaya and seeing the confusion in her eyes. "He is low born and he has... well, he has fae lineage somewhere in his line. His blood is not pure, he is not fully elven" Camellia explained. "He is not suitable."

"But..." Amaya shook her head. "He has a respected position here. Thalian *likes* him. He is important to the realm. He is high enough, surely, and you and Doronion... get on very well." He was a servant, yes, but... it could be allowed, if Thalian were so inclined.

The princess shrugged. "It does not matter. It is just not how things are. He is not a suitable match."

Amaya stopped walking. "Should a suitable match not depend entirely upon feelings?" Surely the king had loved his own wife and gotten to choose her for himself and would not have loved her any less if she'd had mixed blood, so why should his daughter be any different?

Camellia turned towards her, watching her curiously as she wondered why the girl appeared to be so upset about this. She shrugged again, having resigned herself to it by now. Doronion was her friend and that was all. "It is alright."

But Amaya would not be so easily quelled as she quickly shook her head. "No, it isn't!"

Amaya had always been quite the hopeless romantic. Her father said it came from her books, the way she devoured tales of lovers coming together to beat whatever odds were stacked against them, but Amaya knew it also came from the way he had always spoken about her mother. She believed in love and thought it was one of the most precious and powerful things in this world.

To deny it for any reason, especially one so silly, was such a foreign concept to her. It simply felt wrong.

"Do not trouble your mind about it." Camellia said kindly, reaching out to put a hand on her arm with a small smile. She could tell something about it was upsetting the girl even though she could not fully understand. "I have to go and find my brother. I will see you later."

~

When Thalian was finally free of bothersome meetings and paperwork he found his feet leading him in the direction of the library again. It wasn't an entirely conscious decision as his legs seemed to pull him there of their own accord but he did not spend a great deal of time dwelling on it.

When he came to the door he pushed inside, finding Amaya curled up in a corner. However, he immediately sensed a tension as he moved into the room, curiosity as to the cause stirring within him.

Amaya was frowning at the pages of the book that she had not been able to concentrate on all evening, her frustration only growing with each passing moment. However she had no real idea why she was so unfocused. She could not piece together why her mind was so distracted and why she was feeling so irritable when she had been practically on cloud nine after lunch.

Thalian moved to seat himself in one of the chairs, watching her for a moment as he randomly plucked a thick tome from the shelf next to him.

"Enjoying your book?" He asked a moment later. Thoughts of asking how the rest of her day had gone disappeared as her frown seemed to deepen at the sound of his voice.

"Not particularly." Was all she said.

She didn't look up at him, though he immediately dismissed any thoughts about why this bothered him.

He eyed Amaya for a moment, thinking that perhaps she was still having a difficult time with being trapped in the castle. He knew it probably would not just disappear, though he hoped that she would come to feel more at home here with time.

"Perhaps you wish to join me on a walk? The fresh air may do you some good."

"I do not think you need to trouble yourself with what might do me good, my king." Amaya said, standing up and ignoring the way he blinked back at her in bewilderment. "If you will excuse me, I am tired."

Without another word she turned and walked from the room, this time leaving Thalian staring after her in confusion instead of the other way around, grappling to understand what had caused this change in such a short few hours.

~

Her feet carried her on autopilot through the winding hallways back to her room.

Her prison, she thought bitterly, though she reminded herself that not long ago she had started to change her view on that.

Amaya wanted nothing more than to turn around and go back into the library and apologise because, truly, she did not even really know what had come over her.

She had been in a strange mood ever since her conversation with Camellia but she had not stopped to allow herself time to properly think it over, to figure out what about it had actually set her off.

Amaya pushed the door to her room open and stepped inside, feeling her heart sink into her shoes as she suddenly wondered if Thalian would now punish her for her insolence.

Sighing, she turned to go and change out of her day clothes, ready to just pass out and forget this whole evening but she spotted something from the corner of her eye and paused.

Sitting in the middle of her bed there was a package waiting for her.

Amaya sat down on the edge of the bed and carefully unwrapped it. Her nimble fingers pulled back the covering and revealed a book, but not just any old book. It was beautiful, a stunningly embellished cover binding the pages together. It was gorgeous, perhaps the most beautiful copy of any book she had ever seen in her life. It looked expensive. When she investigated further, she could have sworn her heart was about to beat right out of her chest.

It was, unmistakably, the story of Nymeria.

Her favourite tale. The one Vermund had completely ruined. The one Amaya hadn't been able to get another copy of since. The one she thought she might never read again for the rest of her days. The one Amaya had told Thalian about only two days ago during lunch.

Tears began to blur her vision as the realisation of what she was beginning to feel started to descend upon her like a heavy snowfall.

If Doronion was so lowly and beneath Thalian for his own daughter despite all of his overwhelmingly positive qualities and their closeness... what must he think of *her?*

~

Thalian had left the library not too long after Amaya, stalking his way through the halls towards his bedchamber.

He found himself irritated by her sudden foul mood and he could not fathom what had caused it. Undoubtedly *him* but he could not think of a single thing that he had done this time.

Had he not treated her with kindness? Been generous? Allowed her freedoms he probably should not have? Indulged her in ways he would not have indulged many others?

He was annoyed because he had grown to enjoy her company and to be left in such a manner irked him when all he had wanted after the long day of dull meetings and paperwork was to spend time with her.

What could have changed in the hours since lunch? He had not even been in her presence to do or say anything wrong!

Valerian was walking to his own chamber at the same time when he caught sight of his father as he rounded the corner. The prince's smile vanished when he saw the look on the king's face and he wondered what had happened. He had heard no talk of beasts creeping from beneath the canopy of the wood so he did not think it was related to border patrols.

As much as he wished to slip into his room and hide from whatever might have drawn his father's ire this time he stood firm and waited for the older elf to reach him.

"Something the matter, father?" He wondered, watching Thalian look up as if he had only just noticed his presence.

"I am *fine.*" Thalian growled in return, sweeping past his son in search of his strongest wine.

"How utterly convincing..." Valerian muttered to himself, though there was no doubt Thalian had heard him if the venomous look he gave his son when he followed him into the room was anything to go by.

"Father." Valerian said again, softer this time and he watched Thalian's shoulders sag slightly in response to his pleading tone.

"It is that girl." He muttered darkly.

Valerian frowned at the way he was back to not calling Amaya by name. Mere hours ago the two of them had looked to be the best of friends and he was confused by the sudden turnaround. However, as he studied his father's expression, Valerian realised that he too was confused. He was hiding it, of course, but Valerian could see it. Valerian could always see it.

"What happened?" He asked, deciding to tread this road with caution and care, not for the first time wishing that he could just peek into his father's head.

"I do not know." Thalian said, staring at the wall with a deep frown as he turned his own bemusement over and over in his mind.

The prince opened his mouth but then closed it, unsure what to say because he didn't quite know what his father meant.

"What do you mean you do not know?" He asked eventually.

"I *mean* that I *do not know!*" Thalian barked, rolling his eyes in frustration.

His wrath was not really directed at his son, more so at the situation as a whole. At the fact that he could not figure out what he had done this time to upset Amaya - and over the frustrating reality that this even mattered to him at all.

Thalian sighed, softening just a little as he downed the wine he had poured himself and set the goblet back down on the table. "I have obviously done something to upset her but I do not know what that could possibly be."

Valerian blinked, staring at his father for a long moment before he opened his mouth to speak, though was interrupted by his sister's quiet voice from behind him.

"You did not think to ask her?"

Both Thalian and Valerian turned, not having heard Camellia sneak up on them. She was like a ghost. She stood leaning in the doorway, her soft eyes fixed on her father.

Thalian blinked, an incredulous expression spreading across his face, staring at Camellia as if she had just started barking like a hound. "*Ask* her?"

Valerian turned back to Thalian, fighting very hard not to let even the tiniest hint of amusement bleed into his expression. His father's face was an absolute picture. For all his wisdom, the thought had not even crossed his mind.

"Well, yes." Camellia replied. "Simply *ask* her if you have done something to upset her."

"And *if* you have, I am sure you can find a way to remedy it." Valerian added, offering Thalian a little smile. "I will see you in the morning." He turned and walked past his sister, sharing with her one of those secret looks in the way that siblings often did in regards to their parents.

She stayed for a few more seconds, gazing thoughtfully back at her father, before she smiled at him and then disappeared down the hallway in the direction of the door that led to her own rooms.

Thalian watched them go, his eyebrows

knitted together. He thought back to the way Amaya had left the library without so much as a glance at him, making it obvious that she had no desire to be around him and that he must have done something to upset her.

It had not crossed his mind to follow her and *ask* what he had done. He had simply stormed away to stew alone in his own anger as he always did.

He stayed standing there for a long while, lost in thought, before he sighed heavily and turned to sweep out of the room and back down the hallway.

He would never find rest if he did not figure this out.

~

Amaya didn't know why this had upset her so much. It wasn't like she had... *feelings* for him! So why would it matter to her if he thought Doronion was too lowly for his daughter? If he thought *she* was just a lowly human?

Staring at the book she was still holding, she couldn't help the warm feeling spreading through her at the thought of him remembering this was her favourite story, of him seeing her upset at the memory of Vermund ruining her only copy, and of him seeking this obviously expensive edition out and gifting it to her.

That meant he saw her as a friend, right? That he valued her company? That he listened to her? That he... cared?

Amaya felt guilt beginning to gnaw away at her as she realised that she had probably completely overreacted to nothing and lost the one thing that had started to mean something to her in this dark and lonely, albeit beautiful, place.

Just as she thought this, the sound of a knock at the door caused her to jump. She heard her name from out in the hallway in the distinct baritone of Thalian's voice.

A brief spark of fear shot through her veins as her mind jumped immediately to the thought that he might be here to dole out a punishment for her behaviour.

"Come in." She heard herself saying despite her worry, watching the door as it opened and Thalian stepped into the room.

He was silent for a long moment as he moved over to the window, standing there staring out into the night. When he turned back to Amaya she couldn't decipher the look on his face. He still did not speak just yet, simply studied her for another few suffocating seconds.

It was a few seconds too long and Amaya suddenly couldn't take it anymore. "I'm sorry." She blurted out quickly, looking down at the book with a little sigh.

Thalian followed her gaze, his own softening just slightly as he recalled the day she had told him about the book. He sighed. "I thought perhaps it was me who should be apologising to you."

Her head snapped up to look at him and she frowned. "Why?" She wondered, confused.

Thalian merely shrugged in response. "Well, I was rather hoping that you would tell me." He scanned her face, trying to read her like one would so easily read a book. "There must be some reason for your hasty departure from the library this evening." *From me*, the words sat unspoken in his mind.

Amaya realised that he thought that he had done something to upset her and she paused. Had he? He had not said the words about Camellia and Doronion to her himself, she had not even asked him about any of it. She had gone around asking questions and if she did not like the answers, was it really his fault?

"No." She shook her head, sighing again as she looked up at him. "*I* apologise, truly. It was nothing. You have done nothing. I was simply in a bad mood... some days I find myself tiring of the same hallways and the same rooms. It's nothing, I promise. I overreacted."

Telling him the truth might prompt him to question *why* Amaya was so upset about it and she still genuinely could not fully come up with any words that could explain why it did.

Thalian was quiet again as he regarded her for a moment longer. "I see."

He moved away from the window towards Amaya and for a moment she thought he might be about to reach for her hand but he didn't. He looked at the book on the bed beside her and then back up at her face.

"Tomorrow we shall take lunch with a different view." He told her, though did not offer up further explanation.

Thalian then gave Amaya a small smile before he turned and pushed back out of the room, leaving her staring at the empty space he had just occupied as he so often seemed to do.

Into The Wood

The next afternoon, Thalian readied himself and strode down the corridor to Amaya's room to fetch her.

He was still feeling quite unsure about yesterday's... well, it was not an argument but he did not entirely know what else to call it. Still, Amaya said it was no big deal and he decided to believe her.

He did feel bad, keeping her locked away as it were, despite the fact that she had willingly given up her own freedom for her father's crimes. Suddenly going from being allowed to roam wherever you pleased to being shut away would be hard on anybody.

Today, instead of simply lunching in the dining area or the garden, he planned to take her on a ride through the safest part of the forest. He decided to put his trust in the fact that she would not simply run off at the first opportunity. Not that she would get far if she tried, but regardless.

He made his way through the corridors towards her room, passing Elion on the way and falling into step with him to discuss some matters relating to an upcoming festival.

Elion soon took his leave, scurrying over to Myleth who had just left Amaya's room. Thalian eyed the pair for a moment, aware of some sort of shared secret look passing between them but he quickly moved it to the back of his mind. It concerned him not.

Knocking at the door, he awaited her voice allowing him entry and then pushed it open. He had asked Myleth to ready Amaya suitably for riding and she had done as asked, eliciting a nod of approval from him as his eyes took the girl in.

She looked back at him, feeling much better than she had yesterday. She decided that a good sleep had been just what she must have needed after all.

"Afternoon." She greeted him with a polite smile.

"Good afternoon. You look well." Thalian smiled in return, gesturing for her to follow him.

He led Amaya back down the hall and out a door she had never noticed until now. A winding path adjacent to the courtyard brought the two of them to a large stable and she brightened considerably as her gaze roamed the many steeds standing there, chewing hay and neighing softly.

What her eyes fell upon next, however, drew a loud gasp of surprise from her lips.

The biggest deer that she had ever seen stood in the very end stall, contentedly passing the afternoon with the other mounts - made up of a selection of horses and other deer. This particular deer, however, had somehow grown many feet above its peers, far larger than should normally be possible for an animal of its species. Its antlers stood large and proud like an intricate crown atop its head and its hide was distinctly patterned with creamy white splotches against its red-brown coat.

It somehow looked... royal.

When the animal noticed Thalian its entire posture shifted. It seemed to straighten up before Amaya's very eyes, stamping its hooves in excitement. Then she could have sworn it *bowed* before the king. The beast seemed to fully brighten up at the mere sight of him.

Thalian couldn't hide his smile as he stepped away from Amaya and over to the majestic creature, pulling an apple from somewhere deep in his coat pocket and holding it out to his steadfast companion, who took it happily, greedily wolfing the fruit down.

Amaya stared at the deer with wide eyes, having never seen anything so huge in her entire life. Thalian turned back to her with a smile as he noticed the way she was looking upon the animal.

"His name is Agnar." He told her, studying the wonder in her expression. "He has been by my side for many years."

"How is he so... big?" She wondered aloud, her eyes practically glued to Agnar.

Thalian shrugged, looking back at the deer as if he barely noticed the animal's size anymore. "It is normal, for one of his lineage. He is a king of deer, you see."

"Deer have kings?"

Thalian chuckled. "In a sense. Let's just say he has royal parentage." He stroked the animal again. "But he prefers to dwell here these days, not the forest. I cannot blame him... though he much enjoys riding with me through the safe paths."

Amaya tore her gaze from the beautiful creature and turned her awestruck eyes to the king himself. "You... you ride him?" She asked, stunned.

Agnar was *huge*, and yes elves were generally fairly tall, the king towering above her even now, and yet it was still such a wonder to her.

Thalian nodded, amused by her surprise. "Yes. He is my most faithful friend." He reached up to run his fingers down over the deer's snout, his smile growing as Agnar showed his appreciation of the gesture by stamping his front foot.

"You may ride with me." Thalian said, glancing at her before gesturing to the many other animals in the stables. "Or you may choose a steed more to your own liking."

He didn't wish for Amaya to be afraid, after all. Most people worried about mounting such a creature and also about falling off.

She was quiet for a minute as she thought about it, mulling the idea over in her head. She knew how to ride a horse, of course, growing up on the farm... but the desire to sit atop that magnificent beast was overwhelming and she would not be expected to actually take control, she reasoned. Thalian would have the reins.

"I would like to ride Agnar." Amaya said eventually, shuffling forward and hesitantly reaching a hand out for the deer to sniff.

Thalian smiled. "Then let us be away before we lose the daylight."

~

Riding on the back of Agnar was magical. There was no other way to describe it. It was also quite terrifying. He was so large, meaning Amaya was incredibly high off the ground. At first the fear of falling had been too great but Thalian's firm grip around her waist soon eased any alarm.

Amaya wondered why he was taking her out of the safety of the castle itself instead of taking her into a garden as usual but she certainly wasn't going to complain. It was such a nice change, to be properly out, and she was more than a little surprised that he actually trusted her not to run off. Though, with the last few times she had ventured into this forest, she had no desire to go stumbling alone down the dizzying paths that seemed to lead nowhere but into the claws of terror. Besides, even if she *had* wanted to try and escape she knew she would not get more than three steps while Thalian was with her.

When he reached the clearing he intended to show her, Thalian gracefully dismounted the stag and offered his hand to assist Amaya in doing the same. She made a face as she reached out towards him, feeling far too high up, and she wobbled as she swung her leg over the animal.

As she grasped his hand she felt herself slipping and panic seized her but, before it got out of control, Thalian had Amaya in his firm grip. He pulled her gently to the ground, hands moving from her waist to her upper arms to steady her.

A beat passed in which they both sort of

simply looked at each other and then he smiled, stepping back and releasing her.

Thalian reached up to pet Agnar, giving the animal another apple before he moved to unpack the bag of food that the kitchen staff had provided.

Amaya did her best to push past the sudden, strangely cold feeling that had settled over her when he moved away, and turned to help him unpack the lunch though he was quite insistent on doing it himself. Eventually, he allowed her to spread a blanket, causing her to shake her head in amusement as she set about the very simple task.

"Is it alright to be here?" She couldn't help but ask him, looking around at the trees surrounding the clearing. It was very nice in this particular part and the air didn't feel as suffocating as the other times Amaya had ventured into the forest but she wanted to be sure as visions of dirroh and serutluv flickered at the corners of her memory.

"We are quite safe." Thalian assured her, drawing her attention back to him. "This is a little haven that I keep unenchanted. I know these paths like the back of my hand. No harm will come to you. Not here and not whilst you are with me." He said it like a promise and Amaya smiled as she moved to sit down on the blanket.

The two of them passed lunch happily enough and Thalian found himself pleased to see Amaya looking and sounding better than she had the night before. She was engaging in conversation with him again and she was smiling, much to his delight. Maybe all she had needed was a change of scenery; some time outside the confines of his halls. Though this could not be a regular thing, he decided that he would not mind allowing it every so often if it would help her.

The ride back to the castle was peaceful, at least to her eyes. However, Thalian's arm tightened around his human charge just slightly as he noticed a swirling mist closing in. Frowning, he turned his eyes skyward.

He was just in time to see the large claws of a serutluv descending upon the two of them and he urged Agnar into a run, drawing his sword in the same instant and swinging it overhead, slicing the beast into pieces.

Amaya let out a startled yelp as, without his hold, she started to slip again. In the next second though, his strong fingers clasped around her upper arm before she could topple to the ground below and he pulled her back again, pinning her protectively to his body.

Her own hands clutched at his arm, holding onto him in turn as she sank back against his chest and closed her eyes.

Her heart was beating hard and fast, threatening to burst free, but it wasn't fear that had Amaya in its grasp.

No, indeed, her sudden excitement was caused by Thalian's secure hold and his strong body against her own.

The Day In The Snow

Two days later, the snow came.

Amaya stood in the library a few hours after lunch, looking out of the large window with wonder in her eyes as she watched the flakes falling, a blanket of white settling across the ground of the large garden down below.

Thalian entered the library and spotted her instantly, catching the look on her face and grinning to himself as he moved over to join her at the window.

"Why don't you go wrap up warm and then meet me in the garden." He said after a moment.

Amaya turned to him with a big smile. She'd thought that perhaps he would be too busy today to even join her in the library, never mind take her outside into the snow!

"Really?" She asked with excitement.

Thalian nodded.

"Okay, I'll meet you there!" She said, turning to tidy up the books she had been flicking through before rushing to the door.

"Ask Myleth to find you some suitable boots." He called after her, turning back to the window and watching a few birds flit close to the castle walls.

Truthfully, he did have some things that he should attend to. Mainly some issues he was currently having with Lord Haradir's incessant letters from across the sea. The Elf Lord did not know when to give up, it seemed, as every single piece of correspondence he sent went blatantly ignored. For some reason he could not yet pinpoint, he had been toying with the idea of perhaps, finally, penning a response.

But Thalian thought *this* would be a much better way to spend his afternoon. The other elf could wait, just as he had waited for the last thousand years.

He followed Amaya's retreat a minute later, leaving to ready himself to brave the cold. Not that it would affect him quite as much as it may affect her own human senses.

~

Myleth had been over the moon to dress Amaya for a trip into the garden with the king. She always got so passionate and Amaya had grown used to it by now, not blushing quite as much in the face of her child-like excitement. It was a little amusing and it's not like Amaya could ever truly be mad at Myleth.

The female elf found some fur lined boots that would keep her feet warm in the snow and then threw a soft, warm cloak about her shoulders.

Then, for some reason Amaya couldn't figure out, she tied some red ribbons around the strands of her hair that she'd pulled back into little braids that morning.

When it was done, Myleth walked with Amaya down the corridor, hanging off her arm and talking animatedly with her as if they were the best of friends.

When they both reached the heavy doors where the king was waiting, Myleth gave him a little bow and took her leave.

Amaya inclined her own head out of respect, realising that she had been forgetting such formalities the last two days and immediately feeling anxiety pool in her stomach as this dawned upon her. However, in the same instant, she also realised that she had not received any reprimand for not sticking rigidly to these protocols.

There was a pause and when Amaya looked up again, Thalian was looking at her hair with an intensity she wouldn't have expected.

Eyeing him curiously, she wondered what he was thinking but a second later he collected himself and moved, smiling at her as he turned to open the door.

He had been fixated upon the red ribbons in her braids, the colour bringing out her eyes and complimenting her long, dark hair...

Red just so happened to be one of Thalian's favourite colours and he wondered if Myleth had fixed up her hair this way on purpose but he pushed the thought away quickly because... why on earth would she?

He held the door and then followed Amaya outside into the cold. The snow that was coming down had slowed considerably, only the lightest of flakes now falling from the grey sky above.

Amaya stepped out onto the whiteness that

covered the grass and tilted her chin, giggling as snow dusted itself across her nose and cheeks.

Thalian found himself inexplicably enchanted by the sight.

~

Valerian smirked as he looked out of the window, Aurelia at his side shaking her head in mild disbelief.

Myleth and Elion were standing on the other side of the wide window, practically peering out from around the corner so they would have easy access to jump out of sight should the king look up towards them.

Doronion did not seem to care as he stood directly in the middle, shamelessly staring down into the garden where Amaya and Thalian were enjoying the afternoon.

"Can you believe it?" Valerian practically beamed, casting his gaze over the others as he took in their expressions.

Doronion shrugged. "Actually, yes." He said, surprising Elion who turned to look at his friend with questioning eyes.

Doronion spared him a glance, chuckling. "You think I do not spend enough time with our king to see?"

Even Valerian seemed a little surprised, having thought only he and Myleth to be so astute in this situation.

Doronion laughed again, turning his

attention back to the garden below as he watched the two of them feeding a few birds that had been circling overhead moments ago.

"Well, *I* never thought I would see the day." Muttered Aurelia, looking slightly bemused even as she watched the pair in the garden below.

It was not that she thought the king heartless beyond reason. Of course not. He loved his children and his kingdom and cared for everything and everyone in it. She had just never thought of him *this* way, especially not around a mortal girl, who he had always seemed so, for lack of a better word, wary of. She wasn't sure how the two of them could have come together quite so naturally in this way without a much bigger push.

"But isn't it wonderful?" Myleth said, casting her attention over to Aurelia. "Look at her! See how this girl has breathed new life into not only our king but this very castle!"

Aurelia nodded at that because she couldn't deny it to be true. Something had been changing here and it seemed like it had been since Amaya had dared to set foot in these lands.

"Yes." She said. "I have to agree."

~

Back in the garden, Amaya was captivated by the little birds that had come so close. They normally would not be so trusting of humans but with a great king of elves there, any nerves they felt in their little bellies were assuaged.

They landed not far from the pair and Thalian produced some seed from somewhere deep in his pocket, handing some to Amaya and watching her sprinkle it upon the snow for the birds to eat. Then he crouched and beckoned her to do the same, gesturing for her to hold her arm out in front of her with a little of the seed in her palm.

Thalian smiled as he watched, delighting in the sound of her laughter as a bird landed upon her outstretched arm at the wrist, pecking delicately at the seed in her hand, soon joined by another that perched precariously upon her gloved fingers.

Amaya thought it was magical and her smile was bright as she watched the birds flutter off after having their fill. Still grinning, she moved to stand again, having to reach out to steady herself with her hand against Thalian's strong arm as she did so before she turned and followed the birds across the garden.

Thalian watched her go, doing his best to ignore the little feeling her touch had ignited deep within him. It was not the first time he had felt it but he had been doing a very good job of ignoring it. It was something Thalian had not felt in many a century and a massive part of him was not yet ready to admit to himself just what it was.

Amaya, however, was reeling a little. Spending so much time with him was starting to make her feel more and more and it was frustrating to have to come to the realisation that she probably did have - or was starting to have - *feelings* for him. For this elf. Not just any old elf, the Elf *King*.

Amaya tried to keep telling herself it was absurd, it was childish, it was absolutely ridiculous. But it was getting harder by the day.

She glanced back over her shoulder at him and found his eyes already on her, watching. She smiled at him before ducking behind a tree as she felt a familiar heat rush into her cheeks.

"I do hope you are not intending to make me chase you." Thalian's smooth voice carried across the snow-covered grass and Amaya couldn't help but laugh out loud, peeking back round the tree trunk to look at him.

A bird had come to rest upon his head, watching Amaya with curious little eyes as if wondering what the Elf King found so intriguing. It was most amusing but the addition of the bird made him look no less regal. If anything, it only made him look *more* like a king of the forest.

"And what if I were to tell you that is indeed my plan, *my king?*" She teased, unable to help herself as she played along.

"Then I would have to say, my dear-" Thalian spoke again, his gaze pinning her in place as a wide smirk spread over his features. "-you had better hope yourself a fast runner, indeed."

A squeal flew from her lips as he advanced and Amaya fled her hiding place, practically flying through the snow as a roaring laugh sounded from somewhere behind her.

Laughing along, she tore across the garden, the snow making it more difficult than it otherwise would have been. Her heart thundered away in her chest at the knowledge she was being pursued, Thalian undoubtedly not far behind her.

She thought that he would have been upon her by now but, as she chanced another look over her shoulder, she realised that he was drawing it out, making the game last longer. A thrill shot through her as she spun herself around and rushed forward, ducking behind a pillar.

Another rumble of laughter followed Amaya across the courtyard as Thalian paced lazily across the snow, his eyes fixed upon the pillar she had just disappeared behind.

"Careful, little human." He called, grinning to himself. "I *will* catch you."

Amaya laughed as she peeked from behind the pillar and watched him.

Her thoughts drifted back to the first day he had called her *little human* and told her that her manners were lacking. She did not much mind the term falling from his lips this time. It sounded more like an endearment now and it made her feel warm despite the cold air biting at her cheeks.

She ducked back behind the pillar and she heard a low, amused chuckle from his direction as he paced ever closer.

Thalian would have caught Amaya by now if he had wanted to. The game should have been long over but he was enjoying her excitement. He wanted her to be happy here, wanted to show her that she *could* be, regardless of how she had come to be here and regardless of how badly the both of them had gotten off on the wrong foot.

Movement over by the main door drew his attention momentarily and Amaya took her chance. She crouched down behind the pillar and gathered up a handful of snow, compacting it gently in her hands. Then she stood back up and, biting her lip, she brought her arm back before swinging it forward again, letting the snowball go spinning through the air.

Thalian turned his head back just as it smacked off the front of his tunic, exploding against his chest.

He stood stunned for a moment, having not expected it, before he narrowed his eyes at Amaya. "Oh, you had better run now." He practically growled, but his eyes were sparkling.

Giggling, Amaya turned and fled once more, looking for a new hiding spot. She expected Thalian to grab her almost immediately but instead she felt an unexpected pressure push her from behind, sending her crashing down into the snow with a surprised squeak.

A burst of laughter sounded from behind her and she sat up, turning to scowl at Thalian, who had retaliated against Amaya with a large snowball of his own and was now looking very pleased with himself.

He sauntered towards her, unable to suppress his amusement as he extended his arm down to her. "Perhaps you should have run in more of a zigzag pattern." He told her, his eyes dancing with mirth at her unamused expression.

Amaya hadn't been expecting it despite the

fact that she had started it so it took her a few moments to recover. She blinked up at him, finding that she enjoyed how relaxed he looked when he smiled.

She reached out to take the offered hand, pausing briefly as an idea nudged at her. Then, with all the strength she could muster, Amaya pulled him down to the ground beside her.

Thalian had not been anticipating it, simply entertained by the way he had gotten one over on her in this game. He had no reason to be so on guard right here, in the garden with Amaya, offering to help her to her feet.

So when she tugged sharply at his hand, he went down like a sack of bricks as she so obviously intended.

Stunned, he lay beside her in the snow while this time her laughter rang out through the courtyard. Turning to look at her, he surprised himself by letting out another sharp laugh of his own. He was not annoyed, he was pleased! Reaching out he gave a gentle push to her upper arm, still chuckling as Amaya playfully returned the gesture.

"What must our little watchers think of you so easily toppling their king, hm?" He asked, watching her amusement turn to confusion.

He tilted his head, gesturing towards the large window somewhere above them. Amaya turned her face and looked up, catching sight of Valerian, Aurelia, Elion, and Myleth all ducking out of view. Doronion stayed in place, though even from this distance she could tell he had not anticipated her looking up at that very moment.

Her cheeks started to burn as she realised they had probably been there the whole time and Thalian had been well aware of them.

The king laughed again and Amaya turned her attention back to him. She was about to speak but she was distracted suddenly by finding him close... very close. She blinked at him and he looked back at her, taking in her pink cheeks, the flakes of snow on her lashes and in her hair, those blasted red ribbons holding in her braids.

He was so close that he could have tilted his head just a little and pressed his lips against hers. He was shocked to realise that he was fully entertaining the idea but he caught himself and moved away. He stood up then, dusting himself off and reaching his hand back out for her. "Come on. You'll catch your death if we stay out here much longer."

This time Amaya took his hand and let him pull her to her feet, feeling the slightest hint of disappointment over something she could not put a name to.

Thalian led her back inside and she only realised when he pushed into the library with her that he hadn't let go of her hand the entire way.

~

The tavern back in Feardenn was lively that day, full of laughter and music, the smell of ale heavy in the air.

Vermund sat in the corner by the fire, his big dirty boots up on the table as he watched Oeric get completely trashed at a game of darts. "Bad form, my friend!" He slurred, amused.

"Vermund!" The barkeep called over, drying off a few glasses. "Have you seen the old man lately?" It was only this morning he realised that he had not seen Gideon the farmer in a few days now.

Vermund rolled his eyes and didn't bother to hide it. He shook his head. "No." Was all he said, not bothering to mention the elves or following him into the woods. Though if he were to do so, he would absolutely make himself sound like a hero. Like he had fought the elves off instead of just running away and saving his own skin.

He didn't feel too bad about attacking Gideon. He just wondered how he would explain it when Amaya got back from wherever she was and the old man was not here.

As far as Vermund knew, he had been eaten by a pack of wolves or a stray dirroh by now.

He had stopped by the farm when he returned from the forest that day and Amaya had still not been home. In fact, come to think of it, he hadn't seen her since long before he left her father in the Golden Wood... which was odd.

Amaya was usually running around doing something ridiculous. Talking to horses or reading books, or reading books *to* horses. Still, he was certain she was not kidnapped by the Elf King like the crazy old fool had insisted.

"If it will soothe you, friend, I will go over there later." He told the barkeep, acting like the gentleman he was not.

The bartender nodded, his mild worries quickly put to rest. However, at that very moment, the doors to the tavern swung open and Gideon himself stomped inside. He was clad in large fur-lined boots and a heavy cloak to keep him warm against the bitter chill that had been brought in with the snowfall.

Since returning from the forest, the farmer had taken some days to recover again but, so eager was he to find his way back to the Elf King's castle and rescue his daughter, he had soon been on his way once more.

For days he had tried to fight his own way through the wood but he had never gotten far and always had to turn back. It would do neither Amaya or himself any good if he were to get lost. And if he were to succumb to the elements or dangers of the forest, nobody would be left behind to look for his daughter. She would stay lost with the elves until the end of her days.

His angry gaze first fell upon Vermund, who quickly covered his look of surprise at seeing Gideon alive and well.

"There you are!" Vermund cried, setting down his ale. "We were getting worried for you, my friend!"

"Friend." Amaya's father scoffed, shaking his head at the man. "You are a liar, *friend*, a filthy liar."

The whole tavern seemed to draw in a sharp breath.

"What on earth are you talk-" Vermund began but Gideon was quick to cut him off, trudging further into the tavern and turning his attention to the other townspeople around him.

"Vermund attacked me and left me for dead in the Golden Wood!" He cried, angrily pointing his finger at the man.

"The Golden Wood?" The baker sitting over to his left frowned deeply. "What would you have gone into that place for?" He shook his head, eyes moving between Gideon and Vermund.

The day the farmer had burst into the tavern demanding help and insisting his daughter was taken by the elves had been practically forgotten by those who had been there that day.

Gideon was about to open his mouth to speak again but this time Vermund was swift to cut him off.

"We were simply humouring the old man." He said, gesturing towards Oeric. Vermund lowered his boots from the table and stood, rising to his full five foot ten inches, staring down his nose at Gideon before turning his gaze to the other people in the tavern. "You all know it. He has been losing his mind these last years!" Vermund sneered. "And now he says his daughter has been *stolen* by the *Elf King!*"

A chorus of disbelieving murmurs started to go up round the room.

Vermund continued on. "We simply asked him to show us the way he thought she had been taken and then we returned him safely to his farmhouse! Isn't that right, Oeric?" He turned to his friend, who straightened his shoulders and glanced towards Gideon.

Oeric turned back to everyone a moment later and nodded. "Yes, yes. That's right. He was fine when we left him."

Vermund stood with a smug smirk on his face as he spared Gideon a mere momentary glance before his attention went back to the rest of the people, holding his arms out as if to say 'there you have it, he's crazy.'

"I have no idea where he is getting all this from. Me? Attack him! Never."

"Oh, you...!" Gideon, so furious in both his grief and his disbelief at Vermund's cruelty, lunged towards the younger man. He produced a dagger from the pocket of his cloak and went in swinging. However, he was easily caught and held back from the village's beloved hunter, his actions only serving to add false truth to Vermund's words.

"Keep him here." He ordered the others in the tavern. "I shall fetch the doctor."

A plan started to take root in his mind as he pushed out into the cold evening, a plan that would see the old man fully out of his way, and Amaya *his* once and for all.

∼

Valerian was laughing as Elion practically paced a hole in the floor. The poor elf was more or less vibrating with nerves after being caught by the king watching him and Amaya out in the gardens.

"Calm down, my friend." Valerian shook his head, his voice coloured with amusement. "There was no harm done."

"Calm down." Elion echoed in a mutter, ignoring Doronion's little smirk - though to his credit the king's butler did try to hide it by looking away.

"That is easy for you to say." Elion continued. "He is not very well going to punish his son is he?"

"You will not be punished!" Valerian waved off the idea. "None of us will be. Did you not see him? He was simply amused."

"Amused..." Elion moved over to a chair in the corner, slumping down as he tried to calm his anxiety.

Myleth was hiding her own amusement as she returned to the room at that moment with a pot of tea. She had walked with Aurelia down to the kitchens before the other elf had gone off to a meeting about the border defences.

"Come now, Elion, drink this. It will calm you right down."

"There is no need for such displays!" Doronion told him, finally lifting his head back up now that he had rid himself of his smirk. "The king is fine. If he were angry, he would have been up here already."

Valerian nodded his agreement. "Yes. Believe me, we would know."

"Yes, well." Muttered Elion again, shaking his head as he sipped at the tea Myleth had brought, the combination of calming herbs she had chosen to add having an almost immediate effect. "Maybe you are right. He *was* laughing an awful lot out there, was he not?"

Doronion smiled, looking over at Valerian who looked positively overjoyed by the recollection. "Indeed he was. I have not seen the king laugh quite so much in... well, a very long time." He admitted sadly.

Thalian used to have more reasons to, he supposed, back when he was younger and especially when the queen had been alive and well and the kingdom had been a little less dark.

Valerian stood, reaching over to pat Doronion's shoulder comfortingly, as though able to read his mind. "Yes. I must admit, it is good to see my father without such a weight upon him." He said, before he turned for the door. "I should go and check on my sister. She is spending far too much time in her rooms of late."

With that, he left his friends behind, taking his excitement with him and he felt fairly light for the rest of the day, enjoying having seen his father so... happy.

~

"You know..." Amaya ventured, watching

Thalian hang her coat up to dry on a nearby wall hook. "I never thanked you... for saving my life."

Thalian turned to look at her, a soft smile on his face as he took in her earnest expression. "Well, I do not believe that I ever thanked you for saving *mine.*"

Amaya blinked at him curiously. "I didn't even know the bite had venom in it! I did nothing, your healers are the ones who saved you."

He shook his head, walking towards her in two quick strides and taking a seat on the chair beside hers.

"No. Before that." He said softly. "For bringing me back. For not leaving me in the forest. I would not have made it on my own. It would have been too late."

She glanced down briefly at the memory. She had truly been considering stealing that horse and riding off in the direction that would have hopefully brought her back home, but... she just hadn't been able to do it. "I would not have been able to leave you there. It was only right."

"Even though it meant giving up your freedom once more... for somebody so cruel?" Thalian questioned, looking at her almost in wonder. He had never been able to figure it out. Back then, she had been frightened *of* him and repulsed *by* him.

Amaya looked back up at him with a smile, shaking her head. "Somebody *so* cruel would not have bothered to save me from those creatures at all... or become my friend."

Thalian studied her face as her words sank in and then he smiled, reaching out for her hand. He lifted it to his lips and pressed the lightest of kisses to the back of it. "Then I suppose we should simply consider ourselves even."

"I suppose we should." Amaya agreed, looking back at him with barely concealed adoration in her eyes as he stood up again and moved over to the grand fireplace, lighting it so as to make sure that the room was warm enough for her after their day in the snow

A Silence Finally Broken

Three days passed in a fairly similar, comfortable way.

Amaya divided her time between the library, her room, exploring the halls or the gardens, and enjoying the company of those around her. Her main connections remained Thalian, Myleth, and Valerian. Aurelia and Doronion were not too far behind though Doronion was often so busy with the king, being his personal butler. He had a lot to keep him busy even when he was not personally attending to the king himself.

Indeed, with the upcoming festival Amaya had found out about, it seemed that everybody was suddenly very busy. The whole kingdom seemed to buzz with activity and anticipation.

Amaya found herself more and more excited as she discovered what she could about this elven festival. She had learned some of the customs of the elves during her time here and found herself increasingly more curious with each passing day.

Elves were nothing like what the people of her village had always assumed them to be, or the horror stories that had been passed down through the generations. The elves of Thalian's closed off castle being the only ones that her village had come close to in all its years of existence had meant that imaginations had easily run wild.

The truth, Amaya had discovered, was far lovelier. She found herself thinking about how she simply could not wait to tell everyone just how wrong they had been about the elves but, of course, it then hit her that she would never actually get the chance. She was not leaving these halls.

Still, she wondered if perhaps she could bring up the idea of writing her father a letter eventually. She couldn't see why Thalian would deny her the joy of letting her father know she was safe and happy.

Happy?

The word caught her completely off guard but she was quick to dismiss it, distracting her mind with the elven dictionary in her hands which she was currently perusing in an attempt to learn a few words of their language, and it was soon forgotten.

~

On the fourth morning she woke and readied herself for the day ahead as usual.

Amaya had been taking most, if not all, of her meals with Thalian now. Camellia rarely joined her father and brother in their shared dining hall, seemingly preferring to eat by herself, her constant isolation apparently self-imposed. Valerian would sometimes join them, though as time wore on Amaya found him to be more and more suspiciously absent. When she brought it up with him he waved it off as just being busy with his 'princely duties'. She accepted this but she was not entirely sure if she believed him. Still, why should he bend the truth with her? She could see no reason for him to do so, especially about something so trivial.

After dressing, she left her room and trailed down the corridor in the direction of the royal chambers.

When she reached the door to the dining room, Amaya slipped inside and was surprised to find nobody there. By now, Thalian was usually already up and sitting at the table waiting. In fact, usually breakfast was spread out already but today there was nothing. She lingered for a moment, listening, but there seemed to be no noise or movement coming from anywhere.

Slightly unnerved, she turned and left the room again, retreating back the way she had come.

As she made her way down the corridor she spotted Doronion about to turn a corner ahead of her, looking mildly concerned, and she hurried towards him.

"Doronion!" She called out.

The elf turned at the sound of his name and offered Amaya a smile. "Oh, good morning." He said, continuing on his way. "I'm afraid I cannot stop and talk." He seemed a little scattered, which was not his usual manner.

Amaya shook her head. "No, that's okay, I was just... wondering if you knew where Thalian was." It was out of the ordinary and off schedule so she was admittedly a little thrown. Perhaps worried. If anybody would know, surely Doronion would.

His footsteps faltered then, which Amaya

found a little strange because nobody seemed to bat an eye anymore when she referred to the king by his name.

He turned to look at her. "Oh. I am afraid I cannot say, my lady."

Frowning, she tilted her head and regarded him curiously. "What do you mean?" Surely, as the king, Thalian's whereabouts would be rather well known. "Do you mean he has left the castle? Did he slip past the guards? Is he in the forest alone?"

Amaya was beginning to feel a slight panic starting to take hold of her as all sorts of scenarios filled her mind. Though she knew Thalian was a skilled fighter, she could not help her worry.

Doronion gave her a confused look before he caught her meaning and shook his head quickly. "Oh, no! There is no need for concern, he is quite safe. I mean I simply *cannot* say."

Amaya's frown deepened as she blinked back at him. "You cannot?"

He shook his head, turning to start walking again as he was eager to get where he was going. "I am sorry. It is the king's orders."

Amaya stopped walking at that, staring after Doronion as he turned a corner and disappeared from sight, seemingly heading towards Camellia's study room.

The king's orders? Did Thalian not want to see her? Had she done something wrong? Still frowning, Amaya trailed rather glumly down to the dining hall, hoping to catch sight of somebody she knew.

Myleth immediately saw her from the table she sat at and waved her over.

"Oh! I should have come to fetch you, how silly of me." She shook her head as though she had made some sort of mistake and tapped her fingers against her forehead as if reprimanding herself. "No matter, you're here now. Are you hungry?"

Amaya shook her head. She had lost her appetite but she was also confused by what Myleth could mean. "But... you know I usually eat with Thalian, why should you come and fetch me?"

Myleth blinked at her, surprised. "Oh, dearie, did the king not tell you?"

"Tell me what?" She was beginning to get frustrated as the answers she sought continued to linger beyond her reach.

"That he would not be able to break his fast with you today." The elf continued, unperturbed by the girl's slowly rising irritation. "I'm sorry, I assumed he would have informed you and I suppose he probably assumed I would have come to your room before you left it. Miscommunications all round!"

Amaya was still terribly confused as Myleth turned to pour herself some tea from the pot on the table. "But *why* is he unable to dine with me this morning?" She couldn't help but ask, needing to know if something was wrong.

"He is unable to dine with you all day, my lady." Elion stated as he took his seat across the table, glancing at Myleth only briefly but Amaya caught a secret sort of look pass between the two that only exasperated her further.

"Will somebody *please* tell me exactly what they mean and stop talking in riddles!" She half snapped in frustration, looking from one to the other. "Have I done something to upset him? Is that it?"

"No!" Myleth was quick to jump in, hastily shaking her head.

She had absolutely no desire to let Amaya sit with the idea of the king being upset with her, especially not now she had witnessed just how much the two of them seemed to bring out this light in each other where before only darkness had lingered between them both.

"Of course not, no. Oh, dear, do not worry. It is only today. Now, come on. Let's discuss the festival. I think I have found you the perfect dre-"

"Then why?" Amaya cut her off, unable to just let this go. She felt like something was being kept from her and she wanted to know what it was. Especially when it was about Thalian. She glanced at Elion, noticing the warning look he shot Myleth when she turned to him in a silent plea.

"Come *on.*" Amaya said, firmer this time. "Somebody had better start talking."

Myleth sighed and turned back to look at her, ignoring Elion's sound of disapproval.

"My dear, it's just... it is a difficult day for the king... and the prince and princess."

It was only then Amaya realised that she had not seen Valerian yet either and it was quite late into the morning now. He was usually where the others were but right now he was nowhere to be seen.

"In what way?" She asked carefully, looking across the table at Elion who was engrossed in a teacup in front of him, acting like it was the most interesting thing in the world. Though the slight scowl that had appeared on his face said otherwise.

There was a long silence and then Myleth spoke again. "Well, it... it is... the queen's birthday, my dear."

~

From what Amaya had been told, the queen's birthday was a sombre, sorrowful day for all in the realm. Everything seemed to come to a standstill on this one day.

When the queen had been alive, the royal couple had always done something very special on this day. First together, then with their children when they had come along, and then together again as Camellia and Valerian got older and wanted to do their own thing.

Then the Great Massacre was upon them and, after that, the queen had no more birthdays.

With the Elf Queen gone the king had started taking this day to truly remember her. Or, more aptly, to truly let himself drown in his grief. He would take no work and he would speak to no one, shutting himself away in the queen's chambers.

Valerian would disappear into the forest

with bow and arrow under the pretense of hunting but he never returned with any quarry. He simply found himself unable to stay in the castle when his father was like this. Camellia, too, would disappear for the day, not that her absence was felt quite as deeply as it was far more common to not see the princess for several days.

The reason for Thalian's sudden disappearance on this day was only ever officially known by a select few staff members, who were under orders not to further discuss it or his whereabouts with others. Though, of course, rumours had flown over the years and, while not everybody got the reason for the king's absence correct, all ultimately agreed it must have to do with the queen. It was the only thing that would cause their king to abandon them in such a way. Especially with everyone being acutely aware that the queen was so off limits. Her name was not to be spoken. Her memory was not to be acknowledged.

Thalian simply could not stand to talk of her or hear others do so, even his own children. Her memory was brushed under the carpet and stepped over or walked around, everybody acting as though it simply was not there. Nonetheless, her presence was heavy, almost suffocating.

Amaya's legs carried her in the direction of the library, intending to shut herself away for the day as well. However, her gaze fell upon that red curtain that concealed the staircase up to the Elf Queen's rooms and, before she knew it, she had slipped behind the heavy material and was climbing the stairs.

Her last two visits to these chambers flashed through her mind. One horrible, one not so horrible. Amaya wasn't sure which one this would be but she felt as though it didn't really matter. She was set on this course already and no amount of fighting with her own mind would get her to turn back.

She passed the portrait of the queen once more, looking up at the destroyed image of her as she did. She was so beautiful. She had such kind eyes, Amaya thought. It was a shame that she seemed to have suffered such a horrible fate that nobody could even speak of it.

Her curiosity was sky high but she turned her focus towards finding Thalian, peeking into various rooms as she passed.

Walking into what was clearly a bedroom, she found an opened drawer of items had been upended, lots of beautiful jewellery and intricate headwear all scattered across the floor.

Images of Thalian losing his temper in his grief and sending his wife's jewels flying across the room in a rage flickered into her mind.

The thought of it made Amaya feel sad.

Moving into the next room, she went over to the doors that led out to the balcony. From the corner of her eye, she noticed a blackened rose in the middle of a glass case sitting on a little table. She stepped towards it and gently pressed her fingers against the glass.

As Amaya turned to look out of the

window, having caught sight of Thalian down in the garden in her peripheral vision, she realised this dead rose was one of the Starfire Roses. More specifically, the one her father had plucked and killed. The one that seemed to have started all of this in the first place. Thalian had kept it, giving it something of its own little memorial display case.

The sight hurt her heart.

Slowly, she walked towards the doors and pulled them open before slipping out onto the balcony. Thalian didn't look up, he simply continued to caress the roses. She could see them swaying, their movements slow. Even they seemed sad today.

Biting her lip, Amaya turned and walked down the stairs and began to cross the grass. Her heart was practically in her throat as doubt finally began to hit her in full force and she started to realise that this may not have been a very good idea after all.

Would the king just be angry with her? Perhaps her coming here uninvited on such a day, sticking her nose in where it did not belong, would set the two of them back after coming this far.

"This had better be important." Thalian's tone was cold and he didn't move, not so much as turning his head at her approach. His attention remained upon the roses. "I was very clear that I wish not to be disturbed."

Amaya stopped short, her heart practically sinking into her toes. "Oh, I... sorry." A small frown creased her brow and she quickly turned to make herself scarce again.

Thalian looked around then. "Wait." He called, looking at her with a frown of his own. His voice was softer now and she turned to face him again. "I thought you were somebody else." He admitted, having assumed Doronion had come to bother him with something.

He looked at her quietly for a beat before he held out a hand and gestured for her to join him.

Tentatively, Amaya stepped closer and took a seat beside him on the little wooden bench that stood in front of the Starfire Roses. She glanced down and reached out towards one, watching as it turned its attention to her. With a small smile, she turned her attention back towards Thalian. He was watching the flowers again.

Her smile faded away as he glanced up and met her gaze again, attempting to offer her a smile of his own but it fell short and he just looked... sad. It was the only word Amaya kept coming back to, to describe this entire situation.

"Myleth forgot to tell me you would not be at breakfast." She told him quietly, not sure what else to say. She didn't want to overstep and make him feel worse.

Thalian closed his eyes briefly, shaking his head in a way that made it look like he was feeling guilt or regret. "I am sorry." He sighed, opening his eyes. "I must admit, it did not cross my mind to tell you."

"There's no need to be sorry." Amaya assured him quickly. That's not why she had said it.

She'd only been meaning to try and explain her unannounced presence. She understood why it would slip his mind, how could she not? "I really didn't mean to bother you, I just... wanted to see if you were alright."

Thalian blinked at her, finding that it surprised him - the fact that she had thought about how he would be doing. That she would want to seek him out. He knew that they had both become closer, that she had even gone so far as to call him a friend a few days ago, but he still found himself surprised by it. By the changes that had occurred during her time here. By the way Amaya seemed to *care*. For someone such as *him*. It touched him and Thalian found himself reaching out for her hand.

"Thank you. I..." He looked back at the roses with a sigh, watching them curl towards each other. "I will admit, I find this day to be... especially difficult."

The two of them lapsed into silence for a few minutes. Amaya did her best to ignore the butterflies that the touch of his hand gave her, swallowing down the annoyingly present feelings that she simply could not seem to shake no matter how hard she tried.

"Tell me about her?" She ventured finally, looking up at him again. She was quick enough to see the flicker of surprise on his face. He covered it fast enough however, his expression becoming the marble mask that she had grown so accustomed to.

Thalian was quiet for a short time, studying her face as if he were trying to ascertain whether or not she was being serious. When he found no insincerity in her eyes, his gaze softened slightly.

"Her name was Caleniel." He said quietly, speaking her name for the first time in what felt like forever.

It was like a floodgate opened with that name, and so he talked. About Caleniel and the moonlit night they met. About her deep love of the Starfire Roses and his quest to procure the ones in this garden for her. About her beauty, kindness, and strength. Her love of her birthday despite already having seen four hundred and twenty-five of them (yet she didn't look a day over two hundred and nine, Thalian had joked, making Amaya laugh). He told her about what a good mother she was to Camellia and Valerian. And, ultimately, about the war and what happened.

Amaya listened with rapt attention, watching as both sorrow and joy battled together in his eyes as he finally spoke out loud about his beloved queen, and how he lost her, for the first time in nearly a thousand years...

The Great Massacre

In the centuries that followed the war, they called it the Great Massacre. For there seemed to be no reason for it other than to bring death, and the amount of blood shed and lives lost was beyond counting.

The Dark Wizard, Rellik - a fallen and corrupted mage driven by power and greed - had brought into being his own terrifying race of creatures. The grath. Hideous beasts that stood upon two legs, covered in patches of blood red skin, with piercing yellow eyes. Their long grey fangs were riddled with holes from the tiny, spider-like creatures that lived within the cavern of their mouths, gnawing through tooth and gum.

The grath were the most dangerous and relentless killing machines that the world of Amarar had ever seen.

There was not only a legion of grath at his call, however. The Dark Wizard used many of the other foul beasts of this world to fight back against those who opposed him, along with corsairs from across the sea - tyrants with no good in their hearts. There were also those few whose pure hearts Rellik corrupted. A few elves and fae stood beside the wizard, facing their once-allies and fighting them to the death.

Every single kingdom in Amarar came together to fight on the plains of Nezor in those dark days. The Elf Lord, Haradir, led a great host of fighters from the Great Hall in Chakra Woods.

The Fae Queen, Olinda, left her palace in the city of Valcade with her army. Along with King Hamlin of Achnol, ruler of the human villages to the south, and Elf King Thalian from the Golden Isle across the north of the sea. Even the elusive Merqueen, Astaria, came up from beneath the waves, for the Dark Wizard had poisoned the waters around her realm.

It was here that the elves of the Golden Isle had faced one of their greatest losses. A loss that would have aftershocks for centuries to come.

There, King Thalian faced down hordes of foul creatures and evil beings. He took the lives of many that day, cutting down his enemies with grace and skill that the humans on the battlefield spoke of for decades after.

One of the most skilled warriors in all of Amarar, Thalian sliced his blade through flesh with seemingly little effort, moving this way and that, turning and twisting as though the fight were but a dance. However, his attention was soon diverted, for his queen (who had been fighting a horde of slobbering beasts on the other side of the battlefield) was suddenly overthrown.

As the king watched, her life had been snuffed out as easily as if she were but a flower, plucked from the dirt and trampled beneath a dirty boot. A fine soldier in her own right, it was no mean feat to bring her down, but Rellik's grath were the most vicious beasts to ever have existed.

Unable to reach her in time, the Elf King could only watch in horror as she fell. Even from that instant he blamed himself fully for her death, the guilt seeping into his very soul and eating him alive.

Horribly (and irreparably) wounded in his distraction, Thalian turned his fury upon the beasts around him, seeing nothing but red - both rage and blood - as he hacked and slashed his way across the ground towards the body of his wife.

Even as the Dark Wizard was eventually defeated, Thalian heard and saw none of it. The king's guards stood around him as he collapsed on the battlefield, clutching the queen's body to his chest.

For three full weeks, even as her body bloated and began to putrefy, he stayed this way, refusing to let her go no matter who came to try and ease him away. Any who came close got the king's blade pointed at their heart and it was easier to simply let him stay like that until he was ready to leave.

Thalian had not known until the moment that he took Caleniel into his arms that she was once more with child. Only then did he feel it as the dimming light of it reached towards him and he sensed it in the way that only elves can. The tiny beating heart of the unborn being was - from the moment he reached her - the only life still left within the queen until, even as he sat there stricken by grief, that too grew faint and then simply faded away.

From that day on, no elf from the Golden Isle ever left their halls in defence of other lands again.

King Thalian turned his back on the world beyond the Golden Isle, shutting himself away in his castle, looking after his own and no more; all the while locking the jagged, broken pieces of his heart behind thick bars of steel.

As time passed, any magnanimity or virtue that the outside world may have known of the Elf King was forgotten.

So deeply buried beneath his anguish was his kindness in regards to the outside world and the other races in it, that all anyone unlucky enough to come into contact with him could see was a beast.

Moments of Contemplation

Valerian returned from the forest early that evening, striding in the direction of his chambers so that he could bathe and change into some nightclothes.

He was exhausted but that was mostly due to the emotional whirlwind his mind had been in for the entire day. It happened every year and it never got any better. He would wake frustrated and retire in the evening the same way.

This day was always such a dark seeming one in the kingdom, it had been for centuries. Which was saying something when he thought about how generally dark a lot of things in this kingdom had become over these years.

Despite every single shred of his mother being removed and forgotten and forbidden to even be discussed, the heavy shadow of her was ever present.

Valerian barely remembered Caleniel, having still been quite young when the war happened. But he remembered his father's grief. It had been a constant for practically his entire life.

In the beginning, Valerian remembered his father being half unable to look at him or his sister some days. So much like their mother in different ways. Such stark reminders, with his light brown hair and gentle manner, and her freckled cheeks and grey eyes. Living, breathing reminders of the woman Thalian loved most in the world and felt that living without was pointless.

Pushing these thoughts aside, the prince trudged through the hallways towards the royal quarters. He just wished for this day to finally be over once and for all. It would come again the next year far too quickly. One year was such a drop in the ocean to an elf, whose immortal life he felt could often be no more than a curse. It could often feel as if no time had passed at all.

Valerian was surprised to find himself waylaid in the corridor by Camellia. She looked normal at first glance but he noticed a slight flush to her cheeks and she looked a little more wide eyed than she normally did.

"You *have* to see this." She told her brother in a voice that was hushed yet slightly excited, which was perhaps the most startling thing to him, as he was unable to remember the last time he had heard her like that, especially on this day.

Camellia's hands clutched his arm as she pulled him back down the hallway and Valerian allowed her to lead him, though he put on the brakes when they came to the staircase up to their mother's rooms. "Camellia, we cannot. Father…"

The princess shook her head, practically dragging him up the stairs. "Come on!" She urged and something in her tone made him keep moving.

"On this day, he always retires to his own room after dinner, you know this…" She continued. "But he did not come and Doronion was concerned." Camellia pulled him down the corridor in the direction of the balcony window. "So he came up here to look for him, to see if he needed anything..."

Huddled at the window were Doronion, Elion, and Myleth, all turning to look at the prince and princess with expressions Valerian could not decipher. He was frowning now, too drained for games and just wanting to retire to his bed. He could not understand what the fuss was about. If his father wanted to stay up here for the entire night moping then let him!

He came to a stop at the window and stared out of it, taking in the sight of Amaya and his father down in his mother's garden beside her roses.

"She went missing after breakfast." Myleth said to Valerian, watching him closely for a moment before she looked back outside. Thalian was saying something and Amaya was solemnly hanging off his every word. "She was nowhere to be found but I did not imagine that she would have come back up here..."

"Since breakfast?" The prince could not hide the shock in his voice as he turned his eyes on Myleth. He glanced from her to Elion, who nodded, and then he looked back outside.

He watched his father talking and Amaya listening and wondered what they were discussing. He probably would have paid a dragon's body weight in gold just to be able to listen in on one single moment.

For all these years, his father had been a black hole of grief and anger. Not one soul had been allowed up here. Not one soul had been allowed to utter his mother's name or talk about her tragic demise. Not one soul had managed to get his father to simply spare them but one moment on this day.

Until Amaya.

Now, here the king sat. Talking with her in his mother's private garden, on this very difficult day, beside her beloved Starfire Roses.

He did not look angry. He looked a little sorrowful but the weight that always sat so heavily and obviously on his shoulders this day almost looked, to Valerian, a little lighter than it usually did. He could hardly believe what he was looking at but the scene made his heart soar.

"Come. We should leave them." The prince said softly after a few more moments. As big a turning point as he had just witnessed, Valerian was still fairly sure that his father would not take kindly to all of them lingering at the window like spies this time around.

He let Doronion walk his sister to her room, where the pair stayed up talking for a while longer. Camellia felt some strange spark of excitement in her veins for the first time in what felt like forever. A flutter of hope as light as a butterfly's wing yet as strong as an eagle's. Whether this was a false hope or not was yet to be ascertained but the princess smiled, something she never thought she would do on this day, and when Doronion left her to sleep she even dared to press a goodnight kiss to his cheek.

Valerian had, for the first time, retired to his own chambers in a much better mood than the one he had returned to the castle in. It was a strange feeling and, for a longer time than normal, he found sleep evading him.

As they both lay in their beds that night, they couldn't help but hold onto the hope that something in their father could be healing.

~

Once that hard day was behind him, Thalian resumed his duties and was all business as usual.

At least outwardly.

Inside, he was still attempting to quell the rising emotions that he was becoming more aware of with each passing day.

Emotions that seemed to have everything to do with Amaya.

Part of him was still completely stuck on the way that she had come into the queen's chambers as she had, seeking him out only to see if he was well. Why would she do that? He couldn't help but wonder.

He had perhaps seen flashes in her eyes over her time here, during the days that the two of them had grown closer. Brief flashes of emotion or unspoken words. Thalian dismissed them every time, chalking it up to his own imagination. Though, why he assumed his imagination would conjure up such a thing he did not allow himself to study too closely. Still, in the back of his mind, he knew it was there.

Amaya had started to look at him in a way that he could not fully ignore.

There was… yearning.

Sorrow.

Love?

No.

He dare not think that possible.

Thalian told himself not to be so foolish. First, he should not even be entertaining such ludicrous thoughts. Second, it was only a dream… an enchanting little dream perhaps, but a dream nonetheless. Nothing more.

He had become so fraught with rage and despair and darkness since his wife's passing. Amaya had witnessed all of it firsthand many times over and, while she seemed to be a lot more comfortable with him, he could not delude himself.

She could never *love* such a *beast*.

She had come to him as a prisoner (a human, no less) and he reminded himself of the fact he had been so certain he could never again feel for another, not in the way he had for his wife.

His broken heart had been frozen in a block of unbreakable ice for the rest of eternity and it could not be thawed. Not at his will and not by the likes of a little human.

Still, sometimes he found himself entertaining the idea. Even more frustratingly, sometimes he found himself *seeking* the thought out, as if it brought him some sort of comfort.

Thalian could no longer fully understand himself. These sorts of emotions and thoughts had been locked up in a secret part of him for centuries. He had not even recognised them at first, so long had he avoided them - but he was beginning to now.

He did not know how to feel about it.

The king threw himself into his duties to avoid falling into the trap of fully entertaining the entire fantastical notion. He had councils to attend, people to look after, defence of the borders to oversee. Not to mention a feast to ready himself for.

It was one of his favourite things, to see all of his people come together in joy. Dancing and drinking and laughing the night away. Despite his often stony exterior, Thalian very much enjoyed seeing his people finding the light and the love in this kingdom, which had become so dark.

It always reminded him that, no matter what, they would endure.

~

Amaya was excited about the upcoming elven festival. She had managed to deduce that it was a winter celebration.

The snow had almost all but melted away, not having stayed more than a few days after Amaya and Thalian had their excursion into the garden, but winter had not yet given way to the coming of spring.

The name of the festival in her tongue, Amaya was told, was *'Feast Beneath a Winter Sky'*.

No matter how many times somebody tried to teach it to her in the language of the elves, Amaya always forgot it. Still, she was eager for the days to pass and for the festivities to get here. The excited energy she could feel around her was infectious and she liked seeing everybody looking so light and free.

She also could not quite stop thinking about Thalian and the day of the queen's birthday.

Her heart felt heavy every time she did so. Amaya felt so bad for him, losing his wife at all - and his unborn child! But the way he had told her that she died was beyond her comprehension. The way he detailed how he witnessed the whole thing, how despite his efforts to fight his way to her, she had been brutally slain before his very eyes. He had not been able to protect her, or many more of his own people that day.

One had caused him to shut away his heart and one had caused him to shut away his entire kingdom.

Amaya did not think she would have still been walking around, she would be catatonic with grief. He was incredibly strong.

The magnitude of it did not escape her. That Thalian opening up to her had been something incredibly significant.

When Amaya first arrived in this place, everybody had been incredibly quick to draw her attention away from the queen's forbidden rooms but had never stated why. Caleniel's name had not been mentioned at all. Without anybody having to tell her in words, she just knew it was because Thalian had probably forbidden it. If not explicitly, then the sheer magnitude of his grief, the way it made him lash out, would have caused everyone to simply... stop mentioning her. He had been so stricken by his loss - and his guilt, she realised - that his queen could not even be so much as whispered about in her own halls.

It did not strike Amaya as an act bidden from a heart of stone, but that of a broken soul who did not know how to deal with the pain and so shut it out to the best of its ability.

To carry that around for centuries as he must have? She could not fathom.

She had been so wrong in her first impression of the king. He hadn't given her much room to see him in another light, of course, but there was something in him that she simply had not seen.

Amaya understood him a lot more now, and she felt for him. Perhaps in more ways than one.

~

Indeed, it seemed that for the both of them, their first impressions of each other had been so wrong, so far beyond what the reality actually was.

Thalian had seen a mere mortal girl.

Unimportant and of no real use. Perhaps a little below him and his kind. He thought all life precious, this much was true, but when faced with mortal kind Thalian had, over the years, begun to look down his nose just a little.

His lack of trust in those outside of his own people, his own castle, had grown and festered until it was simply too big for him to control. The human race was weak and had little regard for those around them, even their own kind at times from what he had seen and heard. There were some who were noble enough of heart, he knew that, but as a whole they were insignificant, fleeting, and he kept them at arm's length the same way he did now with all races. Fae, mer, witches, wizards, even other elves.

However, Amaya had been a complete surprise. He had looked upon her, at first, as a means to an end. He had wanted her father punished for the attack on his son and for the death of that precious Starfire Rose and it mattered not to him how that punishment was dealt.

Keeping that girl here would obviously hurt her father just as much as if he had kept the man here himself. Thalian had been able to see that right away. The bond between the both of them was a true, deep one.

So he had allowed it. Swapped Amaya out for her father, satisfied in the knowledge that it would indeed still be a punishment. Perhaps, even, a worse one.

Then things had shifted. He couldn't even

pinpoint the exact moment that they had, the moment his own feelings had changed, but they had all the same.

Amaya, too, had at first only seen a cruel, callous dictator who revelled in his own power. A horrible beast of a creature, who lived only to deal out despair and sorrow upon those around him. Who did not listen to reason and who seemed to thrive entirely on spite.

He had frightened Amaya. Terrified her, even.

Then he had saved her from those dirroh and she had saved him in return and... that seemed to have been a turning point.

Then, that day up in the queen's chambers, when he first showed Amaya the roses and explained everything to her, she had felt another, bigger shift.

She had started to feel at home here... at home around him.

They had both seen things in each other that they had not noticed before, simply because neither of them had been looking.

Everything had changed.

There was something there now that had not been there before.

~

Vermund had made short work of fetching the village doctor, practically dragging him to the tavern with a story of how *worried* for the farmer's mental wellbeing he was.

The man had taken one look at Gideon and had one listen to his nonsensical ramblings before he had immediately agreed and, with the help of the townsfolk, he had been taken to the local infirmary and forced into one of the locked rooms where they kept the patients who were a danger to themselves or others, or were a flight risk.

It was not much better than the cell Amaya had traded herself to free him from in the Golden Castle.

Vermund swaggered around the village as though he had saved the day, head held high and a self-satisfied smirk on his face. With Gideon out of the way and the rest of the town in agreement of his madness, there would be no way the farmer's daughter could doubt him.

Two days passed.

Amaya still did not return.

Nobody had seen or heard from her in many weeks and he couldn't understand where she would have gone for this long, especially with no one knowing her whereabouts. Usually, the village was so on top of everyone else's personal business that nothing went secret or unknown for long. It struck Vermund as strange indeed and it concerned him.

It did not *worry* him. It *concerned* him.

He was concerned that if Amaya did not show back up soon then he would be forced to end up looking elsewhere, taking another woman in the village as his wife, and nobody else in this place was up to his standards. But he would *not* be wife-less for the rest of his life. Who would cook his meals? Who would launder his clothing? Who would keep his home clean? Who would tend to his needs whenever the fancy so took him?

On the morning of the third day, Vermund had had enough. He hadn't believed for one minute that Amaya was with the king of the elves but the more time that passed the more he was willing to entertain the idea. After all, elves were known to kidnap pretty human maidens, were they not?

"Oeric." He mused, after he had dragged his friend down an alleyway to dodge a trio of irritating, plain-faced sisters who were constantly vying for his attention. "Do you suppose that the old man might not be entirely insane, after all?"

Oeric gave Vermund a look, shaking his head. "He's utterly mad. You saw him."

"*Yes*, but..." Vermund hummed as they exited the opposite end of the alley, thoughtfully plucking an apple from a nearby tree and then promptly throwing it over his shoulder as though it was garbage. "Where else could she be? She would not have left the old man here alone. She always was rather-" He waved a hand in the air, making a face. "-protective of the crazy bastard." He stopped, folding his arms across his broad chest as he looked down his long nose at Oeric. "I think it is worth a try. I have looked everywhere."

"Why not simply take Thora as your wife." Oeric shrugged, speaking as though the 'who' was of no consequence.

He wilted under the horrified stare Vermund gave him in return.

"Are you as mad as the old man?" He all but cried. "Have you seen that woman's nose? She looks like one of my horses."

The two men guffawed as they fell back into step beside each other, moving off to hunt in the nearby fields.

"No. I think that we should round up the others and leave for the Elf King's castle in two days." Vermund said, nodding very decisively.

And that was that.

Vermund had decided what he wanted to do and everybody else would fall in line.

They always did.

The Winter Festival

Two days after the queen's birthday, the start of the *Feast Beneath a Winter Sky* had come, and Myleth roused Amaya early as she had the whole morning planned.

She had been flitting around Amaya like a little bird for days, determined to dress her up like a doll for the event. It was a little annoying but she stood patiently through it all, letting the other pick out the colours and the style of her dress, her hairstyle, her jewellery, all of it.

It seemed to make Myleth happy and that made Amaya happy in turn, as much as she was not used to being poked and prodded and draped in such expensive fabrics. Myleth had a very motherly aura about her and it had become quite comforting to her.

She helped the girl into her dress and braided her hair very specifically, using red ribbons again as she had already decided.

Amaya had no idea whether or not looking a certain way for an elven celebration was necessary so she quite happily just let Myleth do her thing.

"Are you excited, dearie?" She asked with a smile as she continued braiding a little section of her hair. She had left most of it down to frame her face, pulling a section back into a little bun near the top of her head, with many intricate little braids wrapped decoratively around the bun, tied with the most delicate red ribbons.

"Yes." Amaya nodded but she was a little anxious too and it probably showed on her face.

Myleth smiled kindly at her reflection in the mirror. She finished her hair and gave her shoulders a gentle squeeze. "Don't worry so much, my dear. Just have fun."

She paused, stepping back and appraising her handiwork. "You look beautiful."

Yes, Myleth thought to herself, *the king will be most pleased.*

~

Thalian, too, was being dressed for the ball, though of course he was far more used to being dressed and attended to than Amaya was.

Doronion was at his side, helping him into his heavy clothing and assisting in fixing a splendid crown upon his head.

"If I may speak freely, my king?" Doronion ventured, adjusting an intricate brooch at the front of Thalian's tunic.

Thalian glanced at him, just a little amused. He was certain that his butler already knew that he could practically say whatever it was that he wanted and Thalian would listen. He highly valued his opinion and thoughts. "You may."

Doronion stepped back, appraising the king's outfit for the feast. "I daresay... that the lovely lady will be rather taken with your appearance this day."

Thalian raised an eyebrow, sparing Doronion another glance from the corner of his eye. "And why, pray tell, would it affect me what *the lady* thinks of the way I look?"

Doronion tilted his head a little then, giving Thalian a knowing smile. "No reason at all, my king."

His eyes were shining, however, and Thalian couldn't help but return the smile, somewhat amused because he could quite easily tell that Doronion just *knew*. That he had gleaned his feelings towards Amaya, whatever they may be.

It wasn't too surprising, he supposed. Other than his children, Doronion was the one who spent the most time around him, the one who knew him better than most.

As Thalian turned to take one final look at himself in the large mirror, he found that he did not mind in the slightest.

~

Amaya was a mess of nerves and excitement, the two feelings fighting together throughout her entire body. She felt like she was practically fizzing. She wasn't even sure what she was so nervous about.

Was it that she did not know the customs? Amaya had been assured it was of no matter and nothing was expected of her.

Was it because of Thalian?

Possibly, she grudgingly admitted to herself.

Still, she did her best to push the thoughts away and followed Myleth towards the grand hall where the festivities were to be held. She pushed open the heavy doors and swept Amaya inside by the elbow. No turning back now.

Thalian was seated at the head of a long table on a large chair of intricately carved wood which was almost like a mini throne. He was speaking with his son, who sat upon his right next to Camellia, but he turned his head when the doors opened.

His gaze fell upon Amaya.

And everything stopped.

Without even realising that he was doing it, Thalian rose from his chair. He stood with his eyes glued upon Amaya as Myleth ushered her into the hall. He barely realised Myleth was there. In fact, the rest of the room had seemed to melt away entirely. His son's voice was not even a whisper to him anymore.

Camellia was staring at her father with concern, watching him ignore her brother. After a moment, she turned her head and followed his gaze. Her eyes widened as she saw that his attention had been completely stolen by Amaya's entrance. When Camellia turned back to her brother, he was smirking, having also realised what - or *who* - his father was looking at.

Valerian looked at Doronion, who stifled a chuckle before looking at Camellia, who ducked her head to try and hide her own rising amusement.

She needn't have bothered. Thalian was completely entranced as he watched Amaya coming closer. His eyes took in every little detail. Her hair. Her dress. Her face.

Myleth led Amaya to the king's table, ignoring the confused look that the human girl gave her. She had been spending a lot of time with him, yes, but she had assumed that at such a function as this she would have been seated elsewhere. However, she didn't complain as she watched Myleth move as if to pull out the chair to Thalian's left so she could sit next to him.

He got there first, however, still staring at her as if he was completely starstruck.

Amaya hadn't seen such a look on his face before and she could feel her cheeks starting to heat up as she inclined her head respectfully and took a seat in the chair. Thalian gently pushed the chair in and then stepped aside, finally sitting himself back down.

Valerian coughed to cover a laugh and the spell was broken.

Thalian turned to give his son a deathly glare and Amaya quickly lifted a glass of mulled wine to her lips, trying to hide behind it to cover her blush.

She glanced between the two of them and suddenly realised that the soft golden colour of her dress seemed to match with Thalian's own outfit. Surely that could not have been on purpose?

"You look very lovely." Thalian's voice pulled her attention from the fabric covering his broad chest back up to his face before she had too much time to really focus on it.

She cleared her throat and worked up a smile, mildly embarrassed at the fact it probably looked like she had been ogling him. "Thank you. You look..." How did one compliment a king? A brief flicker of panic shot through her but Myleth's light touch upon her elbow as she walked away to seat herself with Elion and the others calmed her a little. "Very handsome." Amaya finished, before turning to Valerian. "Um. You too. Very princely indeed."

Valerian chuckled. "Why thank you, my lady. I have been told that I, how do you humans put it, *scrub up rather well?*"

He beamed happily as it pulled a laugh from her while Camellia rolled her eyes at his antics.

Thalian lazily reached for his chalice, filled with the spiced wine, and lifted it to his mouth with slightly narrowed eyes. He found he was somewhat disappointed that Amaya had painted both himself and his son with the same compliment. Though he wasn't entirely sure why. So, as with many such things, he decided to simply ignore it.

Still, he could not keep his eyes from the human at his side, sneaking glances at her every so often as the minutes passed. Much to his pleasure, he caught Amaya doing the same and soon he had turned himself to face her properly, suddenly intent on making the most of her attention this evening.

"Relax." He murmured, smiling at her knowingly as she fidgeted with the sleeves of her dress beside him. "You have nothing to worry about."

Amaya chuckled at the fact he had been able to read her so easily. "I have never attended an event that comes anywhere close to something such as this." She told him, scanning the elaborately decorated room and the many heads of the elves who were seated throughout.

Thalian placed a hand upon her arm. "In that case, little human, this shall certainly be a night to remember."

~

The long carven tables were piled with trays upon trays of food and drink. They were full of fruit, cheese, meat, cakes, and a few things Amaya could not even put a name to. The kitchens must have worked overtime for this festival but given the amount of elves that were currently seated in the hall, that was hardly surprising.

The entire room was buzzing with conversation, laughter, and music. All the adults were drinking merrily and all the young elves were playing hide and seek under tables. The hall itself had turned out to be completely open-topped, the clear winter sky shining down upon the merriment below. As the time passed, soon enough they would all be eating and drinking under the stars.

Feast Beneath a Winter Sky, indeed.

Amaya ate good food, drank sweet wine, and very much enjoyed the atmosphere of the room. She talked with those at the table, mostly Valerian as Camellia still seemed quite shy, Doronion was in work mode even now, and Thalian's attention unfortunately seemed to be rather consistently monopolised by those around him.

Amaya tried not to let it bother her of course. She understood that he was the king and he had a great deal of duties, even during a celebration such as this. She had watched him stand to give a speech not too long ago that had officially kicked off the entire festival and he seemed to keep getting caught in conversation with council members, soldiers, and various other staff members.

To anyone simply passing, Thalian was as smooth as ever as he entertained his people and nibbled at honey cakes while drinking copious amounts of his favourite seasonal mulled wine.

His frustrations, however, were simmering in a secret place within him because it seemed that every time he turned his attention to Amaya, to engage her in conversation, he was pulled in several other directions that he simply could not ignore.

At least Amaya seemed to be having a good enough time talking to Valerian and enjoying the food and drink that had been prepared but he would have liked just a moment's peace to include himself into that equation.

It came soon enough, of course, when the

music the minstrels were playing changed into something different. A more upbeat, jovial tune that was intended to get everybody up onto their feet and dancing. It was quite a popular song in elven culture though Amaya would not have heard it before and many elves were eager to begin dancing and singing along.

Her eyes followed various groups of elves as they rose from their tables and turned towards the dancefloor. Amaya watched their bodies move with the music, fascinated. They danced alone, in pairs, or in little groups though this was mostly the much younger ones. They moved more gracefully than she could have ever hoped to achieve but she didn't care as she was suddenly overcome with the desire to join in with them. The joy in the air was palpable and it was as if it was pulling her in.

She turned to look at Thalian, finding him already watching her, and she couldn't hold back the bright smile on her face as she reached out to him. Her hands found his arm and she clutched at the sleeve of his tunic with a childlike excitement he found difficult to ignore.

"Come and dance with me!" She looked towards the floor again before turning back to him. "Please."

Valerian looked up from his plate and spoke her name, drawing her attention. "Alas, my father is not much for dancing at these events, I am afraid." He thought it was better if he got in ahead and told her, rather than his father having to let her down himself, considering how Valerian had seen her looking at him lately. Maybe it would sting just a little less coming from somebody else. "I may not be quite up to standard but I should be more than happy to spare you a dance or two in his place, my friend."

"Actually, Valerian." Thalian cut in smoothly, still looking at Amaya even as his son had briefly drawn her attention from him. Disappointment had started to bleed into her enthusiasm, her shoulders deflating just slightly, and he could not bear it. "I think I can quite manage one dance." He concluded simply, rising from the table in one sweeping gesture.

He extended his arm towards Amaya, watching as her bright smile was renewed. She stood, reaching out to take his offered hand and he turned and led her towards the floor, leaving his children blinking after him in bewilderment.

When Camellia was able to stop herself from staring dumbly at the back of her father's head, she turned to look at Doronion, whose eyebrows were practically touching the heavens. Doronion met her gaze and then, after a beat, the two of them started laughing.

"Well, that is *quite* the development." Doronion muttered, plucking a goblet of wine off the table and draining the contents in one swift gulp.

"Indeed." Camellia shook her head in disbelief. She could not recall the last time she had seen her father eager to dance.

She turned towards her brother, who was

still watching Thalian and Amaya, his stunned expression having turned thoughtful. In a sudden movement, he stood and started to walk away from the table, making his way around the outskirts of the room.

"What are you-?" Camellia called after him but the prince was gone before the question was fully formed.

The crowd parted as the king made his way across the room, a wide space opening up in the very middle of the dancefloor.

Thalian led Amaya to the very centre of the floor and turned to her, inclining his head slightly. Amaya smiled up at him before she gathered the skirts of her dress and bowed low before him.

She lifted her head after a moment, looking up at his face. He was smiling affectionately down at her as he offered her his hand again. She took it, still smiling as if she simply couldn't stop, and he pulled her gracefully back up onto her feet. Then, not breaking eye contact, he pressed a soft kiss to the back of her hand.

A quiet murmur suddenly broke out around the room at the sight.

Just as he seemed to be about to move, the music changed and a much slower tune started to ring out across the hall. It seemed to switch out mid song but Amaya didn't have much time to focus on analysing that as Thalian suddenly pulled her close, needing no such time to recover, his other hand dropping to her waist as he pulled her in.

Her breath hitched as she blinked up at him, all too aware of his closeness. "I-I don't really..." *Know how to dance like this.*

He simply shook his head, seemingly aware of what she was trying to say. "Just follow my lead." He murmured as he began to gently pull her with him across the floor.

The watchful eyes of many curious and stunned elves were fixed upon the near inconceivable sight of a strange little human dancing with their usually detached king, though they all seemed to go unnoticed by the pair. It was as though everything else had melted away completely as all Amaya and Thalian seemed able to look at was each other.

Even Valerian, standing by the minstrels after sneaking over and getting them to change the song to something slower that would force the two closer together, went unseen.

There was a certain energy in the room as the music continued. All eyes were on Thalian, spinning and twirling his human companion across the dancefloor.

It seemed very intimate for those standing on the sidelines, *too* intimate for simply a king dancing with a guest. There was something else there that even those who had no inkling of it before this moment certainly did once they saw the two of them together.

It was a wonderful sight nonetheless. There had been a time, long ago, when Thalian had joined in on these festivities without a second thought. When he would dance and sing and laugh as much as the next elf.

After Caleniel's passing, however, Thalian had simply stopped. He had not had it in him to dance and be merry, not without her. It was as though the very joy had been sucked out of him when the life had left her body. As if he had died too but been forced to keep moving. An empty shell.

Valerian did not actually even remember a time when his father had joined in more than simply giving a speech or rubbing elbows with dignitaries during such events. He was practically buzzing with excitement as he hurried back to the table and seated himself, watching the girl and his father with a kind of reverence in his expression.

He had never thought this day would come. The day he realised, truly, that his father had *fallen in love*. He would not speak it out loud, especially not to the king himself, but he could see it regardless. It was clear as day.

When Thalian had taken Amaya prisoner, the prince had intended to simply look out for her and perhaps use her presence as a way to soften his father in regards to the world beyond the walls of their castle, beyond the shores of their isle even. The way things had developed between the pair of them was something beyond his imagination. Still, it made him feel very happy.

Camellia could remember more than Valerian. She remembered festivals like this when their mother was alive and the way their father danced and got involved happily. She had not thought to ever see it again but, looking at him now, she realised that she recognised this elf moving across the dancefloor, though she had not seen him in a thousand years.

She did not entirely know how to feel about the whole thing, the fact her father clearly held quite serious feelings for a human girl, but the way he looked and the way he had been acting lately certainly made her feel hopeful, perhaps even happy.

Surprising practically everyone who knew him (and himself) Thalian actually led Amaya in one more dance that night, relishing in the joy on her face and the fact he was presented with a genuine reason to be able to have her quite so close. Not that he intended to admit that aloud.

After returning to the table, Thalian made a point of lavishing Amaya with the attention he had wished to bestow upon her when this feast began. Soon enough, they were both talking and drinking as though it were just the two of them back in the library or in his private dining hall.

Amaya's night certainly brightened up, though even without Thalian's dancing and his attentiveness she would have thoroughly enjoyed the whole affair. She decided that elven celebrations were certainly one of her favourite things.

It was just so bright and colourful, full of good food and good music, merrymaking and laughter, dancing and singing. An homage to the passing of the season. The whole thing was simply beautiful and far outshone any human traditions she might have seen back in her village.

The Mirror

Late into the night, after a little more wine than Amaya had intended to drink, Thalian had bidden her to stand and, placing his hand upon her lower back in perhaps the slightest show of possession, led her out of the hall.

Eventually, she found herself standing on a large, stunning balcony that overlooked the forest. She wondered if she could explore this castle her whole life and still find some new room or thing to take her by surprise.

"I trust you have enjoyed yourself." Thalian said, watching her as she took in the view.

"Oh, yes!" Amaya nodded fervently, noting the pleased look in his eyes as she went on. "It's wonderful! And I appreciate you indulging me in dancing."

Thalian's soft smile turned into a grin as he thought back over the way he had noticed everybody eyeing the two of them as he'd actually walked towards the dancefloor with her. The disbelief on some of their faces had amused him. Sometimes he did rather enjoy shocking people, as it were.

"It was no great sacrifice, I must admit." He replied, turning his attention to the view of the trees beyond his castle. "I had rather an enjoyable time."

His grin softened again as he looked at Amaya once more, thinking back to the way he had held her and twirled her around the floor, her body so close and so warm.

She flushed under his gaze, though she didn't entirely know why. There was something in his eyes that she could not decipher and she wished she could peek into his thoughts for just a moment.

"Are you happy here?" Thalian found himself asking suddenly, perhaps randomly.

Amaya hesitated only half a second before she nodded, working up another smile. She thought he wouldn't notice the hesitation, brief as it had been. He did, of course. He also saw something in her eyes. Something he too couldn't decipher. Something that Amaya did not want to admit, perhaps.

"Tell me." He urged gently, voice just above a whisper, as if he was afraid of the unspoken words inside her head.

She didn't look at him for another long moment as she did her best to try and figure out how to put it. She liked being around *him*, she liked the people here, she had fun, and she was basically given anything she needed... but was a gilded cage not still a cage?

"Can a person be truly happy if they are not actually free?" She asked then, looking up in time to see him covering some emotion that had passed over his face.

Amaya wondered if she had upset him. That was the reason she had not wanted to say anything, the reason she was loath to even keep bringing this up. However, she also had absolutely no desire to lie to him.

Thalian frowned, nodding because he supposed that deep down he had known what she was going to say. He'd just wanted to be sure. It upset him to know that she could perhaps never be fully happy here. Over the time he had grown so close to her, he found that it was all he had wanted. For her to be happy *here,* for her to *want* to stay... with him. It pained him to know that he had caused this. Brought such sorrow down upon her.

"If only I could see my father." Amaya sighed, moving to sit down on a little stone chair nearby. She didn't even know why she was saying it but she wanted Thalian to know what was on her mind, to know that she still missed him desperately, even if other parts of her *were* quite happy here in this place. "I just miss him so much."

A silence followed during which she looked up at the sky, watching the stars twinkle overhead as though they had not a care in the whole world. How nice that must be, she thought.

Standing beside her, Thalian quietly mulled something over in his mind as he watched her in turn. She was not hinting to be let go, he could see that quite clearly. No, in fact, Amaya was simply sharing her thoughts with him, her feelings. Confiding in him. Her desire to flee this castle was no longer overwhelming but she was quite obviously torn in two.

"There may be a way." He said suddenly, watching her turn her curious gaze upon him. "Come with me."

Thalian held out his hand to help Amaya

onto her feet and then he turned and led her back inside.

~

She followed him through the winding hallways, back towards the queen's chambers. Amaya no longer felt any apprehension at seeing that crimson curtain at the bottom of the stairs come into view. She easily stepped past as he moved it aside and followed him up.

There was a sort of reverence within her as she walked past that portrait of the queen and down the corridor. She was gone but she was everywhere and her heart hurt for Thalian and Valerian and Camellia, for the loss of such an important figure in their lives.

"I really don't understand." Amaya said as she followed him through to a room she hadn't been in before. What had he meant when he said there may be a way to see her father and how could coming up here help?

He didn't stop, striding towards the back of the room where another curtain fell down. Pulling it back, he revealed a hidden doorway. Surprised, she stepped through after him and looked around.

Thalian had led her into a room that looked as though it had been cut into pure stone. So used to a different sort of look within the rooms of this castle, Amaya stopped for a moment and just took it in.

The room had a slightly ethereal light to it

and, as her attention came back to Thalian, she noticed the small pool of water that he was now standing beside. He was watching her but his eyes looked a little sad. He didn't say so but he hadn't set foot in here for many years. More years than Amaya would have been able to imagine if he had given her a number.

"What is this?" She asked, stepping a little closer and looking from the pool to his face.

Thalian cast his gaze over it, watching little water lilies floating on the glass-like surface of the pool. "This." He said. "Is my wife's mirror. If you wish, you have only to touch the water and it will show you your father."

Amaya blinked in amazement. "It will?" She took a hesitant little step towards the pool, turning her attention down to the water. It was still and clear and had a beauty about it she wouldn't have expected from *water*, of all things.

"Perhaps it can help to settle your heart for this night." He added, watching her with a thoughtful frown, wishing there was a little more he could do here and now to help with how much she very clearly longed to see her father. Thalian had missed her pining somehow, almost forgetting about her father's entire existence, his attention having been more focused on the effect Amaya had been having on *him*. On his *heart*. "I can arrange, tomorrow, for you to send him a letter." He continued after a beat, making her look up at him again with wide eyes. "If you would like." He cleared his throat. "My messenger could wait for him to pen his own response, even..."

She stared at him in silence, a little astounded by his words, unable to prevent the corners of her mouth pulling up into a smile even if she'd wanted to.

"Really?" She was already turning away from the mirror and stepping towards him before he could respond. He nodded, about to give her a verbal answer but found himself completely taken off guard as Amaya threw her arms around his neck. "Oh, thank you!"

Thalian didn't say anything but he returned the gesture with a soft smile, his arms slowly moving around her. He closed his eyes as he focused on the feeling of her in his embrace.

Reluctantly, he pulled back and let go of her. "Would you like to look into the mirror?" He asked.

Amaya looked over at the water again, thoughtful for a few more seconds before she made her decision. "Yes."

Thalian turned his attention back towards the water, moving to sit down upon the stone edge around the pool. "All you need to do is place your hand palm down upon the water." He explained. "Tell the mirror what it is you wish to see... and it shall show you." He looked up at her again as she sat down next to him. "It will show your father to you as he is right at this very moment."

Amaya fixed her stare upon the pool, gazing into the water before she slowly moved her hand out over the surface. It was crystal clear and yet she could see no bottom. She realised that the ethereal look of the room appeared to be emanating from the pool itself, making it obvious this was no regular water. It didn't seem to be filtering in from anywhere either. It was as though it had simply materialised in the stone.

Lowering her hand further down until it touched the cool surface of the mirror, Amaya felt a little nervous though she trusted that it was not dangerous. It just felt like she was continually being introduced to things that were so far beyond her understanding and comprehension and she was not sure she would ever get used to such magic.

"Show me my father." Amaya said as her fingers disturbed the surface, feeling a little silly, as if she was talking to herself but she didn't have too much time to dwell upon any embarrassment as the water began to change before her eyes. A flickering began, so slight at first that she was unsure whether her eyesight was simply failing her. It continued on, an image gradually swirling into view.

What Amaya saw was not even remotely close to what she had expected. She had assumed her father would be unhappy with her taking his place here, sad that she was not with him, and feeling guilty with the belief that she was in danger here, a poor prisoner of a cruel Elf King.

What she did not expect was to see him huddled in the corner of a dirty locked room, his cough clearly returning with a vengeance. He looked almost as bad as he had when she had gotten him released from Thalian's halls!

With a gasp, she jerked her hand away from the water, jumping very suddenly to her feet. She stumbled and lost her balance as she stepped backwards, her foot missing the little step down from the ledge.

Thalian was up in an instant, taking hold of her waist to steady her. He was frowning as he lifted a hand to her face, gently cupping her cheek to calm her frantic gaze and make her look at him.

"What did you see?" He asked softly, his thumb absentmindedly caressing her cheek.

"He-he's in trouble..." Amaya breathed out, shaking her head. "They... they've locked him up! Why... why would they do that? I-I... I don't... Thalian, what am I-"

"Shh, listen. Listen to me!" He urged, beginning to feel slightly panicked himself.

He had seen her angry. He had seen her sad. He had seen her confused. He had seen her scared. However, he had not yet seen her in such a state of distress as this and the sight was making him feel quite helpless. Her eyes were wide and there were tears shining in them. The sight of her like this tugged at his heartstrings.

Before he could even fully comprehend what he was doing, he found himself leaning closer. Whatever thoughts had been swirling and tangling around in her mind instantly ceased as, seemingly out of nowhere, Thalian's mouth descended upon her own.

The kiss, unexpected as it was, was sweet

and tender. His thumb continued to softly skim across her cheek as Amaya subconsciously tilted her head up a little, practically melting into it.

Thalian found himself smiling into the kiss, half amused at how quickly she seemed to have forgotten her worry with one touch of his lips.

Pulling away after a few moments he looked down at her again, studying her face as her eyes fluttered open and focused back on him. He was pleased to see that some of her panic had been swept away.

However, as much as he would like to delve into what had just occurred here between the two of them, Thalian decided that the most pressing matter at hand was her father. He knew that she would not be able to focus on anything else and he did not wish to leave her in despair over somebody she loved. Not when something could be done about it.

Amaya was far too stunned to really say anything for a minute, thoughts jumping from concern over her father and his bizarre imprisonment to the dizzying high from Thalian's surprise kiss.

"What am I meant to do?" She managed, her voice just above a whisper, and found that she truly did not know which problem she was referring to.

Thalian looked back at her with conflicting emotions. Confusion, longing, and unease were all vying for his immediate attention.

"Come with me." He eventually said,

reaching down to take her hand in his and quickly leading her from the chamber. He glanced back once over his shoulder before he stepped out. He did not plan to come in here again.

Thalian led Amaya through his wife's rooms and back down the stairs. "I will take you to him." He said, letting go of her hand as he strode on ahead. "And then... I set you free, you may go where you wish."

Amaya stopped moving altogether then, staring at the back of his head. "What did you just say?"

Her question went unanswered as Thalian kept moving, not looking back.

Part of him felt that if he did his heart may break because despite what had just happened and despite the events that had already led them both here, he still could not be certain whether Amaya would return with him or not and he did not want to see the answer in her eyes. He wasn't ready.

"Harlynn!" Thalian boomed, catching sight of the guard as she was rushing through the halls in their direction. "Ready Agnar, I shall be depart-"

"My king, there is no time!" Harlynn cut him off, completely ignoring the look that flashed across Thalian's face.

"The humans!" She continued, not giving the king any time to admonish her. "They are coming!"

"What are you talking about?" Thalian frowned. His ire was seemingly forgotten as he glanced from Harlynn to the main doors of the castle, where she had just come from, and back again.

Harlynn looked past the king, her attention falling upon Amaya standing like a shadow behind him.

Thalian's frown deepened as he followed Harlynn's gaze and finally looked back over his shoulder at Amaya. The words that came next only served to form a hard knot in his stomach.

"They are coming for the girl."

Enemies At The Door

The journey through the forest had been hard going for the large band of humans who had joined Vermund on his trek through the Golden Wood. None of them had entered this place before, save for Vermund and Oeric nearly two weeks past with Gideon, and most were feeling extremely anxious.

However, when Vermund said something was happening, everybody simply fell in line. He had a lot of control on the people of Feardenn and he liked to keep it that way.

He wasn't used to people *not* falling at his feet to do his bidding, thus over time he had grown more and more frustrated by Amaya and her refusal to wed him. Who would turn *him* down? Only a fool!

Vermund was strong, good looking, and rich as far as their village went. What more could a woman possibly need?

He had come to the conclusion that the girl was simply shy. That she was nervous about living up to his standards and about pleasing him as a *wife* and as a *lover*. He would have to rid her of such idiocies because it was costing him a lot of time.

Once he finally found her, of course.

The longer they walked, the more Vermund wondered if he would truly find Amaya hidden within the Elf King's castle.

Elves had a long legend in their village of being vicious beings who stole into human settlements and carried off maidens and children. Their dark elven magic was said to bewitch and destroy entire villages and crops. They brought misfortune and death. They would curse and kill and if these beasts had the farmer's daughter in their grasp, Vermund would not let it slide.

Amaya was, after all, *his*. Rescuing her would no doubt earn him extra favour with her, too... and her crazy father. Though if he could convince her the old man needed to stay in that room then he would do so.

He found himself beginning to hope that she *was* being held prisoner by this elven monarch. What a prize it would be, to return home victorious with the stolen wealth of the dead Elf King in his possession!

And Amaya.

Obviously.

He hacked his way through the undergrowth of the forest with his sword, cutting away with complete abandon, caring not for the life of the flowers or plants around him.

"This way, men!" He called over his shoulder. "Hurry! And stay close. This forest is evil." Vermund's narrowed eyes were fixed upon the path beneath his feet as he moved, doing his best to ignore the weight of the very air around him as he trudged onwards.

It had taken them since before dawn to finally come to the borders of the forest, near the land where the elves dwelt. Vermund had expected to have been set upon from the trees above as they had come closer to the elven settlement but nothing had come. They had found the place by sending a few scouts ahead to check the area. The men had come back to tell him that the gates were ahead. That they would soon be upon the castle of the Elf King.

He stepped forward into a crouch, peering through the bushes with Oeric at his side, and scanned the area.

Vermund was an incredibly skilled hunter and a very proficient fighter. Oeric was alright and the men behind them could defend their own, he supposed, but they were more used to farming and baking and shoeing horses.

Still, they were the only army Vermund had and they could keep the rest of the elves distracted while he made straight for the king. He didn't really care whether or not the rest of the people he'd brought with him ended up dead. So long as he claimed what was his own he would be satisfied.

"Alright, men." He said, voice low as he stood up and unsheathed his sword. "You know what to do. Go!" He sent them on ahead, charging through the trees, which is when Harlynn and the rest finally noticed the humans approaching with weapons in hand, and knew why they had come.

Then Vermund grabbed Oeric by the collar before rounding up a smaller group of stragglers and gestured for them to follow him. "This way, lads." He muttered darkly, turning and picking his way through the trees. "Follow me."

~

Thalian tore his attention from Amaya and turned back towards Harlynn. "How many?" He asked, snapping back into focus as he started walking.

"Fifty or so." Harlynn told him, glancing at Amaya who was still standing as if frozen, before she turned and hurried after the king.

Fifty people?

Amaya's village, which was the biggest of the three on the isle, was made up of almost one hundred and thirty people altogether. There had been many more before a plague ripped through the community a few months ago but they still boasted the largest population between the three human settlements.

Why were fifty of her people here before Thalian's halls? From the sounds of it they had come armed and were about to launch an attack. Why would they do that? Why would they lock her father up like an animal? Why had Thalian kissed her?

There were too many things happening in her head, and around her, all at once and Amaya couldn't give any of them adequate attention.

Finding it in her to move again, she forced one foot in front of the other and hurried after the two elves, who were now discussing strategy.

"What is happening?" She exclaimed,

coming up to Thalian's side and grasping at his sleeve.

He turned to look at her, taking a moment to study her expression. She looked alarmed and his hard gaze softened just slightly.

"They picked a good time to sneak up on us." He muttered, glaring in the direction of the main doors where elves were now gathering and arming themselves for what looked to be an inevitable fight ahead. "With most of us celebrating, they were able to catch us practically unawares."

He was gritting his teeth, angry at having let the defences of his kingdom slide. It was just one night! He was usually so on top of orders for the guards on duty. He was normally far more insistent there be more on watch at one time. Especially out beyond the entryway, keeping a lookout from the trees. He couldn't quite understand how he had let it slip but Thalian reminded himself he didn't have the time to be self critical.

"Your father must have told them you were here. They are readying to attack." He turned again, striding away from her.

"Wait! Maybe I can talk to them." Amaya said, running forward again and catching his hand with her own.

He stopped and turned back to her. He didn't let go of her hand, in fact his grip seemed to tighten a little. "Talk to them?" He echoed, frowning.

In the back of his mind, his thoughts flickered back to when Camellia had told him to talk to *Amaya*, when he'd thought he had done something to make her unhappy with him. It seemed even less of a good idea now than it had then.

Thalian shook his head, feeling uneasy at the mere thought. "Amaya. They did not come here to talk."

"Yes, I know." She said. "But if my father told them I was being held prisoner and they believe that they are rescuing me... I can tell them it is not what they think!"

Thalian was still unsure as she looked up at him but she continued on. "I can tell them that you are not what they believe you are. Let me try!" Amaya implored, practically clutching his hand for dear life.

The king stared back at her for a few quiet moments, thinking it over. He supposed there was a little logic to it but he could recall what she had told him about the people in her village and their beliefs about the elves. That, plus the fact that they did not seem to hold Amaya in such high esteem, made him worry they would not actually listen to her. That she would hold no sway over them.

Still, as she looked up at him with those beautiful brown eyes, wide with hope and obvious admiration, he found himself relenting.

"Very well. I shall allow it." He held back a sigh, turning to Harlynn. "Stay alert. I do not trust this."

Thalian turned and, still holding Amaya's hand, led her along the corridor. He paused only long enough for one of his people to rush up to him and place his crown upon his head and secure his sword to his hip, before he gave the order.

"Open the gates!"

Intruders

When the heavy, armoured doors opened, the large group of men had reached the end of the walkway, their weapons at the ready in front of them.

They were prepared to run straight into a fight. What they did not expect was to see the Elf King himself walk calmly into view.

What they expected even less was the sight of Amaya walking at his side unbound, looking healthy and cared for. Looking, in a word, *well*. A far cry from all they had been led to believe they would see of her if they were to actually find her here.

Thalian's face was expressionless, blank, far-removed from the emotions battling inside of him. The king would not show it but he was gripped in a state of frantic disquietude. He did not trust that this was simply a group of angry humans worried for the safety of one of their own. If this were the case, where had they been these last weeks? Why had they not descended upon his castle the day her father was returned to them? Why did they look so surprised to see Amaya standing there beside him, as though they had not actually expected to see her here at all?

Amaya made as if to step around Thalian but his fingers closed around her wrist and tugged her back to his side, holding her in place.

She looked up at him curiously. As much as she had felt left out in her village, she didn't really believe that these people would *hurt* her. In fact, she didn't believe that they would hurt anyone once she explained.

"Why do you come through the forest to the Golden Castle armed as if for war?" Thalian's voice rang out loud and clear as he turned his intense gaze back to the group of men at his door.

There was a silence before one stepped forward. From behind Amaya and Thalian, the subtle sound of elven soldiers pulling bowstrings taut in preparation to defend their king was heard.

The man hesitated briefly but when no arrow flew and the elves were still standing like statues, he finally spoke. "Why does the king of the elves hold one of our own hostage?"

"He is not holding anybody hostage!" Amaya cried out before Thalian could say anything else. She wrenched her wrist from his grasp and took a few steps away from him. "Please! You must listen to me! The elves have been nothing but good to me. Nobody is a prisoner here. Put down your weapons, there is no need for any of this!"

The humans blinked back at her, some shifting uneasily in the silence that followed. They were unsure what to believe, what to say, what to do.

Just as the man who had approached opened his mouth to speak again, this time to Amaya, he was cut off.

"Do not listen!" A voice suddenly came from above. "That Elf King has her under his spell!"

All eyes - human and elf alike - shot upwards, where Vermund was standing on high, far up on a balcony slightly adjacent to the gates.

Seeing him, Amaya's expression took on a slight look of panic and she found herself moving a little closer to Thalian on instinct.

Thalian, for his part, was taken completely by surprise. Never before had this happened in his realm, yet twice this season had some mortal man come into his lands and somehow scaled his castle walls undetected. Now, this *vermin* was inside and he was furious.

"Take him down!" Thalian bellowed to his soldiers, anger red hot in his veins.

Immediately, all archers loosed their arrows at their king's command, aiming directly for Vermund's head.

~

Upon leaving the main group, Vermund and his band of men had skirted their way around the castle looking for some sort of weakness in the defences. Some way to get inside.

Vermund knew that with the focus on the men at the front gates, he had more chance of sneaking in undetected. He wanted to get an advantage and he soon found a place he could clamber up to, using the large trees closer to the castle walls to help.

Up, up, up they all climbed until they were standing on some sort of balcony and Vermund was feeling smug as ever as he immediately looked around for something to steal. Before he got very far, his attention was then caught by the happenings down at the gate. At the sight of that elf standing there looking as if he were the most celestial being in the whole of Amarar.

Then Amaya!

His mild elation at having found her at last was short lived. His relish turned to anger as he watched her push forward and... and actually *defend* that... that *beast* of a creature!

The elf had obviously bewitched her!

Vermund had been unable to hold back, shouting down before he could even really stop himself. It pleased him to see the shock on the king's face and he didn't bother to hide it, blatantly smirking down from on high.

When the arrows came he managed to evade them. Vermund was out of the way before they reached him - and though he would attribute it to his skill, it was actually due to his grabbing another man from beside him and thrusting the poor bastard in front of himself as a shield.

The man fell from the balcony, killed instantly, pierced by many an arrow.

Amaya stared into the baker's empty eyes as his body hit the ground a little way ahead of her. A sick feeling of horror took hold of her and she gasped in alarm, reflexively reaching out to grab Thalian's arm. In response he gently pushed her behind him, just enough so that her view would be obscured.

There was the briefest of lulls and then it was as if all hell suddenly broke loose.

"They have killed one of our own!" Vermund hollered from above, pointing down at the dead body of the baker. "They have declared war!"

Never mind the fact that he had riled all of these men up and brought them before the gates of the elven realm for no other reason but to attack. Never mind the fact that it was technically his fault the baker was dead.

"Fight, men!" He shouted. "Fight!"

Thalian was completely rattled, not that it showed. He had far more self control than that in a situation like this, in a fight. However, the sight of humans inside his castle, uninvited and armed, sent a rage through his blood that could not be quelled by mere talking.

The one who was yelling seemed to be in charge and Thalian could already tell that this man had absolutely no honour in him. Using one of his own as a human shield! He was no better than one of the foul beasts who roamed the forest and the king was disgusted.

"Doronion!" He barked as the angry cries from the townsfolk behind him grew into a roar. "Find my daughter!"

At once, Doronion turned and disappeared into the castle, running down the corridor towards the princess's rooms, where she had retired not long before the chaos began.

As his soldiers surrounded their distracted

king, moving between him and the group of armed men, Thalian took Amaya by the hand and all but dragged her towards Aurelia, who was standing by the doors beside Valerian.

Amaya had not noticed either of them come outside in the commotion that had taken over when the humans approached. She'd thought everybody was still in the festival hall.

"Get her out of sight." Thalian said, gently pushing her towards Aurelia before turning to his son.

"Thalian!" Amaya cried out but he spared her no more than a glance as Aurelia began to pull her back into the building.

The king and the prince followed but they veered off in a different direction, towards a staircase so they could ascend to wherever Vermund was.

Amaya's eyes never left Thalian as he raced up the stairs with a group of his people, pausing at the top for just a second to seek her out in the crowd below. Satisfied that she would be safe, he turned once more and disappeared from sight.

Aurelia dragged Amaya towards a different set of stairs that led down instead of up. She could hear the fighting outside at the gates and by now her heart was thundering in her ears. What was happening? This wasn't right, none of this was supposed to happen! Why was Vermund inside the castle? What was he doing?

Amaya turned her frantic attention fully back to Aurelia, realising she had taken her down into what appeared to be a storage cellar.

"I'm sorry." She found herself saying, peering anxiously back towards the stairs they had both just descended.

Aurelia turned to look at her, her eyes full of confusion. "For what?"

"That you have been relegated to babysitting me instead of defending your own home from intruders." Amaya muttered, wringing her hands in frustration. "Intruders that *I* seem to have brought here."

She is a respected soldier! Amaya thought. *This must feel so beneath her.*

Aurelia moved so that she was standing in front of the girl, lifting her hands to her upper arms to hold her in place. "Do not apologise." She said firmly. "It is my honour."

At Amaya's disbelieving expression, Aurelia gripped her arms a little more tightly. "My friend, if the king has chosen *me* to guard you, be assured that you are very important to him. That he thinks you very precious indeed. He would have no harm come to you and he knows that I shall let none."

Amaya didn't realise she was crying until Aurelia reached up and gently wiped away a tear with her thumb. She thought back to the festival, just hours ago. Dancing with Thalian, him sweeping the two of them away from the party to be alone, the mirror, the *kiss*...

She knew he was a great warrior, she had seen it, and she had read many things in the history books in the library over her time here. He was featured in a couple of them, mostly ones that mentioned the massacre. She knew that mere mortals were no real match for him. But she was still worried.

Vermund was here and he did not play fair. Amaya had seen rage in his eyes when he shouted down from that balcony. He had the look of a man who would do *anything*.

Her thoughts were suddenly swept away as the clanging sound of sword upon sword came closer and Aurelia moved to push her behind a large barrel.

"Stay down." Was all she managed to mutter before the cellar was infiltrated.

~

Thalian had taken his son and his closest guards with him up the stairs. He didn't know exactly how many other men this invader had up here with him but he decided that the majority of their force needed to stay at the gate. The amount of men inside this castle could not outnumber the amount that stood before it.

When they reached the balcony, however, it was empty. There was not another being in sight and Thalian was furious. Where were they? He could not allow them to wander his castle unchecked, armed to the teeth, intent on fighting his people and taking Amaya away against her will.

Was it against her will?

He had technically set her free and it had

sounded like her father was in trouble. Perhaps she would not be so averse…

Thalian dismissed such thoughts quicker than he might have in the past, however. He thought back to the way she had clung to him down at the gates. The way she had been so eager to defend him and his people. The way she had seemed to baulk at the appearance of that man.

His thoughts returned to the present moment and he whirled around, stalking back down the hall.

"Find them!" He commanded in a growl, his anger sky-high as his guards scattered to hunt down the interlopers. "Kill them all!"

~

"Where is my father?" Camellia's panic was clear in her voice as she watched Doronion stand guard at the door to her bedchamber.

He shook his head, his ear pressed against the door as he listened to the chaos growing ever closer now the people of Feardenn had pushed their way inside.

"Looking for the humans." He told her. Though he had left before Thalian had gone that way, it was obvious that the king would go himself to take down the castle invaders.

Doronion was pleased that Thalian had asked him to come and protect Camellia. He knew that Thalian sensed his feelings for the princess, or perhaps more than sensed, and while he knew it was not allowed, it didn't make Thalian hostile towards him. In fact, he seemed to use it to his advantage, knowing that Doronion would take good care of his daughter when he needed him to. Thalian trusted Doronion not to act out of turn and he was simply happy to be able to be her friend, if nothing else.

Camellia was quiet for a moment as she tried to quell her growing worry. When Doronion had crashed into her room to tell her the castle was being attacked, she had been taken completely off guard, having been trying to relax after the festival.

Camellia was an introverted soul and she often needed to recharge after large gatherings. Her favourite way to do so was meditation, usually in a garden beneath the sunshine, but in winter she just came to her own rooms. She felt the cold far more than her father or brother seemed to, though of course nothing close to how a human like Amaya must feel it.

The princess had never personally had any dealings with humans until Amaya came. The thought of all these people in her home with weapons, trying to hurt them, was troubling. She knew her father and brother could hold their own but she couldn't understand why the humans would do this in the first place. The elves had never done anything to them! Sure, Amaya had been here as a prisoner... but Camellia could scarcely see her as such now, she was more of a fixture in this place, and the girl seemed to have been enjoying her time here more and more.

"Where is Amaya?" She asked next, watching Doronion shake his head in reply.

"I do not know. I came straight here." He looked over his shoulder at her. "I am sure she is fine." He was worried about Elion, who he had not seen since the festival, but he tried to keep it to the back of his mind.

There was a small silence before Camellia stood up, walking towards him and putting a hand on his shoulder, almost as if she had sensed his worries.

"I know that-" She started, but was immediately cut off by a loud thud against her bedroom door, and then another, and another.

"Stay behind me." Doronion told her as he stepped back from the door and gripped his dagger.

~

Vermund had ordered his men to disperse the moment the fighting had broken out. He needed to find a way to get the king alone and he needed to find Amaya, in whichever order they presented themselves to him.

He needed all the distraction he could get and the men would keep the elves who were no doubt on their way up here busy.

Creeping through unfamiliar hallways, his sword drawn, Vermund was fully alert and ready for whatever came his way.

However, he seemed to rather easily have escaped most of the fighting so far, leaving it to the other townspeople and sending those who had climbed up here with him to their doom to give himself a headstart and a distraction.

Eventually, he came upon a half-hidden red doorway and, curious, Vermund pushed his way inside. Maybe he could find something expensive to steal while he waited for his chance to slay the Elf King.

Vermund could not have known that this doorway was one of the many entrances that connected the king's private rooms to the late queen's. Nor could he know that the blackened rose he happened upon in one of the rooms beyond the door was so important to the king.

He made a face at it before he turned and knocked the whole thing off the table, letting the glass case that enclosed the dead Starfire Rose smash to pieces against the marble floor. Its protective barrier vanished and the rose turned to ash and blew away in the soft breeze that was coming in through the open window.

"You have just made a most grievous error." A low, dangerous voice muttered from behind him.

Vermund whipped around from where he had turned to start stuffing his bag and pockets with the expensive looking jewels he had spotted on the nearby dresser.

Standing there before him was the king himself, armour-less, his long silver sword in hand, narrowed gaze practically hot enough with anger to have burned through Vermund's very skin like the breath of a dragon.

The Confrontation

Aurelia spun in place, thrusting her sword in front of her as a group of men came at her. The humans outnumbered her and yet she fought them tirelessly, moving with a grace that nearly had them mesmerised.

At first she tried not to land a killing blow, under the impression that these people held beliefs that were not entirely their fault, but soon she was focused only upon keeping Amaya safe and ridding the halls of the home she loved from the enemies at the door.

Amaya had ducked behind the barrel when she had told her to but she couldn't resist peeking out, registering some of the human faces as familiar. The horsemaster's son, the butcher's brother, and the baker's uncle.

The whole thing was awful. Why was this happening? Her two worlds had collided in the most violent of ways and all Amaya wished was for everybody to understand, to cease this fighting, to come to peace.

"There she is!" The butcher's brother cried out and, with alarm, she realised that he was pointing directly at her. "Get her! Quick!"

His words were cut off by Aurelia's blade slicing through his leg. A sharp cry left his lips as he fell to the floor but the other men had already heard him and were turning their attention to the girl behind the barrel.

Aurelia, who would let no one near her,

moved to stand directly in between Amaya and the group of men who had started to make for her hiding place. "To the back of the room and out!" She shouted over her shoulder, swinging her weapon and preventing one from getting around her. "Now! Go!"

Fuelled by dread the likes of which Amaya had only felt when Thalian found her that first time in the queen's rooms, she turned instantly and rushed to the back of the cellar. There, behind a stone-grey curtain, she found a doorway cut into the wall.

Looking back over her shoulder for just a moment, Amaya pushed her way past the curtain and fled up the staircase.

~

Thalian stood, the tip of his sword pointed directly at Vermund's chest. He'd advanced slowly, moving with deadly ease, calm and deliberate.

"Who are you, who dares enter my domain? Why come you here, armed with weapons, to attack those who have never done a thing to you and yours?" Thalian's voice was level but there was a dangerous bite to it that was impossible to ignore, even for one as arrogant and conceited as Vermund.

He narrowed his own eyes back at the king, lifting his chin defiantly. A coward though he may be, Vermund had come to see this creature as one of his greatest enemies in so short a time. He had seen the way Amaya latched onto this elven king by the gates, the way her face had fallen when she had seen Vermund himself. She was not locked away in a dungeon as her father had proclaimed her to be. Instead, she walked amongst these *animals* as though she were one of them. She defended them as though they deserved it. As though they were *innocent.*

The evil *sprite* standing before him had obviously beguiled Amaya with his dark magic. He wanted her for himself. Vermund would not allow it.

"One who would slay you where you stand, *elf.*" Came the reply, his tone a challenge all its own. "Vermund, son of Veraith. You will return what belongs to me or I will take it from you. In both scenarios, your life ends."

Thalian continued to look down his nose at this man, the dangerous silence stretching as he regarded him.

Vermund.

Oh, yes, he knew of him alright. He recalled every word Amaya had said about him. The way he sought to own her and hang her like an ornament at his side. The insistent way in which he had badgered her, wearing her down, demanding her hand again and again.

He had seen the disgust in her eyes and, while Amaya had assured him nothing horrific had happened at Vermund's hand, Thalian did not believe this would last. He knew of men such as this.

If there *was* a monster in this room, it was not himself but the man who stood before him.

Vermund had even given him his father's name, as if he was somebody important. As if he was a lord or a king or a nobleman. That sort of thing was reserved for men whose reputation or family line preceded them. Not for insignificant hunters from a little human village that nobody across the sea had probably ever heard of.

Thalian sneered at him, pressing the blade a little harder into his chest. "Big words for such a small man, Vermund son of Veraith."

With that, Thalian prepared to thrust his sword forward. He wanted to end this once and for all. He wanted this filth out of his home - out of his wife's chambers - and he wanted to take Amaya to her father and bring the both of them back to the safety of his castle. Their village was clearly full of deranged imbeciles.

What Thalian did not count on was the other man hiding in the next room, back pressed against the hard wall around the open entryway, sword clasped firmly in front of him. He crept out of hiding as Thalian was speaking and began to approach. It was only at the last moment, as Vermund's gaze shifted minutely to the approaching man behind him and a small smirk crept onto his face, that Thalian realised something was amiss.

He twisted his body into a spin, turning fast and hard upon the man behind him. Oeric raised his sword high, steel clashing upon steel as his weapon met the Elf King's.

Thalian was staring at him with contempt, practically snarling. "And who, pray tell, are *you?*"

"The distraction I needed." Vermund said from behind him, leaping forward and giving Thalian a massive shove, the hardest that he could muster.

The action sent Thalian stumbling forward. His sword moved with him and Oeric's eyes went wide with the pain and shock of Thalian's sword going right through him.

Vermund, seeing his supposed best friend as simply collateral damage in his rearview, turned and fled.

~

Thalian, angry as a thunderstorm, stalked back out to the gates where the fighting had now completely ceased. He saw the remaining humans surrounded by his army but he was unfocused, closely scrutinising the crowd before him.

He was looking for that wretch, Vermund.

After the man had escaped him, Thalian had dragged Oeric's body from his wife's room and then scoured the entire floor, intent on finishing this once and for all. Trouble was, the man was now simply nowhere to be found and Thalian's anger would not be mitigated. He longed to carve into Vermund's flesh and make a feast of him for the crows.

"Father." Valerian approached, holding a

spear as he scanned the crowd.

"Report." He commanded his son, his eyes still roving across the mob of humans now fully under control.

Valerian gave him a brief rundown, assuring him that the upper levels were clear and none of the attackers remained inside the building.

The men that were left were shown some mercy, allowed to live so long as they fled this very moment and never again returned. The Elf King made them understand in no uncertain terms that if he were to ever set sights on any of them again he would personally put an end to their miserable little lives.

He turned back to his son as the humans scattered into the forest, ignoring the fact that they were heading the wrong way. Getting a little lost in the darkness of the Golden Wood was no less than they deserved. Still, he would send a couple of spies after them at some point, to make sure they did not perish. Once he had cooled down.

As they went, he noted that Vermund was not amongst them.

"Amaya." Thalian said her name then, turning from his son to scan the area, seeking her in the crowd. "Where is she?"

The question was directed at Valerian but his son could only shrug, having not seen her. He too turned to look around but Amaya was nowhere to be seen.

"Father!" Camellia's voice rang out then, loud and clear over the heads of the elves. The crowd parted for her as she came running towards the king, Doronion just behind her.

When the humans had invaded her chambers, she and Doronion had fled into the adjoining study, where at the very back there was a secret tunnel that led up to one of the floors of her mother's old rooms. They had both witnessed the whole thing but had been too late to do anything about it.

"He has taken her into the forest!" She cried, as she finally reached her father, her eyes wide.

Thalian's heart nearly stopped altogether as he turned away, unable to hide the dismay on his face as he looked towards the thick expanse of trees.

All that stood before him saw in the king's eyes the heartbreak and the fear that coursed through him at the thought of that monster taking Amaya away.

Those old enough to have been there recalled a similar expression upon his face the day his queen had been ripped from him and he had been unable to prevent it.

Without another thought or word he moved, disappearing into the forest at speed.

Beneath The Trees

After running up the stairs that Aurelia had directed her to at the back of the storage cellar, Amaya found herself slipping through one of three other doorways at the top and, to her relief, came back out into familiar ground.

The Elf Queen's rooms!

She burst from behind a curtain (this one red, which she had noticed all that led to the queen's rooms were) at the same moment that Vermund himself had rushed from a room somewhere down the hall.

Stunned, Amaya stood there, staring at him as his predatory gaze fell upon her. He was moving before she could even really register his approach, so shocked was she at his being *here* of all places. In Caleniel's private rooms.

In the back of her mind she registered that the room he had come fleeing from was the one that led to the garden where the roses lived.

How dare he!

Her anger began to bubble up past the surface then but her time was already up. Just as Amaya opened her mouth, Vermund's large hand had come clamping down over it, his other arm wrapping around her body as he began to pull her with great haste away down the hall.

She struggled against him, of course she did, but she was simply no match for Vermund. The realisation made her blood run a little cold.

She did not see Camellia and Doronion, coming around the corner at the very second she was dragged out of sight, and before she knew it she was outside. She did wonder if she'd heard a voice from somewhere far behind but she couldn't turn her head to be sure, so tight was Vermund's grip on her.

He dragged Amaya out of some back door and away into the forest.

If she had been able to, she would have gone kicking and screaming.

~

Thalian was beyond furious now. He was practically burning with rage as he moved through the forest.

He knew the ways beneath these trees like the back of his hand and following the trail that Vermund's lumbering steps had left was not difficult. A proficient hunter though he may be, all arrogance seemed to override any skill he may have within him.

The king was desperate to find Amaya. Not just find her. Find her *safe* and *unharmed*.

This man had no right. No right to come into his realm armed for a fight. No right to drag her away anywhere against her will.

Thalian had placed Amaya in a cell the first time he met her, yes, but if she had not made the offer of switching places with her father he would not have done so. It was her choice, even if she might have felt that she had none. As bad-tempered and impulsive with anger as he may have been, he would not have put her anywhere had she been truly unwilling.

Vermund had no right to force her into anything, especially this. Thalian could not allow it. Would not.

He had no doubt that this oaf's plan was to drag her back to her pitiful little village and force her into a marriage she had absolutely no desire for. He would rip away her freedom and choice, and cage her in a life that was not her own.

Did he think that Thalian would not come? Did he think that he would let Amaya go so easily? That he would allow this man to disrespect him and his people and simply walk away without punishment?

No, Thalian decided, he was probably counting on the opposite. Vermund had made clear that he wanted to kill him.

The thought caused a grim smirk to appear on his lips as he urged himself to move even quicker through the trees, following the incredibly conspicuous trail.

As if that fool would get a chance to do so.

~

Bursting into a gloomy clearing, Vermund threw Amaya down into the dirt beneath a large tree. Landing hard with a pained grunt, she scowled up at him and then turned to look around, wondering if she could get onto her feet and outrun him quick enough.

"Damn this forest!" He yelled, angry at having become lost once again in this dreadful wilderness, especially with the girl as a burden. He did not wish to come upon the evil beasts he knew lived here.

Amaya shifted, sitting up properly, and he whirled upon her. "You are not going anywhere!" He snapped, stepping towards her threateningly.

"I am not going to lie here in the mud, Vermund!" She couldn't help but snap back despite her panic before pulling herself to her feet. She gritted her teeth, doing her best to ignore the pain in her hip and arm from her bad landing.

"Thalian will come for me. He is probably coming right now." Amaya told him. "You should run, Vermund. You should run far away."

He blinked at her, enraged. "Thalian? What, are you on a first name basis with this creature?" He shook his head, practically snarling at her like a rabid animal in his anger. His fingers toyed with the hilt of his sword as if in warning. "When we return to the village you will marry me and that... that beast's head shall hang above our fireplace!"

Amaya stared at him, utterly disgusted at his words. He meant to kill Thalian and keep his head as some trophy, the way he did with the animals he hunted. She already found *that* rather deplorable, never mind him doing it to an elf, a king no less. Someone Amaya cared for.

"No!" She cried, vehemently shaking her head. The revulsion she held for him, that she had always tried to hide in the past for the sake of politeness, was now clear on her face. "Never! I will never marry you!"

It came then, unexpectedly. Vermund's arm shot out as he backhanded Amaya across the face. Her cheek stung as she brought a hand up to the corner of her mouth, turning her head back to stare at him in complete shock. He had just hit her!

She opened her mouth to give him another piece of her mind, her eyes suddenly ablaze, but he backhanded her again. This time it was so hard that she fell to the ground, her head spinning as she felt the blood flooding to her cheek.

"You will do as I say, woman!" Vermund snapped, standing over her.

When she said nothing, not even sparing him another glance as her anger was now too great she feared the trouble it would get her into, Vermund leaned down and grabbed her by the arms. He shook her, shouting at her, but she didn't hear any of the words. Instead all she could focus on was attempting to thrash herself from his repulsive grasp.

"Unhand her. Now." Came the sudden, icy voice of the Elf King as he stepped from the darkness.

Amaya's breath and senses returned to her at the sight of him, relief immediately shooting through her body. He had come for her!

Vermund turned from her, his shock

written all over his face because he had heard no approach. He pushed her away, causing her to topple to the ground once more, before he stepped back and unsheathed his sword.

"Begone, monster." He spat.

"He's not a monster, Vermund!" Amaya cried, unable to help herself. Her body felt bruised, her cheek stung from his manhandling, but the sight of Thalian emboldened her. *"You* are!"

Vermund did his best to ignore her but he clenched his jaw in response. It wasn't ideal but he didn't *need* his wife to like him. He focused all his attention on Thalian, taking a second before throwing himself towards the elf.

Thalian's arm swung upwards and his sword connected with Vermund's, the sound of clashing steel ringing through the dark clearing.

The fight under the trees raged on in front of Amaya, Thalian blocking every hit the man tried to land on him, Vermund running on fumes as he did his best to keep up with his opponent.

Thalian moved like a swan through water. In comparison, Vermund moved like a creature stuck in a swamp.

"No!" Amaya screamed, as Vermund's blade flashed a little too close to Thalian's nose. She was too caught up in the fear to realise it but the king was in complete control of the situation. He could have taken the man down already but he wanted to toy with him just a little. Watching the dullard struggle to match him caused him an incredible amount of satisfaction.

Vermund wheeled on Amaya again at her cry, full of rage as he glared at her. "You stupid woman! You cannot truly feel for *him!*" He yelled. "Watch then!" He spun back to face the Elf King and then he ran at him. "As I remove his head from his shoulders!"

She watched in horror as Thalian did not move a muscle. He stood there as if made of stone and she thought for a heart wrenching second that he was about to allow himself to be run through.

Just as Vermund reached him, however, his sword buzzed through the air in one swift, graceful movement.

Vermund's own head fell to the ground, closely followed by the rest of him.

"I think not." Thalian muttered darkly. "May you find no peace in death, Vermund son of Veraith."

He then turned to Amaya, moving so quickly to crouch in front of her that she almost didn't even register it. He placed himself in her line of vision, blocking Vermund's body as he looked into her eyes to make sure that she was okay. Then, without a word, he took her face in his hands and captured her mouth with his own.

This kiss was different from the one that came before. It was deeper, more needy, desperate. Amaya could tell how frightened he had been.

She threw her arms around his neck and kissed him back, clinging to him like her life depended on it, until eventually she had to pull away with a slight wince.

She lowered her face but Thalian reached out and gently tilted her chin up so she was looking at him again.

He murmured something in the tongue of the elves, his gaze filling with both sorrow and fury as he took in the cut upon her lip (which was what had caused her to pull away) and the dark red mark blossoming across her cheek.

He carefully moved his fingers and ghosted them over her injuries. A sound of disapproval rumbled in his chest. "I should like to reanimate his corpse if only to give myself the satisfaction of murdering him again." He muttered angrily.

Amaya smiled a little, simply relieved now that he was here with her, that it was over. "I don't doubt it."

There was a silence in which they both just looked at each other and then she leaned in and pressed another soft kiss against his mouth. After a moment he smiled and stood, sweeping her up into his arms before she could react.

"Thalian!" Amaya squealed a laugh as she threw her arms around his neck like she was worried he might drop her.

He chuckled, holding her firmly as he turned to take her from this place once and for all. "Relax, little human. I've got you."

Safe

When Thalian reappeared from the treeline beyond the castle with Amaya in his arms, the relief that fell over the waiting elves was so palpable she could have reached out and touched it.

He gently set her back on her feet once she was safely over the threshold, still feeling protective despite the danger being over.

The doors were shut again, the bodies of the men who had fallen within the castle already disposed of in Thalian's absence.

Myleth came rushing over through the crowd, pulling Amaya into an embrace so tight that it made her flinch slightly, however she didn't say anything. Amaya had last seen Myleth in the hall for the feast and she had hoped that she was safe and well.

"Oh, I was so worried!" The she-elf cried, pulling back a little to look at her human charge. Her hair was a mess, the beautiful dress she'd been put in was dirty and torn from catching on brambles, and the red mark on her cheek made Myleth frown. "Oh, dear. Come with me, I'll have you all fixed up in no time."

"Actually." Thalian's voice said from behind her, turning from where Valerian and Aurelia stood with Doronion and Elion, all discussing the extent of the attack on the realm - the damage and loss. Camellia stood beside her father hanging off his arm like a child, her head resting on his bicep, not really listening to what any of them were saying, just glad that it was over and everybody was safe.

No elven blood had been spilled, thankfully, not that Thalian thought even a hundred human men armed with rusty swords and axes would have been much of a match for his people. Still, he had to admit there had been a few decent fighters amongst those from Feardenn.

"I shall be tending to her injuries myself, Myleth." The king continued, gently disentangling himself from his daughter, pressing a reassuring kiss to the top of her head before reaching past her and taking Amaya's hand in his own.

His actions left no room for discussion as he turned and led her through the crowd and down the hall. Myleth did not try to protest, instead she turned her comforting aura to Camellia, who still looked a little shaken, deciding she was going to make the princess some soothing tea and take her back to her rooms to rest.

As he left, Thalian called something in the language of the elves over his shoulder and Valerian and Aurelia immediately began heading back out into the night.

"What did you say to them?" Amaya wondered as she let him lead her through the halls.

"They are going to your village." Thalian said, leading her around a corner and towards the stairs that led to his own private rooms. "To make sure your people arrive safely, and then release your father from his misfortune and return here with him."

Though he wasn't looking at her directly,

he could see her from the corner of his eye. She turned her face up towards him, blinking in surprise. She was touched that he would even have remembered her father was in trouble, let alone have him ordered to be brought back here, where she now felt he would be safest.

Amaya held his hand just that little bit tighter and his mouth twitched in response as a smile fought its way onto his face.

~

She had been in the room once already but never had Amaya truly taken a proper look around Thalian's bedchamber before and when she realised that was where he had taken her she was filled with curiosity, looking around as if she would discover all sorts of secrets about him.

He led her towards a large armchair that stood beside the window and she sat down, watching him with interest. Her fear had levelled by now, washed away by the feeling of safety that had overcome her the second Thalian stepped out into that clearing.

Her anger, however, was still bubbling dimly beneath the surface. It had nowhere to go and Amaya still could not quite believe this had happened, that her people had rushed in here like that with weapons in hand, attacking the elves for no good reason.

They didn't care about her wellbeing, she knew that already. While she'd thought that they might have listened if she'd told them the reality of the situation, it became clear they were only trying to get her back because Vermund had told them to.

Vermund, she thought bitterly. *Ugh.* That wretched man.

As kind a person as she was, she found that she didn't feel entirely unhappy with his death, nor the manner in which it had come to him. He had brought it upon himself and it seemed Amaya had been quite naive when it came to him and what he was truly capable of.

She felt a sudden stinging on her cheek and she blinked herself out of her thoughts to find Thalian kneeling on the floor in front of her with his hand on her face. It took her a moment to realise he was putting some kind of sweet-smelling ointment on the bruise, so lost was she in his eyes.

The corner of his mouth curved into a smirk, almost knowingly, and Amaya could have smacked him for it.

"Do you hurt anywhere else?" He asked her, carefully dabbing something else on her injured lip that immediately seemed to take effect. She marvelled at the magic of it.

She went quiet for a moment as she assessed herself. Her hip was still sore from where she had been thrown to the ground, as was her arm, though both arms ached a little from Vermund's harsh grip. So she nodded and hummed an affirmative.

"Show me. Remove your dress." Thalian said then, rising to his feet and turning to find the lid so he could put it back on the jar of ointment and return it to the drawer where he kept his healing items.

Amaya stared at him for a long while before her voice returned to her, albeit in stutters. "Wh-what!" A pink flush began to join the quickly fading injury of one cheek to the unblemished skin of the other. "My-? I... *Thalian...*"

Thalian, who was already rummaging around for a different jar, turned to frown at her before he seemed to suddenly remember that it would leave her sitting before him in a state of undress and he hesitated. "Oh. Ah." He lowered his gaze, almost shyly. "I apologise." He cleared his throat. "I will fetch Myleth."

He turned and strode towards the door. Usually only a few select servants would have the leave to enter his most private domain but he would make an exception. Besides, Myleth was one he knew very well. He pulled the door open to ask one of the guards to go down to a lower level and return with her but the sound of his name caused him to turn back to Amaya.

He swung the door shut again at once when he saw she was now sliding her dress down past her shoulders. He swallowed and then he moved back over to the desk, making a show of fiddling around so that she might feel less watched. When he turned back, she had slipped her arms free of the confines of the dress sleeves and eased it down to her waist where the material bunched up. She had a slip on underneath so she supposed it saved her some dignity. However, the fingers of the other hand had hesitated upon removing the garment further, debating whether or not she had the courage.

Though her hip ached, Amaya felt as though she was far too exposed as it was so she pulled her hand back and held one arm out for him to see.

Thalian was no fool. He had not missed the fact that she may be concealing another injury from him, however he dutifully moved to look over her arm. He frowned at the bruises, the redness, and the little half-moon marks from Vermund's fingernails. How tightly he must have held her for those not to have faded by now. He had not been joking before. He should very much have liked to possess the ability to reanimate that man's corpse so that he could have the pleasure of killing him again. And again. And again. And *again*, if that did not satisfy him.

"Don't look so angry." Amaya murmured, watching him. "I am fine."

Thalian looked up to her face. "He *hurt* you." He stated grimly. "When I came upon that clearing, he was hurting you still. It could have been much worse."

"But it was *not*. You stopped him." She said, her hand moving to settle on top of his own in an attempt to offer him some comfort. "That is all that matters."

He looked down at her hand on his and smiled a little. He moved his fingers and took her hand in his own, sitting there like that for a moment as he looked back at her. Neither of them spoke but they didn't really need to. Then he let go of her and turned his attention back to her arms, soothing the hurts on both of them.

His attention shifted to the side of her dress where he'd caught her fingers lingering before. He quickly turned away but Amaya noticed it all the same and she sighed.

He looked up at her face. "Please show me."

"I am afraid." She admitted quietly.

Thalian frowned. "Of me?" He asked out loud before he could stop himself, having intended to keep that worry in his own head. His voice was quiet.

"No!" She insisted quickly, shaking her head. "No, of course not!"

Thalian relaxed slightly but he still seemed a little troubled. "Then what is wrong?"

"It... it is not as if I make a habit of... of dropping my clothes for all and sundry!" Amaya half-snapped out of embarrassment, averting her eyes.

He nodded a little, managing to deduce then that she was feeling self-conscious because she was not used to being unclothed before another.

Not like he, who had servants to help him dress in the many heavy layers he sometimes needed to go around in.

Nakedness was not inherently sexual but to humans he knew that it could often be perceived solely as such. Whether it was their short lifespans that made them so obsessed and unrestrained or something else, he had no idea.

"You have nothing to fear. I am not going to look anywhere I should not be looking. I am not going to touch anywhere you have no injury."

Amaya stayed quiet for a long moment, finding herself wondering what it would be like if he *did*. If he did look upon her properly, fully... what would he think? Would it please him?

She could, of course, never say that out loud and there was still too much to discuss and think about before she could even consider such a thing. So she simply shifted in the chair and gently eased the bottom part of her slip out of the dress and upwards, using the rest of the dress to keep certain parts of herself covered up completely, allowing him to see her hip. She felt a slight chill at the exposure.

When she looked up at his face, he was frowning again. Deeply. His fingers reached out carefully and he moved them, feather-light, over her skin. When Amaya sucked in a little hiss of a breath he looked up at her, worried.

He immediately withdrew his hand. "I'm sorry. Does it hurt very much?"

Her face flushed because it was not pain that had caused the reaction but the touch of his fingers. Amaya pressed her mouth into a line and shook her head, keeping her gaze focused downwards.

Thalian watched her for a moment, like he was looking for something in her expression before another of his annoying, knowing smiles appeared on his face and he returned to the matter at hand.

Her hip was definitely the worst injury, already a nasty dark bruise blossoming across her skin. He probed gently with his fingers, testing the skin just around the bruise and checking for anything deeper.

Eventually, he pulled back and picked up the jar of liniment again, applying a generous amount to the area with great care and then he sat back.

"It doesn't appear you have suffered a fracture or anything deeper." He told her, though she had already been fairly sure it was not overly serious. She just *ached*. However, thanks to whatever he had used on all of her injuries the pain had already begun to ebb away.

Thalian was quiet for a moment, his expression thoughtful, before he opened his mouth to speak again. However, Amaya had done the same and her voice came first.

"What did-" She stopped, having heard the beginning of his own sentence.

"No, you go." He urged gently. Whatever he had been about to say was truly of no importance anyway.

"I just wondered..." She shrugged. "In the forest. What did you say?" When he looked confused, she continued. "You said, *inel...* I don't know. Something in your own language. I didn't know what it meant."

Now it was Thalian's turn to look bashful as he realised what she meant. "*Inellialeth.*" He murmured again.

Amaya nodded. "Yes. Yes, *inellialeth*..." She repeated slowly, testing the strange word with her tongue. "What does it mean?"

He was quiet for just a moment as he looked back at her, his gaze softer than she thought she had ever seen it before. "My beloved."

Many emotions seemed to well up within her at once then. She looked at him in silence as she committed his expression and his tone to memory.

Then, without another word she leaned in to kiss him, feeling much braver than she would have in the past. His desperate kiss in the woods seemed to have banished any nerves she may have held onto about making such a move.

"I..." Amaya pulled back to say something, watching Thalian open his eyes and look back at her with slight concern. The fact he himself looked a little unsure made her feel better somehow and she forced herself to continue. "I love you, Thalian."

Amaya saw his eyes widen, heard his sharp intake of breath, and she leaned back in to press a soft kiss to the corner of his mouth.

For Thalian's part, he found himself rendered speechless. Yes, he had been aware that something much bigger was brewing in between the two of them, and had been for a little while, but he had not quite dared to hope that Amaya would *love* him.

She liked him. She found him pleasing to

the eye. She enjoyed his company. That much was incredibly easy to realise, even for one so repressed as him. She returned the few kisses they had shared with ease and he didn't take that lightly but love? He had not dared to think that the depths of his own feelings might be returned so entirely.

Thalian's voice, when it finally came, was quieter than Amaya had ever heard it and full of a tenderness that made her want to cry. He spoke a few words she could not understand but she didn't need to ask. She could just tell that he was repeating her sentiments back to her in his own tongue.

Once again, she repeated the foreign words carefully, wanting to say such a serious thing as this to him in the language of his own people, even if she was certain she did butcher the pronunciation.

His eyes shone then as he pulled Amaya from the chair, gathering her into his arms, and kissing her until she almost felt that she could no longer breathe.

Reunited

Two days passed and then Valerian and Aurelia returned to the castle with Gideon.

Amaya was in the library with Thalian when the news came. She had forgotten her book long ago by that point, swapping it for the king's lap where she sat curled against him. They had fallen into deep conversation for a while, Amaya delighting in the feeling of his fingers running gently through her dark hair. However, a few moments ago, talk had ceased and she was currently kissing him like he was the very oxygen she needed to breathe.

Valerian suddenly burst into the room and gave Amaya such a fright that she leapt from Thalian's lap like a squirrel into the trees, though not quick enough because the prince witnessed the entire scene - including what was happening just before Amaya moved.

He lifted a hand to his face in an attempt to hide his amused (and shocked) smirk, clearing his throat to swallow a laugh. The look his father levelled at him told him that he noticed.

"I, ah…" He started, recovering himself as quickly as he could. He had the good grace to become a little more sombre as he turned his attention to Amaya. "Your father is safe. We have set up a room and he is with the healer."

"Is it bad?" Thalian asked.

Amaya turned to him, surprised, though

she felt a little guilty for feeling that way. She had become too accustomed to Thalian's disparaging remarks or looks whenever her father was mentioned. She understood it more after learning about the roses and everything else that had happened but it had still felt slightly uncomfortable. Amaya loved her father dearly.

Looking at Thalian now, there seemed to be only genuine concern and it pleased her to see it.

"He will live." Valerian assured them both. "They had him in this place, some type of infirmary I believe it was, but he was just locked in a room and not very well cared for. He has a fever and a sickness in his chest. He is asleep right now but you can see him if you would like."

Amaya nodded instantly. "Yes! Please."

The prince nodded, moving aside for her to leave the library ahead of him.

Just before he stepped out into the hall, he turned to shoot his still ever-so-slightly ruffled father an amused grin. He had not forgotten what he had walked in on.

Amaya followed Valerian to the room they had set her father up in and immediately rushed to the side of his bed. The healer at his other side did their best to put her mind at ease, assuring her that he would recover, and recover well thanks to the medicine and healing powers possessed by the elves.

Still, Amaya hated to see him this way. He had not woken but he seemed feverish, mumbling under his breath every so often as he slept.

She wished desperately for him to wake and yet she also partly dreaded it for the sole reason that the last time he had been here had been terrible and he had not yet experienced the elves as she had.

He had not yet experienced *Thalian* as she had.

~

Three days passed, during which Amaya hardly left her father's side.

Thalian came to check in once on that first day but he had not come again, leaving her and her father in peace. He didn't wish to intrude, though three days apart gave him more than enough time to sit and dwell upon the problem he was now facing.

The problem that was her mortality.

Amaya was a *human*.

Humans, who were there and then gone again so quickly.

The thought agitated him.

He *loved* Amaya.

Thalian had admitted as much to her. Out loud. Despite his many concerns. Against his better judgement.

The days after both of their confessions to each other had been spent in a little bit of a haze. The two of them had been quite wrapped up in the bliss of it all, properly exploring this connection that had grown between them both, that they had both finally acknowledged.

However, Thalian was now succumbing to the reality of the situation.

A human and an elf.

It was unheard of.

He scoffed to himself as he sat behind his large desk, not getting a single bit of work done as his mind tortured him.

Amaya would *die* eventually.

He would *lose* her.

He would be left alone and grieving once more.

He did not know if he could do this again.

~

The sound of her name roused Amaya from her half-slumber. She sat up in the chair and blinked, turning her attention back to the bed, where her father was now awake.

Her immediate joy soon dissipated, melting into confusion as he didn't even look at her, his eyes locked on something across the room. As Amaya studied him, she noticed the wideness of his eyes, the tension in his face... he was afraid.

Quickly, she turned to see what had captured his attention and noticed the Elf King darkening the doorway of the room. He was looking back at her father but he wasn't moving, as if standing very still would make the man less fearful. However, he still looked very intimidating, standing tall with his shoulders straight, chin slightly tilted upwards.

"Father-" Amaya began, turning back to him.

"Amaya!" Gideon cut in before she could continue, reaching out to grasp at her wrist.

She cringed slightly as the very last of the bruises Vermund had left on her skin stung at the contact. Thalian visibly bristled, however he stayed where he was. The man could not know, after all.

"Go!" The farmer continued, looking back at the elf in the doorway, who was now looking at Amaya. The *way* he was looking at her made Gideon feel more scared, more angry. "I do not know how I came to be here but... but you will go! You *must!* I will stay this time. I will... I will pay for my crimes."

"No-" Amaya started again, wishing to explain before he said much more, but this time it was Thalian who cut her off.

"This is not necessary." He said smoothly, taking a few careful steps closer.

Gideon shifted and his grip on his daughter tightened as Thalian's expression finally softened. The man's reaction reminded him of the fear he had instilled in Amaya in the past.

"Nobody here is a prisoner... my friend." He said. "Not anymore."

Amaya watched her father trying to figure out what was happening here. To match the elf before him to the one he had met when he first stumbled across this castle. He couldn't do it and he eventually turned to look at her as if for help.

She smiled at him. It was just so good to see him, finally, to have him right here in front of her. "I have so much to catch you up on." She told him.

Thalian reached out to place a hand upon Amaya's shoulder and she looked up at him. "I only came by to check on you both." He said, ignoring Gideon's expression as he tried to understand what he was witnessing. "I have a meeting I must get to but if you have need of me, tell Doronion and I shall come. If your father feels up to it you might like to show him around."

Then he leaned in and pressed a loving kiss to the top of her head before turning and sweeping from the room.

~

"So, you and... and the king?" Gideon's shock had not lessened in the many hours since Amaya had told him everything that had happened since they last saw each other.

She had taken him on a brief tour of the castle and they were both now sitting on a bench in one of the common areas. He had not seemed the slightest bit surprised when she told him that Vermund had led a bunch of villagers here to launch an attack on the elves.

He scoffed at the mere mention of the man and seemed fairly satisfied to learn of his death. He didn't say so but he felt a sense of gratitude spreading through him when he heard how Thalian had rescued Amaya from that fiend's clutches.

"Yes..." She felt heat rush to her cheeks and she ducked her head, nudging her father with her elbow as he started to laugh at her. He was feeling more comfortable now that she had told him what had happened, how things had changed here, though he still had a few of his own concerns.

"It is good to see you up and about!" A voice floated towards the pair of them and when Amaya looked up she saw Valerian coming towards them.

She smiled brightly at him. "Well, there is much to be said for the wonders of elven medicine."

She turned back to her father, her smile faltering as she realised he'd gone a little pale and was looking down at his shoes. "Are you okay? Are you feeling sick again?" She panicked, placing a hand on his arm.

He shook his head and stood, looking up at Valerian a little timidly. "I... I just wanted to say that... that I am so sorry. I never meant-"

Valerian shook his head and stepped forward, reaching out to clasp Gideon's shoulder in a gesture that said more than words somehow could. "It has long since been forgiven."

A weight seemed to fall from the man's shoulders and he offered the prince a smile of his own, nodding gratefully.

Valerian turned back to Amaya, still smiling. "My father wondered if you would both like to join us for dinner tonight."

It was the slightest bit strange just because she had grown so accustomed to no longer being asked to join them in the royal dining hall but she realised that Thalian was probably doing his best to show her father respect. It made her smile more even though he wasn't there.

It was agreed that they would all meet for dinner. The three of them talked a little longer and then Valerian took his leave while Amaya showed her father around a bit more and introduced him to some of her friends. Myleth was especially keen to meet him, though Amaya was pretty sure the elf exhausted her father further with the way she talked his ear off.

~

When dinner came, Amaya found that she was nervous for some reason. Myleth had come and dressed her up in a beautiful gown that seemed a little too grand for the occasion but she didn't complain about it even as she tripped over the ever-so-slightly-too-long hem while leading her father towards the royal quarters.

He was kind of awed at everything around him, though she could tell that he was a little worried to see the king again.

He needn't have been as Thalian was oh so very gracious. He rose from the table to greet them and seated both of them before he re-took his own spot and the meal was started.

A surprisingly easy conversation passed as

the rest was caught up on and Gideon finally told the tale of how he had ended up locked away again in the first place.

Amaya felt a little responsible for where he had ended up but she reminded herself that everything was okay now. It had worked out and he was safe. They were all safe.

However, as she sat there passing the meal with them all, she began to feel that something was a little off.

Whenever Thalian would meet her gaze, he would immediately look away and, if she didn't know any better, she would have said he even looked a little uncertain.

She focused on talking to Camellia, whose presence had been a surprise, and who seemed to be in a much better mood since the attack on the castle. Though sometimes it was difficult to tell as the princess could be such a reserved sort of soul.

Once the meal was done, she stood and offered Thalian a smile. He smiled back but he seemed distracted as he gestured towards Gideon before the other man could stand. "I have a few things I wish to discuss with your father."

"Oh. Okay." Amaya said, hesitating before turning to look at her father. "Should I wait for y-?"

"That will not be necessary." Thalian said and she frowned a little, feeling as though she was being dismissed.

She did her best not to pout, wondering if something was wrong as she simply nodded, smiled again, and turned for the door.

"If anybody needs me I will be in the library." Amaya said as she left, figuring that nobody would.

The Question

The door of the library creaked open a few hours later.

Amaya jumped, a little startled, having been quite lost in her thoughts. The open book she had been staring at on her lap was forgotten as she turned her head, watching Thalian as he stepped inside and walked over to her.

She stared at him, suddenly aware that she had not really seen him in a few days, since her father was brought here. She missed him. The thought made her feel warm and for a brief moment she forgot the worries that had taken root in her over dinner.

"Reading anything good?" He asked, coming to stand beside her, peering down at the pages.

She closed the book so that he could see the cover. It was the copy of the tale of Nymeria that he had gifted to her - it felt like so long ago now, with everything that had happened since.

He hummed, smiling, and Amaya studied him for a moment before she spoke again. "Is something wrong?"

Thalian looked from the book to her face, tilting his head as he took in her expression and her quiet tone. He realised then that she looked unhappy.

"No." He shook his head, crouching down by her side as he reached for her hand. "No, of course not. What would be wrong?"

She shrugged, looking down at her hand in his with a little sigh. "I just... I thought maybe..." She didn't really know what to say, what she'd thought, so she trailed off for a second before continuing. "You seemed distracted. At dinner."

"Ah." He nodded, his mouth twitching then as he looked back at her. His eyes were bright and she blinked, wondering at the slight change in him.

"No." He assured her quickly, leaning in to kiss her. Amaya relaxed somewhat, allowing her eyes to drift shut as she kissed him back. If he was sending her back to her village and ending this whole thing he wouldn't be kissing her right now, would he?

"I thought maybe..." She said as he pulled away, lifting his hand and tenderly brushing some strands of hair out of her eyes. "You might have been having second thoughts."

"About what?" He asked quietly, studying her face closely.

She looked down. "Um... about... maybe you wanted me to leave."

Thalian's brows knitted together and his mouth dropped open just slightly in surprise. "Why would you think such a thing?"

"I don't know." Amaya said, feeling foolish as she squirmed under his gaze in the silence that followed.

When she looked up to meet his eyes, she thought she saw tears. She straightened immediately, feeling slightly panicked. "Oh, no!

No, don't be upset, I... I'm sorry! I was just being-"

He swiftly cut her off with another firm kiss. Amaya melted again as she wrapped her arms around his neck.

When he pulled away this time, he was smiling. "You were being silly." He finished her sentence for her, raising an amused eyebrow. "I have no wish to send you away. In fact, I want nothing more than for you to stay with me." He paused just briefly, his voice dropping. "I *need* you to stay with me. I was not shutting you out, little human, I was making sure everything was perfect."

"What do you mean?" She asked. Her voice was quiet but she was smiling now too, his words making her feel much better.

"I wanted to do it all properly. So I... I asked Myleth to find you the perfect dress and I was asking your father..." He trailed off then, glancing back down at their hands.

Amaya waited, tilting her head curiously before prompting him to continue. "What?"

Thalian sighed. "Well, this was not where I planned for us to be when I did this." He let go of her hand and he reached into the pocket of his overcoat, pulling out a small carved wooden box. "I was asking your father..." He paused again. Amaya was not used to seeing him so unsure. "If, now he knows the full story, if he would be okay with me asking for... for your hand in marriage."

She was not sure what she had been expecting but she knew with absolute certainty that it was not that and so, for a long minute, she simply stared at him as if completely stunned.

Tears began to blur her vision as Thalian opened the box, revealing a ring wrought of silver with tiny ruby coloured gems entwined around the banding to look like little roses. He took it from the box and held it in between them both as he looked back up into her eyes.

"Would you?" He asked, voice practically a whisper, sounding suddenly so very unsure and so very unlike himself. "Would you stay here? And marry me?"

Amaya laughed then because how was it even a question? "Thalian." She breathed, reaching up to brush away the tears that had started to fall. "Of course I will. I... nothing would make me happier!" She cried, shaking her head as she practically threw herself at him.

He laughed, gathering her into his lap and kissing her senseless.

The old Thalian would have allowed all of his doubts during their days apart to control every single one of his actions. He would have drowned in them and never resurfaced. He would have twisted it into anger and he would probably have done what Amaya feared and sent her away before locking himself inside the castle once more. He would have stayed in his bubble of misery and denied himself every happiness.

The Thalian sitting here now had been changed. Her arrival had changed him. Every day that he had encountered Amaya since had changed him. She had challenged him in a way he had not been challenged in a long time.

He had grown to understand that denying this happiness because of a future pain would only double it.

He wanted her with him and that was all there was to it right now. Yes, they would both need to talk, there was still a lot to discuss, but right now he didn't want to think about any of it.

"You have made me very happy." He told her when he finally pulled away, sliding the ring onto her finger and then moving to stand.

He offered his hand to help her up but then swept her off her feet and into his arms, chuckling as she squealed in surprise.

He carried his little human through the hallways of his castle, oblivious to all the watchful eyes he passed by, and swept her back up the stairs.

Doubt

In the days that followed, the entire kingdom was buzzing with excitement.

Plans for the wedding had already begun, though Amaya had no real care for what type of flower adorned the banquet hall or the ceremony aisle.

Much to Myleth's dismay, she didn't even mind what dress she wore. She was too wrapped up in Thalian and how happy she felt, to no longer have to suppress her feelings for him. To finally be *his*.

Truthfully, she would have been fine carrying on as they both had been, without a wedding or anything official.

Amaya had no desire to take the place of his late wife and at first it had worried her, that his people would think badly of her or the situation itself. It was rare for the races to mix in such a way, to love and to marry. Friendships were forged often enough of course (though not on the Golden Isle since Thalian had shut his realm off) but this? It was not common, if it happened at all, and she knew that some in this world simply would never approve.

Thalian, however, had assured her that nobody here would think anything of the sort, that from what he could see and hear everybody was more than happy to see their king take her as his bride.

Amaya did not want to be a queen in the official sense and she made that explicitly clear. She only wanted to be his and Thalian had taken this very well, as though he had already assumed as such. As a human, she couldn't have much of a say in elven politics anyway, married to him or not.

All Amaya cared about was what came after all the formalities. She just wanted to be with Thalian forever.

Well... for the rest of *her* life.

The thought stopped her in her tracks on the fifth day and a pain struck her heart as it suddenly fully dawned on her that she would die long before him, if he ever did.

Amaya would age and die and leave him behind.

Her thoughts drifted again to Caleniel. Her chambers up that forbidden staircase. The way Thalian had locked away every memory of her. The way every mention of her name and her death had been forbidden while he drowned in his grief and misery. The way he'd locked his kingdom up and forsaken all the lands beyond.

With tears in her eyes, Amaya sought him out, finding him in his grand throne room.

He was surprised by her rather abrupt appearance and, seeing the stricken look on her face, quickly dismissed the advisors he was meeting with and stood, hurrying towards her.

"My sweet girl, what is the matter?" He asked, taking her face into his hands and caressing her cheeks with his thumbs.

Amaya felt ridiculous for coming to him this way, especially when she realised that she had interrupted his work.

She leaned forward, pressing her forehead against his chest as she wrapped her arms around him. He held her close, running a hand up and down her back comfortingly, tangling his fingers in the ends of her long, dark hair.

"Tell me." He spoke again a few moments later, pulling back and tilting her chin up with a long finger, forcing Amaya to look at him.

Worry was written all over his face and she felt horrible to burden him with this, to make her unhappiness his own, but she knew she would only dwell on it and pull herself deeper and deeper into despair.

"I just realised..." It felt silly to say that she had suddenly realised it when it was so very obvious.

On one hand Amaya knew that it had always been somewhere in the back of her mind. How could it not have been? It was just that, in all this happiness, she had sort of pushed it out of her head altogether. All she had been thinking about was that she would stay here with him and her father was safe and everything seemed to have fallen into place.

"Realised what?" He prompted gently, brushing her hair back behind her ears as he studied her. Thalian didn't say it but he was worried that Amaya had changed her mind.

She forced the words out. "I realised that I...

that you... Thalian, I'm a human! You are an elf!"

"Yes." He said gravely and he nodded, sighing as he looked back at her. It wasn't difficult for him to catch up just by what little she said. It had been ever in the front of his own mind, after all.

"Does that not bother you?" She asked in a half sob that made him gather her back into his arms and hold her close.

"Shh... oh, my darling." He sighed again, shaking his head as he held her for a while longer and then let go, taking her hand and leading her out of the throne room.

"What about-?" Amaya started to ask, turning back to look over her shoulder, gesturing to the room. He had been busy ruling his kingdom!

Thalian waved his hand in the air, shrugging as he led her away down the hall. "It doesn't matter." She was more important right now.

~

Thalian led Amaya to the Elf Queen's garden, where he knew no one would disturb either of them and where he knew Amaya would find some comfort. She had grown to love the Starfire Roses and it brought him great joy.

He let go of her hand once they were sitting in the garden by the roses and a small silence fell over the both of them.

Thalian watched her carefully as she dried her tears and reached out towards the flowers, a few of which had woken up and shifted their attention towards her as if sensing her sadness. She touched their petals with the tiniest little smile but it did not quite reach her eyes.

"I do not like to see you in such despair." Thalian said quietly.

Amaya turned to look at him with a small shake of her head. "I don't want to leave you."

"It would not be for many long years yet." He said softly as he tried to reassure her.

She gave him a look of disbelief. "The turning of the seasons of my life are nothing to an elf." She turned back to the roses as she felt fresh tears threatening to spill from her eyes. "It will be long for me but not so for you. What if-"

She fell silent again, abruptly cutting off the rest of what she had been about to say. She sat silently caressing the petals of the flowers as they stretched their stems towards her, seeming as distressed at her sorrow as the king sitting beside her was.

Thalian watched her with a sad frown, able enough to fill in the gaps. "What if I once more become the monster I was when you met me." It was not a question.

"You weren't a monster." Amaya said quietly but firmly, lifting her face and looking up at him. "You have suffered greatly. You were grieving. You grieve *still*. I will only add more."

"Why should that mean we forsake the happiness that these years will bring?" He asked, reaching for her hand again.

The roses watched on quietly. If Amaya had looked at them for too long she might have said that they seemed to be thinking.

"Will it not just make it hurt even more?" She asked, another sob catching in her throat.

Thalian pulled her to him once more, unable to handle seeing her so crestfallen. "*You* are worth any pain I will have to endure." He said, kissing her head.

"I don't want to be the cause of *any* of your pain." She told him, sniffling against his chest, her fingers clutching at his shirt.

"I am afraid, my little human, that it is far too late for that." He murmured, rocking her gently.

It did not matter now, after all, whether Amaya stayed or left. There was no choice she could make or unmake, no way in which he could lose her, that would not cause him pain.

The little Starfire Roses watched, listened, and then - when Amaya and Thalian had finally retired for the night - they talked together beneath the stars.

Loose Ends

Two days later, Amaya had finally stopped crying at every opportunity.

She had half wondered if she should flee the kingdom and spare Thalian the pain of watching her wither and die before his very eyes, but she knew that it had never actually been something she was seriously entertaining. Merely the panicked scrambling of a mind scared to break the already fragile heart of the one it loved so deeply.

Leaving Thalian now had never been an option, not really. Amaya could not have lived with that and it was true that it would cause him pain just as much as losing her at some undetermined point in the future would.

She did not wish to hurt him at all but doing it right now felt far more cruel, especially when he had finally blossomed into this wonderful being who had learned to open up and feel things freely once more. When she could see joy in him when before there had been only misery. Light where there had only been darkness.

Besides, Amaya was quite selfish and she could not now be without him. So she accepted, a little reluctantly, that she loved Thalian as he was and he loved her as she was - a mere human - and she was going to marry him and live out her days in his realm before one day, far too soon, leaving him to mourn her beneath the very same trees that grew upon his doorstep today.

Her father had been able to tell that

something was wrong, of course, but Amaya was loath to talk about it with anyone else in case she started sobbing again. She assured him it was fine and he accepted it even if he did not fully believe it.

He smiled and laughed more in the days since he awoke and she found great joy in seeing him interacting with the elves, even with Thalian who he had once feared and wished to rescue his daughter from.

She walked in on the two of them one day, her father laughing heartily over a glass of strong liquor and Thalian lounging in his chair holding a glass of his own, an amused chuckle leaving his lips.

"What have I walked in on here?" Amaya asked with a laugh as she sat down at the other side of the table, propping her elbow up and resting her chin on her hand as she looked between the two.

Thalian was the one to speak, her father too busy trying to get his laughter under control. "Well, your father was regaling me with stories from your village." He raised his chalice to his lips and threw back the rest of the contents, his brow quirking in amusement as he set it back upon the table. "However, I fear that the alcohol is much too strong for him, considering that he has been laughing over something he is certain he said out loud to me, but in fact only said in his own head, for the past twenty minutes."

Amaya shook her head as her eyes turned on her father. "Oh, for goodness sake!" She tried to scold him but it didn't quite hit the mark and it wasn't long until he looked as though he might fall asleep at the table any moment.

"Doronion!" Thalian's voice beckoned to the elf he could sense lingering outside the door. Amaya smiled kindly at him and he seemed in fairly high spirits himself as he returned the smile.

Thalian gestured to her father. "Would you be so kind as to escort our friend here to his room? I fear he will pass out any second."

Doronion assisted Gideon in standing, the man putting his arm around the elf's shoulder and leaning in close as though he were about to tell him a secret, but all that came out ended up being a jumble of nonsense.

Doronion looked a little concerned as he walked Gideon from the room and it was all Amaya could do not to laugh.

She turned back to Thalian as the door closed and found he had risen from the table and gone over to a desk at the back of the room. When he returned, he laid out a little box in front of her and opened it up. Curiously, Amaya watched as he unveiled a collection of beautiful looking rings. She tilted her head as she looked up at him, silently asking what they were for.

"I would like you to choose one." He explained, gesturing a hand towards the rings on the table. "I have chosen yours. It is only fair, after all."

"You want me to pick a ring for you to wear?"

Thalian nodded. "Once we wed I shall wear

it, as a symbol of our love." He paused so briefly Amaya nearly missed it. "For the rest of my life."

She gently bit at her bottom lip, glancing back down at the rings. They were all so beautiful she didn't know where to begin. She wondered what he would prefer but he offered no assistance, wishing it to be entirely her decision.

She looked over each ring very intently for a time. Eventually, she settled on one of silver to match hers but instead of ruby coloured gems set into flowers, this had emerald coloured stones twisted into little leaves. He seemed satisfied as he put all the other rings away, smiling as he studied the one she had chosen.

"What ring did... did Caleniel choose?" Amaya asked after a long pause, unsure if she should mention the queen at all.

He had told her all about Caleniel the day of her birthday, when she had sought him out after he'd shut himself away with the roses, but still. Amaya was not sure if it would be too far of her to bring her up out of nowhere.

While he hesitated, he did not seem upset or angry. His gaze dropped to his hand with a tender smile and he held it out towards her, slightly wiggling one of his fingers. "This one."

She reached out for his hand, brushing his skin gently as she studied the ring. Silver coloured stones set against a gold band, almost like stars.

"She had a good eye." Amaya said softly, smiling as she released his hand.

"Well, yes." He shrugged, pulling his hand

back. "She took *me* as a husband, did she not?" He joked, smirking as he poured himself some cordial from a nearby pitcher.

She blinked at him and shook her head, trying to look far less amused than she actually was though the twitch at the corner of her mouth likely gave it away. "You are terrible."

"Yet you love me." He teased, watching her over the rim of his glass as he lifted it to his lips.

Amaya shot him a scathing look but ended up laughing despite herself. She rolled her eyes. "I do. Ego and all."

Thalian feigned a look of indignation as he placed his cup back down and leaned forward in his seat. "Hmm." He hummed and Amaya shivered slightly as his lips brushed the shell of her ear.

Her eyes drifted shut and she leaned into him, sighing as he kissed a line from her ear down her jaw and to her throat.

A knock at the door shook them from the moment and she heard Doronion's voice again on the other side. "My lady? Myleth is looking for you. She wishes to go over your dress one more time."

Amaya groaned softly. "I cannot wait to wed you but I fear I have become Myleth's personal doll."

"One more week, my precious little human." Thalian chuckled against her skin, pressing one last kiss to her throat before he pulled back. "Just one more week."

∼

"Why can I not look at it?" Amaya asked with a heavy sigh, her head tilted backwards, her eyes on the intricately carved ceiling above her.

Upon entering the room, Myleth had (as seemed to have become routine) made her close her eyes and turn away from the large mirror.

"It's a surprise." She said, shooting her a look that she wouldn't even see, but Amaya knew her well enough by this point to realise she'd done it anyway.

"It is just a dress." She muttered childishly.

"Excuse you!" Myleth playfully smacked her hip from her place down at the hem of the dress she had helped Amaya put on blind. "That attitude is exactly why you are not seeing yourself in this dress until the day you are presented as the king's bride."

Myleth had full faith in the fact that Amaya would change her mind when she actually saw herself all beautifully dressed up on the day. And, she told herself, she would be gracious enough not to throw it in the girl's face!

Amaya had grown used to the other dressing her up by this point and, as someone who had never grown up with many dress options, she'd never spent much time fussing over what she wore or putting much thought into it.

She didn't fully care what she got married in, truthfully, for it wasn't as important as *being* married, being *with* Thalian. While she did want to marry him and be his bride, this was in some way merely a stepping stone. She just wanted to get to everything that came after.

She briefly thought of Vermund and how angry he would be if he could see her now. A small, uncharacteristically cruel smirk tugged at her lips. He would absolutely hate this. Good.

"Do you have much more to do?" Amaya asked, bored of studying the ceiling. She wanted to check on her father and then go and finish the book she was reading.

"No, just... a little... there!" Myleth stood back, smiling. "All done." She took a moment to study the dress, her gaze softening as she thought how lovely Amaya looked in it. "Alright. I'll help you take it off now. Close your eyes!"

~

When Myleth finally released Amaya from her evil seamstress clutches, she made her way down the hall in the direction of her father's room. Just to check in on him before she went to the library to read the rest of the afternoon away. There was still so much to get done but today Amaya did not wish to do any of it.

Rounding a corner, she suddenly came upon Camellia sitting alone on a bench in the quiet hallway.

The princess saw her coming and immediately stood, pasting a smile onto her face but Amaya had noticed her quickly wipe away a tear. She frowned and quickened her steps.

"What is it?" She asked upon reaching the

princess, putting a hand on her arm.

Camellia shook her head quickly, simply continuing to smile at her. "No, no. Nothing. Don't worry! Everything is well."

"It doesn't look well." Amaya replied, not believing it for a second. "You can tell me."

Camellia was quiet for a minute as she bowed her head, looking down at her shoes as she seemed to wrestle with the decision of whether or not to talk to Amaya about whatever was on her mind.

When she looked up it seemed that she had decided on the latter.

"Do you remember the conversation we had before?" She asked quietly, looking around as though afraid of being overheard.

Amaya paused a second as she thought back and then nodded. "About Doronion?" She asked, thinking about the day she had left Thalian in the library, upset about the way he seemed to look down upon Doronion in regards to courting his daughter.

She recalled the way she had fled the library after he entered it and the way he had come to try and offer an unsure apology later on, however her ire had waned by that point. It was the day Amaya found that copy of the story of Nymeria in her room.

Camellia nodded, her cheeks turning slightly pink. "I am afraid I lied to you." She murmured and Amaya knew what she meant.

She was saying that she did not simply see

Doronion as just a friend, but as more, and Amaya had already known it. Camellia had not outright denied it but she had not confirmed it either.

"Why were you crying?" Amaya asked her then.

"Well, I... I..." The princess floundered briefly, not wishing to say anything to upset the girl or make her feel bad, not when she was so happy and everything had fallen into place. She was happy for Amaya and she was happy for her father, of course she was. She had seen and felt the changes and nothing could be better for him, or this realm and everyone in it, including her... and yet.

"It is... it is just the wedding. All the talk and the..."

Amaya immediately nodded in understanding. She hadn't thought about it but it was probably difficult to see it, especially if Camellia was fighting feelings of her own. Maybe she was having similar thoughts as Amaya had had on that day. Maybe seeing Thalian marry a lowly human made her wonder why Doronion would not be deemed good enough for her.

"I see." She said softly, studying the princess's face for a moment. "Camellia-"

Camellia shrugged quickly and turned from Amaya before she could continue. "No. Forgive me. Please, I am alright. I must go, I have things to attend to."

She fled before Amaya could say anything else and the girl was left blinking after her for a while, even after she had turned the corner and was out of sight.

Then she turned and hurried back the way she had come, making for the stairs that led her back to Thalian's chamber.

~

Thalian looked up in surprise as the door burst open and Amaya came barrelling into the room.

He stood from where he'd still been seated at the table, work in front of him forgotten, and studied her face, trying to figure out what was wrong just by looking at her.

"Why do you not allow your daughter the happiness you have allowed yourself?" Amaya asked once the door clicked shut behind her.

Thalian blinked, taken off guard. Of all the things that had gone through his mind, this was not one of them. "What?"

"You heard me."

"Indeed, I *heard* you, yet I did not understand the question." He said in a slightly sharp tone, eyeing her as he stepped around the table.

"I see the way she and Doronion look at each other." Amaya said.

At this, the king rolled his eyes and turned away again, suddenly understanding what it was she was getting at.

"There!" She said, moving closer to him.

"Thalian! If you can marry a lowly human, why can't your daughter marry a half-elf?"

He whirled back around to look at her with a deep frown. "What are you talking about? Who said that?"

"Camellia." Amaya scanned his face. "Do you remember the day in the library? When you thought you had done something to upset me?"

He nodded. This was something neither of them had spoken of since and he had to admit that he was still curious because he was not sure he truly believed the reason she'd given. "Of course."

"I had asked Camellia about... about her and Doronion because I had seen things and I thought they were... well, together. She told me that you would never allow it. That his blood was not pure enough and he was not of royal breeding, simply not suitable for her."

"What does this have to do with you fleeing the library?"

She hesitated for a second but figured that there was no use in secrets between the two of them now. "I thought that perhaps, if you thought that way about someone like Doronion, then what must you think of *me.*"

He tutted a sound of disapproval and took a step closer, taking her face into his hands as he looked back at her. "I insinuated something along those lines to my daughter once, yes." He sighed and Amaya could see in his eyes that he did regret it. "But I did not mean it."

"Then why say it?"

Thalian was quiet for a long while then continued, his expression thoughtful, almost a little sorrowful. "I just wished... to keep them apart."

"Because you don't think him good enough?"

"No." He said firmly. "Because I am not blind either. I have seen their stolen glances for years upon years. I have heard their familiarity and their inside jokes. I have seen her light up for him in a way she does not for others. I have seen them grow close... too close."

"But *why?*" Amaya implored, unable to understand anything he was saying. If it was not for the reason that Camellia (and maybe even Doronion) believed, then... why?

"To spare them!" He snapped, frustrated by her prodding, though he was not actually angry at her. She could tell that easily enough. He did not want to have to admit it, to say any of this out loud, but he knew that he had to, now that he was faced with her.

She blinked up at him, lifting her hands to cover his own, still on her face. Her thumbs brushed against the back of his hands. "Spare them from what?"

"My suffering."

He did not need to say any more, for Amaya understood his meaning immediately.

He dropped his eyes from her face to the floor and she shuffled closer, removing her hands from his and wrapping them around his neck, pulling him to her. He let himself sag against her with a heavy sigh, his arms going round her in response.

Thalian had said what he had to Camellia all those years ago, he had kept himself in between her and his loyal butler like a wedge, because he knew that what they shared was *real*. And that a loss of that magnitude was catastrophic. He had striven to keep them apart, whether rightly or wrongly, to spare them the pain that he knew came from it. The pain he had been drowning in all these long years.

It was another cruel act from a shattered heart, Amaya realised.

They stood like that for a minute before Amaya turned her head to kiss the side of his face. "It is like you said the other day." She said softly. "Why should a future pain or a perceived loss mean we forsake the happiness that these years before will give us?"

Thalian inhaled a shaky little breath as he pulled back to look at her. He managed the tiniest of smiles and a brief nod before he leaned in and pressed a kiss to her forehead.

The Big Day

The day of the wedding came quickly and Amaya found that she had woken with more nerves and anxieties than she had anticipated. For some reason, she'd thought it would be simple. She would walk through the formalities and then... she would be married. She would stand beside Thalian and support him and, most of all, she would love him. *For as long as she was able.*

But Amaya realised she was shaking as Myleth weaved her hair into a beautiful tangle of braids and curls.

The elf smiled kindly at her as she carefully tied a red ribbon through the strands. "Breathe, dearie." She was doing her best to suppress her own intense excitement, Amaya could tell, and it almost made the girl laugh.

Amaya had grown to truly love Myleth during her time here. She had made those first few horrible days and weeks so much easier for her. She remembered how scared she had been then. How apprehensive and distrusting of everyone. And now she was marrying the king she once feared and despised! Who'd have thought? Certainly not her.

Next Myleth helped her into her dress and, when Amaya turned to look at herself, she was struck for a long moment.

For having next to no input in the entire thing, she found that she absolutely *loved* it. Just as Myleth had known that she would. She knew Amaya so well by now, of course she would find something that was utterly perfect. Something so utterly *her*.

"Oh..." Amaya breathed out, blinking back a few tears as it hit her that this was actually happening.

The door opened behind her but she barely registered it until she heard a soft gasp and turned to see her father staring at her.

"You are a vision, my girl!" He beamed, moving to embrace her.

~

Elven customs were different from those of humans but Thalian and Amaya had decided that they would sort of merge the two together, considering they were joining from two separate worlds. Amaya hadn't thought she minded either way but he had insisted upon it and she found that she was glad for it as she neared the hall with her father.

Gideon would be 'giving her away' as it were, walking Amaya towards Thalian where they would do some kind of ring exchange and then there would be a feast and there was also something later about the planting of a sapling. It was apparently supposed to grow alongside the passage of their union. It was a beautiful thought and she tried not to think about the passage of time and the growth rate of an oak tree compared to the lifespan of a human.

Walking into that hall was the most

nerve-wracking moment of her life even though she could feel her father's reassuring presence as she clung to his arm.

However, it all got a little bit easier when Amaya actually saw Thalian. He was standing waiting and he looked almost as uneasy as she did but setting his sights on her seemed to have the same effect as it did her.

Everything else seemed to melt away as she neared him, though her legs were still shaking beneath her with what was practically the entire kingdom watching them. Amaya still held some small concern that they would not like this but she felt no such emotion emanating from the crowd and it eased her further when she even heard a few scattered cheers from some after the king kissed her in front of everybody.

Even Camellia was in higher spirits than Amaya had ever seen her as they all finally sat down at the long banquet table.

Amaya wondered at the change in her until Thalian leaned in and whispered in her ear that he had had a long, fruitful discussion with her after Amaya burst into his room. And that Camellia and Doronion finally had his blessing.

It made her heart soar that he would do that and she felt a surge of emotion, rewarding him with a kiss on the cheek. Every time Amaya thought she could never love him more, he surprised her.

The rest of the evening passed in a whirl of good wine, plenty of food, and lots of singing and dancing as it seemed the elves were so very fond of.

Amaya danced with her father and wept on his shoulder when he told her how proud he was of her, and how proud her mother would have been.

Then Thalian cut in and the music had changed again, to the same slow tune that had been playing that night of their first dance, during the *Feast Beneath a Winter Sky*. This time it was not Valerian who changed the song but Thalian himself.

All eyes in the room were fixed upon the pair of them as he spun Amaya across the floor but once again they hardly noticed, only seeming to have eyes for each other.

Ever After

"Slow down!" Amaya laughed, clutching Thalian's hand in a death-grip as he dragged her along behind him. "I am going to trip over my dress!"

He chuckled. "Is my bride so drunk on wine that she can no longer walk properly?" He teased.

Amaya shot him a withering look, though her heart quickened at the loving expression on his face as he looked back at her. He looked quite drunk himself but she knew it was not the wine that did it.

The two of them had slipped out of the banquet hall early, making their escape so that they could be alone.

Amaya had not complained as Thalian dragged her from the room and up the stairs through the queen's chambers to her garden.

She would always think of this as the Elf Queen's rooms, though she knew that she was technically King Thalian's 'new Queen' (especially to those outside the realm). However, she did not wish that role upon herself in any other way than by some vague reference and he did not seem to care about that.

Caleniel was the queen here and Amaya had no desire to take her place in any way.

She smiled as he pulled her down the garden path. Nobody would bother them here, she knew, though she was sure nobody would have dared tonight even if he'd taken her elsewhere.

Still, she found this garden incredibly comforting so she did not mind staying out here for a while yet, sitting under the moonlight with him. It was full in the sky tonight, the moon, and she was as glad as ever for the little pockets of outdoors within these castle walls.

"Look." Amaya said, pointing to where the Starfire Roses lived.

The flowers were sleeping, tucked away into little buds. They did not stir when the two of them came near, so deep was their slumber. She smiled fondly at them and did not disturb them, turning back to Thalian as he sat beside her.

"I am not sure what they are so tired for." He sniffed, eyeing the roses almost suspiciously. They were usually awake at this hour.

"Well, perhaps they have had a busy day! Don't judge them!" Amaya nudged him and he chuckled.

She thought she saw one of the roses twitch just a little at the sound of his laugh. It was nearly imperceptible and, a moment later, she decided that she had imagined it.

The feeling of Thalian's hand, his thumb brushing over the back of her own, made her turn her attention back to him with a soft smile.

"I cannot believe we ended up here." She murmured, gazing into his eyes. They looked so *alive.* So full of love and life. *Joy*, she realised. She could recall the cold way he had once regarded her, none of which remained as he sat with her now.

"It is a wonder to me as well." He said, with a slight smirk. "That you could ever have fallen for my beastly charms."

Amaya laughed, leaning in to kiss him before she rested her head on his shoulder and closed her eyes, breathing the moment in as she felt his head come to rest lightly upon her own. "There was never anything beastly about you, Thalian. Not really."

They both fell silent for a while, enjoying each other's company. It had been such a perfect day and Amaya did not want it to end, though she couldn't tell if it was because it was so lovely she wanted to live in it, or whether every days ending would bring her a little sorrow now - as it would bring her closer to leaving him in inevitable heartbreak. Perhaps it was a little of both.

Then Thalian placed a finger under her chin, tilting her face up so she was looking at him again. He looked a little more serious, though his eyes were still bright.

He cleared his throat, glancing down at the new ring on his finger before he looked back up at her face. "I never did thank you."

She frowned at him and tilted her head, reaching for his hand. "Thank me? For what?"

His gaze was tender and full of emotion as he regarded her for only a brief second before he spoke again. "For bringing me back to life."

It was at that very moment, a mere half second after Thalian's admission, that the roses suddenly all burst open, stretching their petals and reaching out towards the bench where the two were sitting.

There was barely time to react to the awakening, so quick was their movement and so huge was her shock, for Amaya had never seen them move so fast.

Thalian, too, was quite stunned. The poignant moment was almost forgotten as his attention moved to the shining little flowers.

As they burst forth, the very air around them seemed to take on a shimmer that was as ethereal as their own sparkling red petals.

Amaya blinked, dumbfounded. "Thalian, what-?"

"I do not know." Was all he could mutter in response.

The shimmering continued as she stared, watching as it seemed to come out from the flowers themselves, moving directly towards her. She shifted on the bench but she was too astonished by what she was seeing to actually move out of the way.

"What are you doing?" Amaya whispered to the roses.

They danced in response and only continued on until she was wrapped in a glimmering haze that, to Thalian's eyes at least, made her look as though she were made entirely of starlight.

He was gaping at the scene, completely aghast, feeling utterly powerless to understand or do a single thing. He had never before seen the roses do anything close to this.

A soft humming seemed to come from the very leaves of the plants, almost as if they were singing.

The glimmer continued, wrapping around Amaya before settling upon her, and then seeming to evanesce away into her very skin.

As quickly as it began, it was finished.

Silence descended.

Amaya stared at the roses, watching them sway gently before her, appearing to be looking between both her and Thalian. The king was still staring at her, frozen, feeling as though his senses had completely left him.

She had to admit she was not faring much better. "I, uh... they..." She swallowed hard, looking from the roses to Thalian. She had never seen him look so perplexed.

Suddenly, he seemed to come back to himself, turning his attention swiftly from Amaya to the roses. He frowned at them and they merely shivered in response.

"They... they look tired..." Amaya managed, once she had it in her to actually look at them properly.

They seemed to have become sleepy again, almost as if they had used up all of their energy.

Thalian moved then, kneeling in grass before them in one swift movement, reaching his hands out towards them. They turned fully to him as well, allowing his fingers to brush their petals, sharing with him their message in the way that most plant and animal life could converse with the elves.

When he turned again, to look back at Amaya in amazement, there were tears shining in his golden eyes.

"What?" She asked, her tone practically pleading at this point. "What is it? What's *wrong?*"

"Wrong?" He shook his head, shuffling back towards her, still on his knees.

Oh, if his people could see him now, Amaya thought at random.

"Nothing is wrong. Nothing at all. Oh my..." He lifted his hands to her face and looked at her like he was studying her, every part of her, and Amaya could only frown back at him in confusion. She couldn't make much sense of his actions or his words.

"Then why are you crying?" She asked quietly, her voice breaking slightly as she looked at him, watching a tear travel down his pale cheek.

He shook his head, his mouth curving into a soft smile. "These are... they are *happy* tears, little human."

"I don't understand." She told him, raising one of her hands to his face and brushing the tear away with her thumb.

Thalian only leaned in and kissed her with a fervent passion and, though Amaya was still confused, she let him. He seemed to be at a complete loss for words.

Finally, he pulled back again, sitting on the heels of his boots with his hands in her lap, fingers entwined with her own.

"They were fast asleep." He said, and she nodded, still not understanding. His smile only widened. "They were fast asleep and they have been since last we were out here with them."

"This whole time?" Amaya gasped, glancing past him towards the roses, which still looked drowsy from their odd display. "Are they sick?" She was suddenly worried but then she realised that couldn't be it because he would not be happy as he'd said he was.

Thalian shook his head. "They were resting. They were gathering their strength. All their strength. As much as they would need."

"Need for what?"

He paused, eyes shining again with fresh tears as he looked back at her. He was practically clutching at her hands for dear life. "To bond with you."

Amaya stared at him in silence for a second, trying to make his words make sense. "What?"

"They linked themselves *to* you, *with* you."

"I... okay, but..." Her eyes moved between Thalian and the roses before settling back on his face. "But what does that *mean*, Thalian?"

He saw she was growing frustrated with the lack of information and suddenly felt bad about his apparent lack of ability to communicate, but this was a thing such as he had never encountered before in all his long years.

"It means, darling, that as long as these magnificent little roses bloom... so, too, will you."

He lifted her hands to his mouth, kissing them both. "They have tied themselves to you, and you to them. You will live as long as they do."

Amaya could only stare at him. "Wait. You mean...?" How was this at all possible and why would they do that? "How long do Starfire Roses live?" She asked him then.

Thalian nodded, his eyes filling again as his smile only grew bigger. "They live... for as long as they are not cut or picked."

The entire truth of it dropped on Amaya then, as heavily as it had for him. Neither of them said anything else but there was no need to. They both understood now.

Promptly, she burst into tears and fell forward to join him on her knees on the grass, wedding dress be damned.

He laughed and kissed her tears away before pulling her down with him and lying there with her on the grass, gazing up at the sky, practically glowing in the knowledge that Amaya could now be with him *forever*.

Though, through all his joy, he did make a mental note to double the guards on this side of the castle lest some vagabond broke in a *third* time.

After watching for a few moments, the roses sighed in contentment and then began to curl back up as they drifted off together into another much needed, and very well deserved, sleep.

They had seen and heard Amaya's fears the other night and they had seen and heard Thalian's own echoed in his responses. It had been a very long time since they had seen the Elf King in such a way.

Long after they had both left the garden the roses had talked together, whispering beneath the night sky, and it had not been difficult for them to come to a decision.

For they had promised their beloved queen that if anything should ever happen to her, they would care for the king in any and every way they possibly could.

And so Amaya would live on, tending and nurturing the selfless, wonderful little flowers that had bestowed upon her such a precious gift. She would live on, at Thalian's side. Human, but unchanging as the years passed by.

Thalian, too, would live on. No longer a creature hiding in darkness nursing a broken soul and shutting the rest of the world out. For he had found happiness and love again in the most unlikely place and in the most unlikely person.

One who had, despite all the odds, seen the beauty buried deep within the beast.

~*~

Printed in Great Britain
by Amazon